Chapter 1

Slowly the mighty huntress sneaks through the environment, her silent footsteps staggered to break up the motion. Ducking low, she waits for the moment to strike, her hand reaching out for the prey's young. Careful...careful...now! With sudden violence, the huntress snags the young, then makes a mad dash for the-

"Victoria Marie Blythe, you will put those cookies back right this moment."

Ducking my head, I turned and put the two cookies in my hand back on the tray, while a partially eaten conquest hid my smile. Seeing the treat in my mouth, Emma smiled and shooed me away while snagging one of her own. While Emma might act like my mother, she was the same age as my sister, just two years older than me. Chewing the remains of my cookie quickly, I gave her a lopsided grin then I tramped through the servant's hallway back to the family wing. Ms. Northrop hated whenever I used the servant ways, but if I wanted to stay away from her, then they were my best option.

Leaving Emma working industriously to make the lunch meal, as well as baking treats for dinner, I stopped at the back stairway to listen for the sound of heels and the swish of petticoats. Leaning on the dark oak handrail of the narrow stairs, I strained for the sounds of Ms. Northrop's stern voice. I wished to avoid her at all costs. I had been free for the last few hours from her comments, her scowl, and her cutting ways. It wasn't that the Governess was evil or abusive, I couldn't stand that we had a Governess assigned to us at all. We were nearly adults - the wedding of my sister was to be the day after tomorrow- but still, our father had appointed someone to watch and control us. Though, given the fading faculties of Owen, it was not that surprising that Father had wanted a woman assigned to us. We wouldn't want tongues wagging back in London after all.

Slinking up the stairs, I waited at the top to see if the distant voice of Ms. Northrop was in the family wing tea room, or closer to the sitting rooms and bedrooms. When her voice faded on my ascent, I smiled and then made a soft-footed rush to my room. Closing the wooden door to my room, I started to gently spin around in my bedroom with my arms held out at the joy of outwitting my watcher. Not that my escape from my lessons had been some significant adventure. With my sister to be wed shortly, I had become a low priority victim of Ms. Northrop's verbal lashings. The thought of what I would experience when my sister lived with her new husband, though, filled me with dread. Ms. Northrop's wrath over my 'silly childish acts' and 'brutish and uncouth behavior' were already long-winded tirades. I doubted her recriminations would shorten when my sister was no longer a target.

Quickly, I reached my limit for spinning. It was mostly knowing that it would be disagreed with rather than the act itself, that I enjoyed. Still, my smile almost split my face as I ceased then opened my wardrobe and reached for my pride and joy. Hidden in the back of the closet, tucked beneath the hanging dresses, was a medium sized chest usually reserved for accessories like belts and pins. Struggling with the cumbersome box, I pulled my treasure chest out of the wardrobe and onto the floor. I waited, listening to see if I would hear someone approaching, this was the most critical moment. Being caught before, or after, would matter little, but being found with my secret exposed, that would be my undoing.

Finding nothing to suggest an imminent visit, I pulled on

the small metal design on the outside of the box. Opening the chest, I removed the false bottom and exposed the treasure hidden inside. Reaching in, I smiled as I grasped my pride and joy. The pants I pulled loose from the depths of the chest were ugly. They had no lace, no frills, and the thick linen was rough against my skin, but they meant more than all my pretty dresses combined. These pants were cut to my exact figure and hid my feminine curves while allowing for a full range of motion. With these, I could run through the forest or climb the hills and trees. I wouldn't be forced to sit daintily sipping tea on a picnic outing, no, I would be free to explore and adventure. Well, as much experience as I could obtain in the small woods a mile from our summer mansion. Combined with the loose white, buttoned-up shirt and cap, I could pretend to be some young man out on a lark.

Pulling out my pants and tucking away the chest with its secret compartment, I stuffed my adventuring clothes under a pile of fabric within the depths of my wardrobe. The design of my pants came from reports of what the women of the Dress Reform Movement wore. That is, what little I could glean from the paper's scandalized comments on the style.

The plan was to wait for Robert's arrival tomorrow, with whatever invention or curio he was sure to bring, and then sneak out as everyone else was tied up with preparing for the wedding. Given the rushed nature of the marriage -Robert's family needing a sudden influx of funds because of a failed shipment of tea- the few people here would be unlikely to notice my absence. I frowned as I thought of Robert and his less frequent visits.

I still yearned for the days of our youth. Annie, Emma, and I would play in the garden while Emma's mom Sophia would watch us. We would dance and sing together as if no social caste separated us. Robert would join us while his uncle would trade tall tales with Father. We grew up together, playing as if we were all the same. It wasn't until Father was called back to India by the Queen, and Sophia died that things had fallen apart. Suddenly, Emma was no longer a friend, but a servant expected to take her mother's place as the head maid. Sure, it was a prominent position, and it meant Emma was clothed and fed, and in the future could find a husband, but it also meant Annie, and I could no longer talk to her as an equal. The change in Emma's station was worse for Robert.

Sniffling, I dabbed at my eyes before turning away from the past and what was. Quickly I checked my dress, smoothing out any wrinkles which might have formed while kneeling to remove my treasures. Finding my appearance was appropriate; I decided to see if I could manage to sneak back to the library without Ms. Northrop being the wiser. Opening the door to my room, I listened, then exited and dashed into the hallway, passing Owen without slowing. Owen just smiled, his back bent slightly and his balding head shiny under the lights of the oil lamps. While Owen had slowed down and become forgetful of late, I still could see the friendly butler of my father hiding within the older man. With Father posted so long in the Indian colonies, Owen practically raised us in our teenage years or failed to, given Ms. Northrop's view on the subject.

My silent dash was almost interrupted by Northrop's voice changing in volume, but I managed to turn the corner into the library before the Governess entered the hall outside the library. Quickly utilizing the key for the gas lamp on the wall, I tucked my dress under my legs and sat in front of the large oak desk in the library. I pulled the tome on the history of dressage closer; its weight and tight penmanship making the book a difficult chore to slog through. Flipping to any page near the middle, I hunched over slightly and pretended to read, trying desperately to calm my breathing.

"Victoria, I will thank you not to rush about the house and skip your studies. I do not have the time to deal with your flights of fancy. Your sister is soon to be wed, and she is still failing to make many important decisions," said Ms. Northrop as she entered the library, seemingly uncaring of my apparent studying.

"I am studying Ms. Northrop, and I will have you know, I find your accusation distasteful," I said with my most prim and proper voice.

Frowning, Ms. Northrop marched across the library, her light blue dress swishing and emphasizing the sounds of her hard shoes on the wooden flooring. Stopping before me, she smiled tightly then pulled a handkerchief from her sleeve and wiped a bit of cookie crumb from my lips. I couldn't help but frown at both the evidence of my guilt as well as the way she treated me like a child. Yes, I was sometimes childish, I knew it, but I was sixteen, and capable of studying at my own pace without being watched and brooded over.

"Now, I can't distract myself with your antics. Your father wishes for this wedding to go forward and your sister has no one else to stand for her in her mother's place. I will be focusing on her needs, and I do not have the time to deal with your games. For your sister's sake, behave, please," Ms. Northrop asked, her voice becoming more mothering and sweet by the end.

She wasn't fooling me.

While she could sound sweet and kind, it was no more than her skills in acting. I had watched her over months slowly whittle away at the household's staff. Instead of ten people caring for the summer mansion and another ten for the London home, the two locations had a workforce of six spread between them. Her sarcastic comments and vile treatment had cost us butlers, cooks, and maids. Poor Emma was working as both Head Maid and Cook alone; how she planned to prepare such a large meal for the wedding was beyond me. While the wedding was small and 'intimate,' rushed because of the financial struggles of Robert's family, it was still going to seat more than twenty guests from his family alone. The real tragedy was that Father would not be here; Annie was instead to be given away by Robert's Uncle. Colonel Markus Collingwood was a dear friend of the family, loved by both of us, but he still wasn't Father.

Staring me down as if waiting for a response, Ms. Northrop waited for an uncomfortable time before turning with a swish of her dress and leaving the library. The worst part of Northrop's lessons was how remote they were. I wasn't to learn about dressage, no, I was to learn about the history of dressage. I didn't learn natural philosophy, no, I was to learn about the people involved in the study thereof. It was always one step removed from the exciting bits. I learned the history of Nobility, but never the stories of the battles they fought in. Unlike Father's or the Colonel's stories, those focused almost solely on the action.

I tried to return myself to my studies, but my attention was drawn to the window and the courtyard outside. The sound of a horse and the Colonel's customary booming voice had me flying from my seat and out of the library. Flinging myself through the hallways and to the entranceway, I threw back the large double doors and myself down the stone stairs. My mansion slippers crunched along the crushed stone courtyard for the few paces needed until I could toss my arms around the Colonel. I snugged my face under his chin, his right arm holding his sword cane to the side while he roared his usual laugh of greeting.

"Oh, Victoria, my girl, you're growing. Soon your hugs will knock this old man down!" he roared with his usual bellow. His hearing was nearly gone with his many years leading the cannon division under Father which left him as a loud and boisterous man. A limp from a stray musket round and hearing loss were his only real injuries from his military service. He would often joke that he was glad for the leg wound since it gave him his 'wife,' 'Eloise,' the sword cane Father presented to him upon retirement.

"What are you doing here, Colonel? I thought you and Robert wouldn't be here until tomorrow? Isn't Robert afraid of the 'impropriety'?" I asked while hanging off Colonel Markus Collingwood, watching what Robert was pulling from the top of the carriage.

"That's why I'm here. With Ms. Northrop and me as chaperones, no one could claim any such thing. It's not like this mansion isn't large enough for a whole brigade of us with room to spare, we never need even rub elbows with such a bunking!"

When Robert pulled down from the carriage a metal frame and then two wooden wheels, one with a set of peddles and the other without, I gasped in delight. Robert just smiled as he continued to pull down trunks and additional baggage. Rufus, the son of our stablemaster, was directed to the frame and wooden wheels and told to place them in the barn. Following behind Rufus was the old barn cat Buttons, an animal more motivated by food you could not find. The animal had learned early that leaving partial mice at the stablemasters door had his diet supplemented with milk. I found the behavior distasteful, but Rufus claimed his father thought that it was an incentive to hunt for further mice. I felt it incited the cat to leave both halves at different times instead.

Phillip, Rufus's father, climbed up on the carriage and led the horses into the barn. I was almost unable to contain myself at the sight of the wooden frame and the two large metal wheels. I had heard stories of the newer version of the device but had been afraid I would never see one, but as usual, Robert delighted in everything technical and had procured one for demonstration.

"Is that the French style Velocipede? You know it has been nicknamed as the 'boneshaker'! Please, can I ride it? Please!" I wheedled.

Robert smiled at me, his arms full of a luggage trunk. Before he could promise me a try at the new style bicycle, my hopes were dashed by Ms. Northrop.

"Heavens, no! That device is most unladylike. It would be one thing if it were one of the four-wheeled devices, those can be used in a most lady-like manner, but a dandy-horse? No."

While the Colonel made small talk with Ms. Northrop, and Robert carried his and his uncle's luggage inside, I stood there and gazed forlornly at the barn. It would be wonderful to watch his demonstration with the new conveyance, but I itched to ride it myself. I knew it wouldn't be a comfortable ride, the nickname of 'boneshaker' made sense with hard wooden wheels and little suspension, but the very nature of it would make it an adventure. I could almost feel the wind through my hair as I flew around the courtyard in my mind.

When Rufus placed the frame against one of the stalls inside the barn, just within view, I decided. I would wait until everyone was distracted inside the house, then I would try my hand at riding the velocipede.

Chapter 2

Nearly instantly, my plans to ride the bicycle were thwarted. Everyone withdrew to the drawing room, taking tea as well as some of the cookies I had stolen earlier. Emma must have heard the arrivals, figured out that everyone would need a moment of relaxation after the trip, and prepared the tea for that precise reason. That was Emma, prompt, prepared, and filled with forethought. If I didn't love her to death, it would drive me insane.

I noticed that Ms. Northrop marked the prepared tea as well, she had probably been waiting to berate Emma. It seemed that lately, she was waiting to swoop in and harangue any of the servants at any moment. If Father were here that would never be allowed, but then, if Father were here, many things would be different. Robert and Annie had been preparing to wed for years, but Robert's medical studies had been a higher priority up till now. Combined with Father's absence, and other issues, they would have been happy to remain unwed for years still.

Everyone settled down for a spot of tea, while mine was quaffed the moment attention had drifted away; I was prepared to exit the conversation as soon as possible. My plans hadn't counted on Annie leaving her room. Entering the room, she performed according to her training. Smiling with her head held high, she paused at the entrance to the lounge before stepping into the room. The Colonel, of course, pulled himself to his feet without hesitation, bowing at the waist stiffly, his hand held white gripped on his beloved cane. Even while he strained to bend at so low an angle, he made every appearance that it was a simple maneuver. Annie managed to smile at his action even as small lines crinkled at the edges of her eyes. I could tell she knew what the act had cost the Colonel in pain, but then, the man had fought a battle with a bullet in his leg, he was familiar with both suffering and duty. Requesting he not bow to save him the pain, was something no one in the room would do. He had his pride and his honour, and we all cherished him for it.

Robert, on the other hand, shot to attention at Annie's entrance, his bow deep and florid. The returning gentle head bob hid the slight upturn of her smile as well as the continuing frown hidden in her eyes. I was not too fond of the way she would hide behind the formal rules and etiquette. When Father told us he had been requested by the Queen to return to India, she had followed all the politeness required. She had smiled, she had said the opinion Father had expected, but she couldn't keep the tears from falling. I could see the sadness even now, her smile being far less an indicator of her feelings than her eyes.

After the usual pleasantries about the trip -good weather, pleasing to be free of the London smog, and so on- the Colonel explained their early arrival before the rest of the party. Not that it was such an arduous trip as all that, merely a couple of days by carriage. He first presented his congratulation card for Annie, while Robert politely slid the bag of gifts to Ms. Northrop. The requirement to gift the servants of your host had been one etiquette requirement I had always thought appropriate. I would have to try and peek at the contents later, maybe see what Robert had set aside for Emma.

The Colonel, in his usual boisterous and roundabout manner, explained that the two were here to greet us privately before the rest descended upon us, as well as to assist in any preparations which might be necessary. The last was said politely, and I knew the two had no ill will, but Ms. Northrop was finding it difficult to contain her sour look at the pronouncement of the family requiring assistance. If she hadn't fired so many servants, something that was supposed to be Owen's job, not hers, then it wouldn't be necessary. When I made such faces with guests, she would run me through polite conversation behavior later; somehow, I didn't think she would be forced to do the same.

I wanted to go outside. I could practically hear the call of the bike. I wanted to see how the frame worked and connected to the wheels. Was the structure like the older models, made from cast iron with the wheels bolted directly to the frame? Could it reach half the speed of a horse with a peddle configuration? What would it feel like to go that fast by my efforts alone? I had been so distracted that I had missed Emma's entrance, but the men rising roused me from my daydreams.

"A light luncheon has been prepared in the dining room. We have light vegetable soup with cucumber sandwiches. If there is something else you would like, I would be happy to oblige," Emma said as she avoided eye contact.

Robert nodded to Emma as he offered his arm to my sister, but his eyes never left Emma's retreating form. The Colonel, of course, led Ms. Northrop into the dining room. I was tempted to sneak away, but there was no way that my absence from lunch would be missed. After lunch, though it was likely that our guests would require light entertainment like cards or such, I would be able to escape. A quick trip for my adventuring clothes, a little time spent attaching the wheels, and I would be off and up and down the front drive. As a bonus, the game room was an interior room and had no windows. If there had been more men present, then the plan would have never worked, they would have retired to the study leaving the ladies together.

While lunch was light and enjoyable, there was a sour note to the whole affair. Twice during lunch, Owen entered the dining room then exited again to retrieve food which had not been requested. While no one commented on the head butlers slip up, they had all noticed it. Annie was barely able to keep herself from crying, and even Robert looked uncomfortable. He had spent nearly as much time around Owen as a boy as my sister and I had. The only one who could spend any time caring for him lately was Emma. As much as the social strata separated us from our childhood friend, it also allowed her to care for Owen without interference.

"A toast," the Colonel said while raising his teacup in a self-deprecating manner, "to the joining of our two families. I've considered you ladies like daughters for many years, and I'm glad that soon, Annie will be a Collingwood."

With a few murmurs of agreement, everyone sipped at their tea. Robert's cup hid his frown, but it was still clear to anyone who knew him. Which, of course, meant Ms. Northrop missed it entirely.

Turning to Robert, she queried, "Tell me, Mr. Collingwood, what are your plans for after your marriage? Will you be taking up residence within the Blythe estate or will Ms. Blythe be moving to the Collingwood home? Given the current distastefulness and your studies, that is."

If a mouse had decided to run through the attic, I would be afraid that everyone would be able to hear it at that moment. To discuss finances, even so obliquely, at a luncheon was crass beyond words. To have a woman initiate such a conversation was worse, but to do so in such a direct and frankly offensive way? Crass. I could have run through the room in my adventuring pants and not generate the same level of silence. Our Governess was technically only included in the luncheon as a pairing for the Colonel. Ms. Northrop's social standing was no higher than Emma's, and she would never have asked such impertinent questions.

Gamely, Robert responded, "Hmm, I do believe that Annie would prefer to stay with her sister for the time being. I will be finished studying at Oxford within the year, and then I will be setting up a practice."

At that, Ms. Northrop relaxed in her seat, and the conversation continued, but I couldn't get the moment out of my mind. I was sure none there would talk of it, the marriage was in the best interest of the Collingwood family, but her rude behavior was so very unlike the Governess. Annie seemed to find her fiance's response to her liking as well. My sister gave a small tight smile to me and then a subtle nod to Robert in thanks. No one missed this little exchange, but it was ignored for further polite conversation.

After finishing our lunch repast, the men rose to go to the game room. Both men wore evening black, so did not need to change, but my sister, Ms. Northrop, and I could not say the same. Emma's timing was perfect as ever, planned, and meticulous. There was not a second where she was alone with Robert, nor a moment where he could greet her as she crossed his path. The dance of avoidance was so perfect it almost appeared as if by chance, except for Robert's frown and Emma's careful blank-faced sadness.

My heart ached to see my friends so hurt, but there was little which could be done about it. I had told Annie that she should refuse to go through with the marriage, but she would hear nothing of it. Where I had found my taste for adventure from Father's military stories, she had found her sense of honour. Where I had found a resolve to explore the world, she had found the shackles for her own life within Father's wishes. Robert was just the same; his family came before all. The two of them were of a type. Such similarities made them stalwart friends. Emma had a different sense of honour, one tempered by practicality, entirely unlike the other two.

While Annie and Ms. Northrop softly discussed which dress to change into before returning to the game room with the men, I slowed to let the other two drift ahead. If the Governess failed to notice my absence, then on my return I could claim to be returning to my reading. Humorously enough, I would be changing just as the others were. My outfit would be unlikely to meet Ms. Northrop's approval though.

Softly I closed the wooden door to my room and crossed the antique floor rug to my wardrobe. With little care I ripped off my pre-luncheon dress, my dark tresses caught momentarily within the lace of the dress. The sting of the pulled hair was oddly pleasing when compared to the mild numbness of my days. Yanking on my pants first, I checked to be sure the thick black belt was sitting at the proper length. I had measured, and cut, and trimmed, but I had no chance actually to assemble the outfit in its fullness. The white dress shirt was buttoned up quickly, the unfamiliar arrangement of buttons on the opposite side made the process awkward. An unladylike snort of amusement burst from my lips as I fumbled the alignment badly enough that I had to unbutton and rebutton the last few. Topping the outfit was a thick folded cap, oversized and almost ridiculous with my long curls hanging behind. The last item was my riding boots, high ankle, and low soled.

With a kick, I knocked my discarded dress across the floor in a careless manner. Marching down the hallway and out the backway, found me exiting the mansion on the far side from the barn. My exit left me with a short trip in the shadow of the building to the stable area. I listened, but I didn't hear either Rufus or Philip. Odds were that Philip had decided to get some of the grounds cleaned up and was employing Rufus for it as well. I felt guilty over that. Philip was not a groundskeeper; he had been hired to manage the horses. Father would have never allowed such a disruption of the servants as Ms. Northrop had caused, but Father wasn't here, and she was. Philip was probably willing to suffer the indignity to avoid being fired. Jobs were scarce at the moment, at least jobs which included room and board for a man and his son.

Arranged with two main areas, one side for the storage of carriages and the other outfitted with stalls, the stables were often used as a place to store large and bulky items. It was likely that the bike would be in one of the empty stalls in the back. The horse stall was probably not the best place to store such a device, it was massive and of heavy construction in wrought iron with wooden carriage wheels. Poor Robert had barely been able to lower each piece down from the roof of the carriage with both hands, and the man was in excellent shape. Little Rufus had struggled when moving it and had stopped to rest more than once.

The last stall had the heavy metal frame and wheels. Struggling, sweat already breaking out on my face, I managed to drag the frame from the hay. Hauling on the frame, I lifted the nearly sixty-five kilogram wrought iron structure upright. Inside the stall, I found the front wheel, the one with the peddles, and pulled it out and arranged it next to the frame. The front half of the structure would need to be lifted and then set down on the wheel before the locking nut applied, then the process would have to be repeated for the rear wheel. The direct wood to metal construction without a spring, like in a carriage, was what gave the bicycle its signature nickname. Together, the entire device would weight in excess of ninety kilograms.

Returning to the stall, I heard the clatter of the frame falling and the crunch of snapping wood. The sound of the breaking device, a conveyance that was expensive and was likely purchased solely for my amusement, had me frozen in horror. My eagerness had caused the velocipede to break. Hopefully, it was just the wheel, and a cooper could fix it, but either way, it would be an expensive proposition that was entirely my fault. Before I could exit the stall to check, I heard the crunch of boots on gravel.

"Rufus! Look at it! You were told to put that fool device

away!"

The sound of Philip berating his son had me ducking down in the stall. The two had returned just in time to notice the broken bicycle, leaving me hiding in shame in the stall. I couldn't keep hiding here, it wasn't Rufus' fault, and I wouldn't let Ms. Northrop remove Philip for my actions, but my shame had me hesitating. The sound of a slap propelled me out of the stall and between Philip and Rufus.

"Wait, he didn't do anything; it was my fault. I'm sorry!" I said.

Philip was red-faced, his large hands clenched in anger, while he backed away. His eyes raked over my clothing, his eyes locked for longer than was appropriate to my pant covered legs. When I turned to check Rufus, his eyes were averted, but his pointed avoidance of looking at me made me aware that my rash protection of the child had left my rear directly in his face. Being alone with a man, even with his son present, especially in such compromising clothing, had me flushed red in embarrassment. Worse, I would have to explain to Robert what had happened and entreat him to protect Philip from any reprisals from Ms. Northrop. Everything would be much easier if Robert could be enlisted to handle Father's financials -preferably with Ms. Northrop no longer employed- but his studies and his families financial issues made that unpalatable.

"Excuse me, Ms...I didn't know that you were...uh. That is, me and Rufus here will uh," said Philip Nye as he tried to find the formal response to the situation. One which did not have him or his son staring at his employer's scandalously dressed daughter.

"I'll go tell Robert that I have accidentally damaged his property. I will make it clear that Rufus had nothing to do with my actions. Excuse me," I said.

Annie had an overdose of honour and responsibility, but I

didn't lack it. I just tried to temper it with adventure and fun. This situation was one I had to own up to. Likely, Robert would be annoyed but forgiving, the bicycle being mostly an exhibition to entertain me in the first place. Annie would be upset, probably worse than the situation warranted, but it would be a safe way to let out some of her sadness. Ms. Northrop, though, she would use this mistake in every diatribe from here out.

Kicking a few of the larger stones on the walk to the mansion, I tried not to stomp. Pulling open the large mansion door, I cringe when I noticed Owen at the foot of the stairs giving me a curious look.

"Hmm, an interesting clothing choice," he said before he smiled and continued down the hall.

I planned to change out of my adventure clothes and into 'appropriate' stable clothes which would avoid at least one diatribe. Before I reached my room, with my hand in the air reaching for the door handle, the world stuttered and stopped.

It was as if the air became a cage and locked me in place. It was more than just the air, my muscle locked up, my eyes remained focused ahead, and the breath in my lungs became stone. Even my heart lay silent in my chest. Panicking I strained my muscles to move but nothing shifted even minutely. The dust suspended in the air, shining in a stray shaft of light, remained perfectly frozen.

While I was in that world of a static moment, a large blue box with a square, evenly spaced writing, appeared in front of me.

Chapter 3

Everything I was screamed that I should be dying, my heart didn't beat, my lungs didn't pump air, and the whole world was silent. The only thing I had to focus on beyond my frozen existence was the box of text hovering in front of my eyes.

This simulation has been sold to eX-Tre Entertainment and will become the basis for 'Age of Victoria!', an old school immersive MMORPG set in the Victorian Age upon a backdrop of a magical apocalypse and the return of the Old Ones.

The Old Ones have found a crack within the Veil. Magic has returned to earth, and the collective unconscious has awoken. Unfiltered and unconstrained magic has engulfed the land, giving rise to Monsters of both Creatures and Men. Can you survive the horrors of the Old Ones?

As an NPC within the beginning of 'Age of Victoria,' you will be given limited options of freedom and advancement. Your initial class has been selected by the Overmind AI as 'Warrior' due to emotional or significant actions taken within the last twenty-four hours. Your activity was:

Protecting NPC 'Rufus Nye' by drawing Agro.

<Warrior class selected>

Warrior's are masters of armor and weapons, skilled at protecting their team members and providing defensive buffs through war-cries. The signature skill of the warrior is [Taunt] and its derivatives.

Warriors have no limitation on their weapons or armor.

Warriors can wear cloth, leather, chain, or plate armor, though usually, they wear only the most massive and durable of plate armor.

Warriors are not restricted in weapon selection. Warriors may use the smallest dirk to the greatest two-handed sword.

Warriors can learn all defensive skills.

Warriors do not have mana. Instead, they have Rage, a resource which rises as the warrior takes or delivers damage.

Warriors do not gain many of the damage increasing skills of other melee classes. The signature DPS advantage for warriors is the ability to wield a Two-Handed weapon in the primary weapon slot while also wielding a one-handed weapon or shield in the secondary weapon slot.

Warriors are suggested to work with groups. Warriors are rated as 'Weak' soloers.

Currently, 'Victoria Marie Blythe' has been set as a Zone-Locked Combat NPC. Zone-Locked NPCs are restricted from leaving their zone and are predominantly responsible for Quests and Shops. Zone-Locked NPC's have ten days to reach level ten to remove the zone lock restriction. Zone-Locked NPCs have a slow respawn rate, and if the Old Ones encroach on that zone, they no longer respawn. After the tutorial, the event 'The Great Cleansing' will start, any NPC who fails to survive the event will be permanently deleted.

Reading the text was odd. I couldn't move my eyes, but my vision was focused on the next word that I was trying to understand. It was like trying to focus on a bit of text caused it to shift to be in the center of my vision. I had never believed the women who had claimed to suffer from hysteria. The idea of something could be so upsetting that it would cause them to scream and faint was laughable. If I could move at this moment, I would be diagnosed with hysteria in a moment. Was the world ending? Was the apocalypse at hand? I was no longer a minor noble but was now a warrior? What did that even mean? The last line though was chilling, I can't imagine why they would phrase it that way -deleted- but not surviving was a very clear message. Before I could work myself into a tizzy, a new box appeared that was much like the previous one. This box was titled 'tutorial,' while the previous box had been untitled.

In the upper left-hand corner of your vision, three bars should exist. The top red bar is your health, when it reaches zero from injury or spells, you die.

Sure enough, three bars appeared. The topmost bar was red and full, inside the bar of red was two numbers with a divider between them; sixty-five and sixty-five. Below that was another bar, but this one had five odd bubbles inside it, none of them were full, and this bar had no numbers. The final bar was yellow and said one-hundred percent.

The second bar is your Rage Meter. Each bubble is a Mark of Rage which a warrior can use for their skills. A Warrior increases their Rage through taking or delivering damage. With skills a warrior can increase the number of Marks of Rage they have. Currently, you can have a maximum of five Marks of Rage.

The fact that the tutorial felt the need to inform me that I could have only a maximum of five marks was infuriating, I was perfectly capable of seeing it with my own eyes. It felt like whoever was writing the text was looking down on me. They were like every tutor who thought that women did not deserve to learn particular subjects, the things I was most eager to learn. Whoever wrote that text would probably be good friends with Ms. Northrop.

The final bar is your stamina. During a battle, stamina regenerates at a slow rate while attacking and a faster pace while defending. Outside of combat, stamina will regenerate at high speed.

Running and walking have no stamina cost. Non-standard movements will experience a stamina cost relative to their difficulty: swimming, crawling, jumping, climbing, crouch-walking, etc.

That was an intriguing message. The idea of being able to run as long as I wanted without feeling tired was interesting, that is if this entire thing was not a stress-induced hallucination. If this was an apocalypse, and especially one with monsters, then being able to run non-stop without tiring was a good thing.

A moment after I finished the message in the textbox, something new floated into view in the upper right-hand corner of my vision. Trying to look at it caused it to swing out into my vision further and ignoring it caused it to swing back above. The same happened with the three bars, something I hadn't noticed before.

In the upper right-hand corner of your vision are a compass and minimap. Quest markers, areas you have explored, and areas of interest will be displayed in this area once you have visited them.

The circle of the minimap looked useful. There was a bronze looking loop, marked with an arrow which was pointing off to the North-West, while inside the loop was an image of the layout of the mansion as if seen from the sky. In the very center of the minimap was a blue dot, which I thought was supposed to represent me. Far to the North-East on the minimap, almost to the edge of it, was a marker of a cave centered in the clearing in the woods.

Now think 'character' to display the character screen.

I was going crazy. I had to be. The content of one's soul and mind was inviolate, yet this message wanted me to think something and command it. The chances of me merely being insane and talking to myself, most likely reduced to paroxysms of tears and gibbering, were rising. When I finally broke down and tried to think 'character,' a new window appeared before me.

It had a little model of my body, rotating within my view, and there were slots for each item I was wearing. The knowledge that the creator of this text could see down to my underclothes and likely beyond left me faint.

The tutorial didn't care how I felt. It waited until I had overcome whatever had delayed me, then it continued. It went on to show me how to open my inventory, assign stat's (giving only the most basic of descriptions), how to join groups, and send chat messages. It went on and on, but finally, the text ended. I wanted to take a deep breath, but I was still locked in place.

To my horror, everything around me started to fade away. The darkness slipped across, from the edge of my vision until only the smallest dot of light was at the center of my view, and then, it was gone.

The return of the light caused me to blink wildly in confusion before I realized I *could* blink. More than blinking, I could breathe and move and look around. The ground was a flat grey stone without any distinguishing feature. The sky above me was black, but where I stood was in a circle of light which seemed to cut off at thirty feet leaving a ring of light surrounded by the dark. But the nightmare was not over. The 'quest window' opened at that moment and filled in with a simple objective, 'finish fight tutorial.' After I read the objective, a bright flash of light covered my body. When the light faded away, I wore a chest plate and was holding a large sword and shield. A chest plate like this would have cost a fortune and been worn only by the strongest of men, but for some reason, I felt comfortable, the armor felt light and easy to move in. Swishing the sword back and forth I could tell that I would be able to wield it effortlessly. I had no skill, but the sword itself felt less like a five-foot-long bar of steel and instead light like an umbrella or cane. That is when the squeaking behind me drove me out of my distraction.

Whipping around, I crouched slightly, pulling the large plate of the shield in front of my body with the sword held up right next to my chest. I had no experience with the sword, but I had fantasized about being a dashing knight more than once. My favorite daydream was of saving a princess from a dragon, then imagining her look of annoyance when her savior turned out to not be prince charming and that instead I had only wanted the dragon's gold horde.

From out of the darkness, a giant black rat slunk into the light. With a head the size of a grapefruit and long black whiskers, the rat's nose twitched as its beady eyes squinted at me. The claws on the rat's paws were sharp and scratched at the stone ground, its tail whip-like and trailing into the darkness even as the rat's body entered the light. Hissing once, the monster charged. The hiss and charge unnerved me, but I only took one step back. From there, I tucked the shield in close and raised my sword slightly as I prepared to bring it down and end the rat's life.

At the last moment, the rat jumped and tried to scramble its claws across the metal of my shield and over to attack my face. My sword flew through the air, almost without any effort of my own, and the edge sliced into the side of the rat. The impact threw up a small red five which floated away from the rat. Suddenly in my mind's eye, the combat log window appeared, and my awareness was drawn to try and understand the unnatural event.

Victoria [Warrior lvl 1] slashes training_rat_1 for 5 damage.

I smiled as the recognition of my achievement scrolled away within the text, even as my vision was unhampered by the combat log window. Somehow I was reading the log, but not actually seeing it. My distraction caused me to fail to notice the rat had recovered from the injury and was prepared for another attack. The only part of my body with armor protection was my chest and what I could cover with my shield. The rat went for my neck, and it connected, its outsized incisors latching on to my throat and tearing away without a splash of blood but with my body convulsing in pain.

Traing_rat_1 critically bites Victoria [Warrior lvl 1] for 3 damage.
All damage nullified during the battle tutorial.

The thought that I wouldn't die from such a wound was uplifting, but the idea that such a critical attack was only three damage and that it felt so horrible that I had feared for my life, left me shaky. My distraction cost me again, the rat rushed forward and tried to bite me on the ankle. His teeth grabbed my pants and missed the flesh of my leg, a white zero floated away from the miss. Screaming with rage and fear, I retaliated, swatting the rat away with my shield.

Victoria [Warrior lvl 1] shield bashes training_rat_1 for 1 damage.

Once I found the rhythm of the fight, it was over rather quickly. Another two points of damage had the rat dying shortly. Once the rat died, a golden one hundred floated away from the rat's corpse and into my body. Another golden fifty appeared from the quest window and drifted through me as well. Finally, a new objective appeared in the quest log that I needed to 'loot' the rat. Reaching down to the rat, the brush of my hand and my intent caused a new window to appear with only rat whiskers on the rat's corpse. When I had the intention to loot the whiskers, they appeared in my inventory, and the window vanished. That finished the final quest objective, and another golden fifty filled me. My log said I needed another one thousand eight hundred experience to reach level two. Standing there, the corpse of my enemy slowly fading away, I just breathed deep. My lungs pumping air like a bellows and my heart pounding in my chest, my skin oddly without sweat. While the entire time, a smile spread from one side of my face to the other.

While I was standing there breathing and recovering from my conquest, my body froze again, then faded away as it had before. When the light bloomed from my chest and expanded again to fill my world, I found myself frozen where I had stood before, in my adventuring clothes, with one hand reaching for the door handle of my room. With a stutter, the world continued, and screams of horror started from downstairs. Spinning around, I dashed down the stairs and rushed towards the game room, the entire time a smile spread across my face.

Chapter 4

The game room was paneled with dark wood and dark tones, it was one of our father's favorite places in the house. Most summers when father was home we would find him sitting in one of the giant stuffed chairs, smoking his pipe while reading some thick leather-bound tome. This and the library were the only rooms in the house that father allowed smoking, a leftover from mother's rules. The scent of the smoke had impregnated itself into the chairs, and the rugs, even the thick oak card and chess tables had a faint whiff of the thick pipe smoke. The scent reminded me of father making this a difficult room to stay in, it was like he hid in every chair, but was nowhere to be found.

Ms. Northrop was on her knees, her ankle-length dress disheveled and untucked laying around her as she screamed and hid her face in her hands. Her screams were interspersed with gasping sobs, her voice cracking in distress. The Colonel and Robert were both standing over her with careful, watchful eyes. Annie was sitting listless and confused in one of the stuffed chairs. The oddest part of the scene was not the screaming, it wasn't Annie's glazed gaze at her cupped hands, it wasn't even the Colonel's unsheathed sword. The oddest part was the words hovering over each of their heads.

The Colonel
Markus Collingwood

Annie Blythe

Robert Collingwood

Rebecca Northrop

As I slowly moved around the room, my gaze focused on the words, the text over each of their heads shifted and turned so that it was always directly over them and visible to read. At one point, the words over the Colonel's head should have moved through a support pillar, but the text didn't, it remained in front of it and readable.

The text was odd, but it appeared to be harmless. It was interesting that the white words over the Colonel's head had his title. Looking above I noticed that I lacked any kind of floating text which confused me.

Ms. Northrop eventually stopped screaming and was reduced to whimpering and crying about the rat.

"It just kept biting me. It hurt, oh god, it hurt!"

I realized that Ms. Northrop had fought a rat the same as I had. Both the Colonel and Robert seemed unsurprised which had me turning to Annie.

"Did you fight a rat also Annie?" I asked.

At my question, Annie seemed to come out of her confusion and looked me in the eyes. With a slow nod, my sister held up her left hand in a cupped motion. Before I could ask her what she was doing, her eyes narrowed in concentration, and a ball of glowing flame appeared over her hand. The ball of flickering death slowly rotated above her palm, the air roiled away from the fire, but Annie remained unmoved. Smiling at me while holding the ball of flames outstretched in front of her, she closed her hand and snuffed the fire out.

"How did you do that Annie?" Robert asked, his mouth hanging open in astonishment.

My sister's face was beaming as she stared at her hands and at

Robert's approach she looked up and answered, "The text said I was a wizard. I...have spells for the elements. I just...knew how to throw a fireball. I wanted it burnt, and I just did it. My important event was lighting the lamps in the morning. I've always liked to light the lamps since I was a little girl; I love the warm glow. So now...now I'm a wizard."

Annie sounded both excited and concerned. I matched her concern. Seeing my sister, thin and weak, fearlessly handle a ball of fiery death with a near-manic smile of discovery had been deeply disturbing. Before I could ask further questions, Emma appeared in the door of the game room. Emma was pale and upset, but she still wore her usual reserved look. Once she noticed Robert was there and unharmed, she moved forward but stopped next to me and assessed if anyone was injured.

Emma also had the bright white text floating over her head. It was odd that everyone had the floating words except for me. When I mentioned the disconcerting difference to Robert, the following discussion became even more concerning. Everyone could see the name floating above everyone...except for their own text. While discussing the weird labels, our voices were starting to rise, the confusion and upset being evident among us. When Owen walked in, our voices again moderated down to a lower tone. Owen had always brought a sense of calm to a room, and since his decline, no one had wanted to cause him distress by being loud or boisterous.

During our discussion, the Colonel stalked around the room, his limp exacerbated by his speed and his failure to sheath his sword-cane. His movements were hypnotic, back and forth, his actions like the lion in the cage at the London fair I had seen as a girl. My staring caused a new text window to appear before me.

The Colonel
Markus Collingwood
Warrior - Lvl 3

This would be a difficult opponent.

The final line was in a bright yellow text. Experimenting, I focused in the same way on Ms. Northrop, and the results left me surprised.

Rebecca Northrop
Rogue - Lvl 1
This would be an even fight.

The last line was given in a white text similar to the rest, but the real question was why Ms. Northrop was a rogue.

"Why are you a rogue?"

I hadn't meant to ask out loud, but my question could have been a pistol shot for the sudden silence it caused. Ms. Northrop silenced her mutterings, her surprised eyes staring into my own then glancing around at everyone as they stared at her. I could tell the moment that the Colonel had figured out how to get the same information window to appear. He marched forward like an unleashed beast, his sudden grip on Ms. Northrop leaving the woman gasping as he yanked her to her feet.

"I'm a warrior, I think of my battles every day. Annie lit lamps to become a wizard. What. Did. You. Do?"

The rage in the Colonel's voice was unlike anything I had heard from the man I thought of as an unofficial uncle. This voice was the sound of the military man I had always known him to be. This was not the boisterous and cheerful man, the loud and jolly cheer which signified safety. This was the sound of violence made manifest.

"I…oh god…it was…Owen wasn't taking care of things, so I did it," Rebecca said, her voice starting frightened and ending with the usual confident self-assurance in her own righteousness.

"So you steal from the Lieutenant-General while you were

supposed to be protecting and teaching his daughters?" The Colonel asked as he threw Rebecca away from himself.

The Colonel leaned over Rebecca, his large frame seeming to grow even larger as he hovered over the prone woman. Without warning a deep tone strummed out as if a giant bell was struck within my chest. For a moment the world hung in silence, then a new text appeared in front of me. From the edge of my vision, I could see everyone else shift or straighten, telling me that they got the new text as well.

Start of New Global Event - The Great Cleansing!
The Veil has torn, mana has entered the world again. Collecting at points of importance to the collective unconscious, mana forms into the creatures of myth and legend. These monsters and agents of chaos have been tainted by the malignant aura of the Old Ones to act against humans and further weaken the veil. The Old Ones have focused the first tide of mana to create an initial wave of death and destruction. Will you survive the Great Cleansing?

Objective:
Survive three waves of monsters. Levels and numbers depend on the density of the population in the Zone.
Wave 0/3 Survived.

The words 'Wave 0/3 Survived' flashed for a moment then shrunk to hover directly below my compass. Each of us stood silently, waiting for something to happen. The calm was broken with the sound of shattering glass and howling coming from the entrance hallway. The Colonel lunged to the doorway, pulling me unceremoniously behind him as he strode forward. He cast a quick glance down the hall which had the sounds of screaming rising in volume. Robert grabbed one of the giant stuffed leather chairs and shoved it into the doorway while the Colonel backed up to make room, his eyes flashing around the room before he returned to staring at the door.

Unconcerned with the stuffed leather chair, a warty green little man grabbed the back of the seat while nearly vaulting over and in through the door. The green man-thing landed awkwardly, one leg on the seat and the other on the armrest. In one arm he carried a crude sword with notches in two places while in the other he held a small buckler made of wood. His body was distorted, with arms too long, legs too short, head too broad, and bald with large ears. Above the monsters head was the floating text the same as everyone else.

Goblin Raider

When I focused on the monster, as I had when looking at Rebecca, an information window opened.

Goblin Raider
Warrior - Lvl 1
This would be an even fight.

While I was confused trying to make sense of this new world, the Colonel stepped forward and drove his unsheathed sword cane into the eye of the goblin. A red number fourteen popped from the goblin's head and floated away. The disgusting creature screeched then fell, but his death failed to slow his brethren. The next monster appeared much like the one before, his head slightly different in shape but generally he seemed a clone of the goblin before him. His actions also mirrored the first, grabbing the back of the chair he tried to throw himself over only to receive a slashing cut from the Colonel's sword. This time a red ten rose from the Goblin, the injury leaving no mark and seemingly wholly ignored. Before the Colonel could recover from his initial swipe, the goblin swung his own sword into the Colonel's side. Grunting the Colonel reached for his wound, but finding no injury, he roared out his anger and returned the blow to the goblin.

While the goblin had caused a red three to leave the Colonel, the Colonel's return blow delivered a red eleven and death.

Three more monsters attempted to climb the chair, now overloaded by corpses, but before they could vault the obstacles as the others had, Robert chucked another chair at the entrance. His makeshift barricade was lodged awkwardly into the door, but it's usefulness was unlikely to last. The monsters wildly swung at the chairs, their blows leaving leather slashed, wood breaking, and bits of the cushion flying.

All I could do was stand there watching as the Colonel fought as a man possessed. I was frozen in fright, entirely unlike with the giant rat. I had no weapon, no spells like Annie, and no armor. This wasn't like the ring of darkness and light where I could pretend to be someone else and act out my dreams, this was my family home, and monsters were fighting through the door to kill us.

Robert looked as frightened as Annie, Rebecca, Emma, and if I was honest, as frightened as I probably looked as well. The difference was that Robert was doing something. He wasn't as capable as the Colonel, but he was doing something. With a wild look on his face, Robert reached into his double-breasted waistcoat and pulled his Webley pistol and took aim. When Robert pulled the trigger, the gun and his hands flashed red, and the weapon fell through his grip and to the ground. Robert's mouth gaped wide, his eyes staring, his hands held out and clenched while the pistol sat on the rug. Robert repeated the action twice more while the Colonel struck at the small creatures as they pried their way through the blocked doorway. After the third time pulling the trigger and the gun falling from his hands, Robert cursed and reached for the card table which he lifted into the air and slammed into the ground until the table broke. Grasping one of the broken legs he joined his uncle at defending the doorway with heavy blows of his impromptu club.

After a few more minutes of battle, the monsters were dead,

most of the bodies faded while two remained. When Robert touched one of the corpses, a crude shield appeared in his hands before the body faded and disappeared. The Colonel looted the other corpse, it's body yielding a small hard leather cap.

The sudden silence was loud, each of us breathing quickly in fear, the sound of our panting the only noise any of us could make. Before we could calm, the quest objective updated, the zero becoming a one. The moment dragged out, each of us looking to the others as we recognized what the change in the objective list meant. Our fears were confirmed when a roar, louder than the howls of the goblins, broke through our stillness.

Chapter 5

The roar from outside had us ducking and preparing for another attack from the door. For a brief moment of silence, we paused, not even daring to breathe. The silence was broken by a loud crashing sound followed by a child's scream. There was no hesitation, without discussion we all rushed towards the door, the Colonel flinging the stacked chair barricade away with two wild swings of his free hand. In passing, I grabbed Robert's pistol, knowing somehow instinctively that I could use it though it was in some way a weak weapon. Going outside was a dangerous idea, going unarmed was foolishness. None of the others followed us out, they each huddled around Rebecca.

The Colonel rushed down the hallway like a rampaging injured bull, his momentum only slowing at the doorway to check the field of battle. His sudden stop caused a flinch to ripple across his shoulders, visible even from down the hallways. The Colonel's pause was only for a moment, and then he turned and lumbered towards the barn. Robert, fast on his uncle's heels, led with his shield held in front, crude club following. I loved Robert to death, he had been a friend since childhood, but compared to the expressive masculinity of father and the Colonel, he had always seemed wishy-washy. His show of bravery changed my mind.

Audibly gulping, I followed in the wake of the two defenders.

The stables had been built so that a small stablemaster's apartment was above the tack room. Fully updated with a water closet, it was the most significant perk of the job. The door to the apartment was shattered with pieces of the door strewn about. Climbing the stairs was the back side of a sizeable greenish brute dressed in cloth rags. The humanoid monstrosity was so tall and wide it barely fit in the doorway. Turning its body sideways slightly it started to climb.

Focusing, I tried to read one of these monster's information. With a bit of practice, I could imagine this would become second nature.

Orc Pillager
Warrior - Lvl 2
This would be a difficult opponent.

The difficulty line was yellow as it had been when inspecting the Colonel. The orc was trying to climb further up the stairs, but its forward progress was blocked by its compatriot in front. The apartment had been modernized, but the narrow stairway remained the same as before it had been updated. It appeared that this was an unexpected benefit. Three of the orcs were crammed into the stairwell. The lead orc was trying to bash through the door at the top of the stairs, but its efforts were hindered by the awkward angle and lack of bracing.

The Colonel grasped the strategic advantage of this situation and ruthlessly exploited it. Lunging his large body forward the Colonel's sword drove through the knee of the last orc on the stairs. Above the orc's head, two floating images appeared. One was a dripping drop of blood and the other a leg with manacle. Yanking his sword from the injured orc's body, the Colonel stabbed the orc in its unprotected side, killing it. The red thirteen which floated out of the orc didn't block the next orc in line. This monster was facing the Colonel and had the high ground, in its hand was a large knotted club. Before the Colonel could retreat the orc slammed his weapon into the Colonel's head. A floating image of a man's face with stars and a duck rotating around his head appeared. The weird image was joined by a red thirteen. The Colonel stumbling backward forced Robert to the side of the doorway. The Colonel's knee-high boots thumped on the flagstone entranceway as he nearly fell prone. The orc never hesitated in giving up its height advantage, it rushed through the doorway after the Colonel and pressed its advantage. Robert found himself behind the bruiser with access to the beasts unprotected head.

The loud sound of the orc's skull cracking rang out from Robert's full body swing. Robert had played cricket when he was younger, and his experience showed.

The first orc's body faded when it died, but this one remained. The sounds of the third orc's rampage above stopped. The silence had me squeezing the pistol's grip with white knuckles. I had never fired a gun before, but if the need occurred, I would. While Robert and I stood and prepared for the third adversary, the Colonel recovered from the stun he had received. Beyond a small mark on his forehead, he appeared amazingly healthy.

From within the entranceway, we could hear loud snorts; these were the sounds of the beast sniffing the air. Robert moved forward with his makeshift club and prepared himself to attack the final enemy when a loud inhuman roar of sheer rage started from above and lasted for seconds. All of us recoiled from the animalistic noise and scrambled further back in surprise as a loud crash came from inside. The sound of shattering wood was followed by bodies tumbling down the stairs. From within the entranceway appeared the orc with Philip Nye straddling him. An image of a screaming red human floated above the stablehand's head, his muscular arms cloaked in blurs of red as he pummeled the orc with fists grown massive and grotesque. The orc took blow after blow, his arms trapped uselessly under the stablemaster's knees, red fives and sevens floating away in a flurry of destruction. Soon the orc was dead and disappeared moments later.

Breathing heavily Mr. Nye stood, his body shrinking back to its standard size. Above his head, a new image appeared of a man trudging wearily under a load of weight.

"Rufus, get down here. Hurry!" called the Colonel as Robert helped a now staggering Mr. Nye.

My habit of focusing on everyone and anything showed me Mr. Nye's information.

Philip Nye
Berserker - Lvl 2
This would be a difficult opponent.

Philip Nye was a berserker. That would certainly explain the explosion of rage and violence that he delivered upon the monster.

With a repeat of the horror from before, the one in the quest objective became a two. Two waves survived, and shimmering into view in the courtyard was the third wave. The monster which coalesced out of the air was seven feet tall, a dark woody tan, and wearing only a loincloth. Its colossal body had scars and marks from numerous battles, and its belly was bulbous. The monster's arms were as thick as my waist, and it hunched forward allowing it a four-limbed gait. It appeared to be a melding of a rotund man and a gorilla.

Young Ogre
Berserker - Lvl 5
Prepare for death.

The brilliant crimson text describing our imminent death caused me to whimper.

The ogre's head whipped up, our eyes meeting. The pinprick black pupils floated in orbs of blood red. Nostrils flaring, the ogre opened its oversized jaw, the lips pulled back showing yellow and cracked teeth. With a howl of anger, the young ogre charged. I couldn't move, my body froze as death hurdled towards me. The Colonel never hesitated, he charged then braced as he extended his sword like a pikeman breaking a cavalry charge. The Colonel's movement altered the ogre's trajectory, but his sword failed to slow the beast. A red twenty-five floated away from the sword now embedded in the ogre's eye. An image of a man with an eye patch appeared over the beasts head along with the bleeding image, but its injury did not stop it from stomping over the Colonel. The red thirty which floated from the Colonel's prone form told the tale of how damaging that charge was.

The ogre stomped forward five or six paces before it slowed and turned, the embedded sword swinging around like a macabre weather vane. A small puff of a red five floating from the monsters head failed to distract it.

Baring its teeth the beast knuckle-walked forward to finish the beating of Markus' body. When Markus rolled over and stood, the ogre paused then hollered and swung at the Colonel's head. The Colonel took the blow across the jaw, his head whipping to the side. A ten floated away from his head; his health must be close to empty by this point. According to the tutorial, in this new world, zero health meant death.

Strange words flowed from Robert's mouth, a deep echo resonating from his tones. With Robert's words rising to a crescendo a white light appeared around the Colonel before a green twenty was sucked into his body.

The young ogre dropped the arm raised to beat the Colonel and turned on Robert. Leaning forward the beast froze and let loose a holler as the image of the screaming red human appeared above its head. A small bar over the image began to fill as the monster screamed. If the monstrosity performed the same crazed attack that Philip had, none of us would survive.

While the monster continued its rage-induced yell, I stepped forward and pushed the pistol into the ogre's ear and pulled the trigger. The gun kicked back as a red twenty-three drifted from the monster's ear. Multiple images appeared over the monsters head, a torn ear, a return of the swirling duck and stars, along with a large number two on the blood drop. The monster's roar was halted, and its head wobbled as it tried to turn toward its new attacker.

The presentation of the Colonel's sword was all I needed. Without thought, I dropped the mostly useless pistol and wrapped my hands around the sword and shoved with all my might. The red twenty-five was the last act needed to end its life. The golden one hundred and fifty floating into my body was anti-climatic compared to the fallen corpse. Reaching down I looted a chainmail armor from the monster, the shiny ringed tunic dropping into my inventory instantly.

"How did you do that Robert?" the Colonel asked.

Robert refused to meet our eyes. He held his club loosely in his hand while he stared at his shield. Before we could continue to question him, the quest objective updated.

The Great Cleansing!
Objective:
Survive three waves of monsters. Levels and numbers depend on the density of the population in the Zone.
Wave 3/3 Survived.

Reward: 1000 exp, class specific item.

With that, the event was over and the exp, the golden number one thousand, floated into my body. A flash of shimmering golden light swirled around my form, and I could feel a sudden burst of power ripple through me. Wondering what had happened, I brought up the log window as the tutorial had taught me.

Level up!

Victoria [Warrior lvl 2] - at level 10 NPC's will no longer be zone locked.
New Skills!
Gained Skill - Block.
Gained Skill - Kick.

Once I closed the log window a new window appeared, this one titled 'Reward.' Inside was a large sword, more meat cleaver than the refined lines of the Colonel's cane sword that he had nicknamed Eloise. Once I accepted my reward, the window disappeared and the weapon transferred to my inventory.

Rounding up Rufus we returned to the mansion. Despite the lack of a door, it was the sturdiest built building on the property. With some care, we should be able to block off the entrance using some of the larger furniture. It might not stop an ogre or even goblins, but it would give us enough warning to prepare to fight. While Rufus peppered his dad with questions, I stared at Robert's information.

Robert Collingwood
Cleric - Lvl 1
This opponent appears weaker than you.

While the last line in light blue text drew my eye, the word 'Cleric' answered at least a few of my questions. For whatever reason, it appeared a cleric could heal using the magic words Robert had spoke. Out of curiosity, I focused on Rufus and his information made me chuckle.

Rufus Nye
Beast Tamer - Lvl 1
This opponent appears weaker than you.

Rufus loved animals, and so the question of what he did to gain his class was easy to guess. More than once I had caught him feeding the barn cat Buttons.

My musings were interrupted by yelling and screaming coming from the ladies we had left behind while Owen just stood silently next to Annie. Our return silenced the screaming match. Emma looked over each of us from head to toe, but I noticed her eyes lingered on Robert more than anyone else. When she caught me watching her, she blushed and focused on the Colonel.

Resheathing 'Eloise,' the Colonel leaned on his cane. His movements had been better while fighting, but he seemed to be coming down from the battle rush that had allowed him to fight. The clothing the Colonel wore had a few smudges and wrinkles, but he remained almost pristine compared to the battle we had just fought. None of us appeared to have suffered more than a superficial wound during the fight even as we had taken damage which drove us nearly to death. Even the small bleeding headwound the Colonel had sported during the battle with the orcs was now gone without leaving a stain.

"Me and Robert will barricade the doors. We will huddle here and wait for our family to arrive, if they have survived the trip that is," the Colonel said.

Annie bit her knuckles in concern at this pronouncement, and well she should. With the doorways we had been able to fight our enemies one at a time, two at worst, the terrain acting to hinder the monsters movements and attack. Out in the open, the young ogre had bulled the Colonel over with little fanfare. If we had been mobbed by all of the goblins at once, we would have all died in short order. Our location had played as much in our survival as the lucky access to weapons.

Everyone agreed that we should huddle down and wait for rescue.

Glancing around I said, "I'm going upstairs to change."

The Colonel just nodded, my attire being scandalous but less important to him than the defenses. While the men turned to harvest material for a makeshift barricade, I raced to my room.

I had no intention of waiting for the others. The world had changed, and the rules were different. I had ten days to reach level ten or I would be stuck in this 'zone' forever as a merchant or 'quest giver.' That life wasn't for me. I wanted to explore. I wanted to see father again. I wanted more of the feeling of gaining a level. The rush of conquest at the moment I shoved that sword into the young ogre's face was like the thrill I felt as a young girl hearing father's war stories. I was the Warrior now, and the icon of the cave in my minimap told me exactly what I needed to do.

Chapter 6

"What are you planning Vick?" asked Emma as she stood in the doorway to my room.

I ducked at the sound of my nickname, like a little kid caught with their hand in the cookie jar. I had always hated the diminutive form of my name, 'Vicky,' it always seemed to me like someone was calling me a little girl. The three knew that, and they always called me 'Vick,' something that polite society would find distasteful and crass.

"Emma, you called me 'Vick.' You haven't called me that in a year at least," I said, trying desperately to distract Emma from my plans.

Emma's face scrunched up in a frown, her little nose wrinkling in the unfamiliar facial expression. She was holding her arms clasped around her chest, and I didn't think it was just the attack and the windows which was the cause. She had been upset when she entered the game room as well.

"I…I buried a dead mouse from the pantry this morning."

The nonsequitur threw me for a moment. It was a very 'Emma' thing to do, she had always felt strongly about animals and had even buried two barn cats when they died. But that didn't explain why she was upset. Focusing on Emma, I brought forth her information.

Emma Raines
Necromancer - Lvl 1
This opponent appears weaker than you.

Necromancer, a death mage, that Class said it all. Little Emma, the most stoic and lovable of all of us, always there to help with a scrape or a bruise, was now a mage of the dead. Robert had never been much for religion, he went to church, and he mouthed the words but had never espoused the faith in private, but this might be a step too far. Worse he was now a 'Cleric,' we didn't know the rules in this world, but he might be required to avoid her or fight her or some other craziness.

"Oh Emma, why did you bury a mouse hun?" I asked. It made no sense, I knew she cared for animals, but it was a mouse!

Emma seemed to shrink in on herself, her hands held tight to her chest, as silent tears ran down her cheeks.

"Ms. Northrop has been saying for weeks she was going to get rid of me the moment she found that I had done anything. She kept saying she thought I was a thief. A dead mouse in the pantry, that's my responsibility, she would say I never cleaned or something, she would blame me, but I couldn't just throw the poor thing outside, it was so tiny and looked helpless, all skin and bones," she rambled, with her chin tucked into her chest.

Like a flash of light, I could see what the plan was. Steal from the family, accuse Emma, and blame more and more of the servants she had fired. Then leave with whatever she had stolen. If she planned it right, it would place the crime on Emma and she might have been able to continue as a Governess somewhere else with none the wiser. Except for anyone who had ever met Emma that was. We would have known that she would never have stolen from us. Rebecca's plan would have failed right at that moment.

"Emma, hun, none of that matters now. She isn't in charge, and none of us care what that 'Rogue' says. You need to go down and talk to Robert. You need to find out if this changes anything," I said, trying not to let the guilt of manipulating my friend show in my voice. If Emma hadn't been so upset, she would have figured out that I was distracting her. I couldn't let them stop me; this was my only hope to escape from this place and to see the world. I thought of the pleasant feeling from when I gained a level; I wanted more of that.

With a bit more encouragement, Emma agreed to talk to Robert, a conversation I was hoping not to be around to hear.

If I was going to fight monsters and gain levels, I needed to check what armor and weapons I had available. In my inventory, I could see the sword quest reward and the chainmail shirt I had looted from the young ogre. With a bit of intent, I moved the sword from my inventory and into the right-hand slot in my character window. Much to my surprise, the sword didn't suddenly appear in my hand, but the moment I thought of it, I was grasping the sword. The blade was as long as my leg, thick and blocky, the edge a large curve of metal with two notches. The incredible thing was its weight. Huge and heavy, yet I could move it quickly. The weapon felt like it was an extension of my body. Different movements and how to use the blade flashed through my mind, how to slash and jab, how to use its weight to help with dodging as well as how to block using the sword. I could even tell that blocking with the blade was more difficult than with a shield, the nature of skillful blocking was just there and hovering in front of me.

Shaking my head, I let the combat forms drift out of my mind. Focusing on the blade, I looked for its information.

Noob NPC Warrior Blade
Non-Tradeable
One-Handed Slashing
Dmg: 5-15
Speed: 35

There was that term again, 'NPC,' I didn't know what it meant, but I understand that it was how the blue text frames referred to people. The other word was not one I knew. 'Noob,' didn't sound like a term of endearment, but beggars couldn't be choosers. This blade was for Warriors, and I had earned it. The other terms were just as confusing. 'Non-Tradeable' was odd, but it seemed to imply the sword couldn't be given to anyone else. 'One-Handed Slashing' seemed to imply the type of weapon it was, something I understand that Warriors didn't have to worry much about since we could use any weapon. The last two lines though were harder to guess the meaning. Was 'five-fifteen' good? Higher numbers were probably good, that is if 'Dmg' meant damage as it appeared to, but what about speed? Was thirty-five good or bad? Was a higher speed number good or a lower speed number? I would have to wait and find other items before I could figure it out.

Knowing more about my new world was important, but it's nature seemed to be all numbers. Without context though, the numbers were almost useless. Clenching my jaw, I focused in on the chainmail.

Fallen Champion's Chainmail
Non-Tradeable
Armor Type: Chain
AC: 13

The last clue to a champion's fate.

The last line floated below the information about the chest piece. Its horrific nature was muted by the fact I had watched the young ogre appear out of thin air earlier today. Had it been somewhere else and killed someone else and been hauling the armor around somewhere hidden inside it? Who and how? The more I learned about this new world, the less sense it made.

The notification window also liked to repeat information. The Armor type was chain, which presumably meant chain-mail, which was blindingly obvious by the name itself, not to mention in the inventory window it was an image of a chainmail tunic. The real concern was the 'AC' of thirteen. A greater number was likely to be good, but what exactly was 'AC'? It was probably an abbreviation, but of what? Armor something? With a sigh I resolved to figure it out later, I had nothing in my armor slots, and instead, I had my clothing in my 'casual' clothing slots. It was likely that I could switch between one and the other like I had with the sword, but I would have to test it to be sure.

Dragging the chainmail onto the chest slot next to my rotating image had the chainmail appearing on my body. The problem was the chainmail wasn't a tunic when I wore it. Looking down I nearly screamed at the sight of my naked arms, stomach, and upper chest. The only thing on my upper body was metal links which formed the top half of a corset! The chainmail failed even to establish a full torso of metal, only the 'cups' of the corset and the shoulder straps existed. How was this armor? Let alone something for a 'fallen champion'!

I agreed with the Clothing Reform Movement, pants were comfortable and allowed for movement when necessary, a reasonable position. This garment though was entirely about titillation! If I were seen wearing this, I would be scorned as the lowest harlot! Grinning, I moved carefully to see how bad the cups pinched. To my surprise the metal felt like the softest cloth on the inside, the metal even helped with lift and contained the movement of my bosom. The vision in the mirror took my breath away. My breasts were uplifted and proud, almost bursting out of the material, but nothing below the armor could be seen. Trying to look through the rings all I could see was a metallic grey blocking my view. A careful hop had my breasts bouncing most obscenely, but the feeling was less than I had felt when in full corset while riding side saddle. The dissonance between the appearance and the feel was disconcerting.

Shaking away the odd mental image of fighting goblins in such naked attire, I looked around to see if there was anything else I could use to hide my body. A riding cloak quickly rounded out my appearance. While it fit on the back slot in my inventory, the material was thin and listed as cloth and an 'AC' of one. That confirmed that 'AC' was an armor value and higher was better.

Down the stairs I went, walking on the edge of the step closest to the wall to avoid creaking noises. Sealing the busted door was an upended sofa. The ornate wooden furniture was tipped up and covered most of the doorway. Biting my lip, I reached out to see if I could tilt it away slightly to make my escape. I was worried that the sofa would be too heavy to move, but amazingly, it seemed almost simple to lift it out of the way. The bulky furniture was more awkward to handle than it was heavy. Another change to my understanding of the world which beggared belief.

Outside, the world seemed calm, like a typical summer afternoon right before dinner. While it was peaceful, it was also a bit eery. The savage violence of earlier didn't match the natural calm the summer mansion had always exuded. Turning North, I walked into the grasses which surrounded the estate. Nothing seemed to have changed, the goats which roamed the property had chewed the grasses low, and somewhere around they were wandering. Currently, though, it appeared that the large open area to the forest was free of monsters and it would be a short hike to reach the woods and then the cave. I wasn't sure the cave had my salvation, but it was the only thing on my minimap, so it was worth examining.

The sound of loud clicking and movements from the grass in front of me halted my hike. Glints of shiny black and yellow moved in the ankle-high grass as something approached. Flying out of the grass was a beetle, twice the size of my hand, the appearance so surprising that I failed to act before its large mandibles grasped onto my stomach.

The monster beetle pinched into my flesh, but the mandibles failed to do more than compress the skin it gripped. Falling free from my stomach a red one floated away from the unmarked surface. Yelling, I used the new skill I had earned from leveling; kick.

The tip of my riding boots smacked into the beetle, the blow taking it across the mandibles and dealing five damage. Flipping twice through the air, the beetle landed on it's back. An image of the outline of a man falling with arms windmilling for balance appeared above the floundering beetle. Focusing on the pictogram the image's information appeared in front of me.

Debuff - Broken Stance
Increases damage taken.
Reduced ability to dodge.
Reduced ability to block.
Duration: 2 Seconds

While I was watching the information window, the image disappeared above the beetle, and it flipped itself over and charged at me again. This time though I was ready. When the beetle tried to jump and bite me, I moved to the side. When it landed, I brought the sword down on its head. A large red fifteen floated away from the beetle, but other than the number it appeared unharmed. Lunging forward the beast pinched my wrist, luckily the one not holding the sword and it delivered another single point of damage. My forehand blow, well practiced by playing battledore and shuttlecock, had the beetle on it's back and legs twitching into death. My strike had delivered a sixteen and had emptied the monsters health.

A golden ten floated out of the beetle and into me. Inspecting the remains explained the ease of the fight.

Grass Beetle - Dead
Rogue - Level 1

This opponent appears weaker than you.

It made no sense that the beetle was a rogue. The level though offered clues. The text below compared my level to whatever I was looking at and told me the relative difference. A level one was weaker than a level two, and a higher level still was more powerful. I would be cautious in thinking this was absolute, but it appeared that levels told the tale in combat.

Looting the beetle, I was presented with a beetle's mandible.

Beetle Mandible x 1

The odd thing was that the text for the item was grey and the image in my inventory was also greyed out. Everything else had been white. I was sure it meant something, just as everything else in this text system meant something, but what it said wasn't clear yet.

The real issue was the ten experience I had gotten from killing the beetle. It had taken more than a thousand experience to go from level one to level two, and neither Robert or Markus had leveled from their fights. I had killed the young ogre and gained the experience while they hadn't, why wasn't clear, but still, it appeared that each level would be harder to earn than the last.

With my eyes searching out over the grass they were drawn to the small movements which I had missed before. I thought about how many beetles I would have to kill to reach level ten. My shoulders sagged, and I could feel my eyes watering at the extent of the impossible task before me. Straightening, I gripped my sword tighter and started marching towards the forest. I might not be able to fight and kill enough beetles to level to ten in ten days, but the cave was different, it must mean something, and it was my only real hope.

Chapter 7

The blow came from behind. I had just finished off a beetle and was reaching down to loot when a stabbing agony hit me at mid waist. Sprawling forward from the pain and the awkward position, I barely had the presence of mind to try and kick away whatever hit me. My kick barely struck whatever stabbed me, the red one said I had hit it, but the red thirty from the stab was a more significant concern. Whatever had struck me, removed a significant chunk of my life in one go. If it did it again, I was in deep trouble.

Rolling on the ground, the moist grass and dirt pressing into my skin and clothes, I tried to avoid my attacker enough to rise. I had little talent in tumbling; my roll was like a drunken sailor on a ship at sea. When I reached what I felt was enough distance in my frantic flopping, I pushed my self onto hands and knees only to have a beetle lunge for my face. A red ten, a critical hit message, and a beetle nose ring were my rewards.

Gritting my teeth, I stood as I slapped the new jewelry away, the blow causing me as much damage as it did the beetle. While the beetle flopped on the ground trying to upright itself, I looked around to find the more dangerous assailant. The beetle could wait until the real foe was dead.

When I was a child, I had watched a barn cat be startled by a dropping acorn. Jumping back and forth the cat looked all around trying to find the enemy which had surprised it. I found myself reenacting the cat's movements. My feet set wide and arms held out. With my head swinging back and forth in jerky motions and hopping in circles, I tried to look in all directions at the same time. I found nothing but the beetle which had finally righted itself.

With a careless swing, I swatted the jumping beetle out of the air. The motion being routine for me at this point. Waiting for the beetle, I smacked it on its jump as if it where a return serve in shuttlecock. I paused while looking around, wondering if my assailant would try for me again while I was trying to 'loot'. To my mind the term was still odd, but it was the one the window and the tutorial had used. Bringing up my combat log I checked to see what had made the attack which had done so much damage, damage without even a critical hit.

Grass Beetle backstabs Victoria [Warrior lvl 2] for 30 damage.
Victoria [Warrior lvl 2] suffers from Broken Stance!
Victoria [Warrior lvl 2] kicks Grass Beetle for 1 damage.
Grass Beetle critically bites Victoria [Warrior lvl 2] for 10 damage.
Victoria [Warrior lvl 2] slaps Grass Beetle for 2 damage.
Victoria [Warrior lvl 2] suffers 2 points incidental damage.
Grass Beetle suffers from Broken Stance!
Victoria [Warrior lvl 2] slashes Grass Beetle for 14 damage.
Victoria [Warrior lvl 2] slashes Grass Beetle for 12 damage.

The text of my combat log had me glancing around carefully. There hadn't been another assailant. It had been an ordinary grass beetle. The term 'backstab,' along with the blow to my kidney from behind, hinted that it was only an attack that could be done while I faced away from the beetle. My real concern was if it could be done quickly and repeatedly. If the beetle could strike like that again and knock me down, then repeat its act, I would be near death in moments. Glancing towards my health bar I was surprised. My health bar didn't say sixty-five was my maximum health, and it now said my maximum health was ninety-three. The added life meant I could take around three of those backstabs before death, instead of two. I would rather avoid even one if it were possible.

I tried fiddling mentally with my health bar, trying to figure out how I could have gained some twenty-eight life, but nothing seemed to happen beyond changing the way the bar was displayed. My options were with numbers, with a percentage, or both. I decided to leave it with both since it seemed the most appropriate. My only guess was that my life went up when I gained a level, another argument for fighting rather than hiding.

Continuing my appraisal of my combat log, I noticed the listing of 'debuffs' as the system called them. I should probably keep the log open while fighting so that I could keep track easily of who is hitting whom and what is being done during combat. It didn't block my eyesight so it wouldn't be a problem in that way, but it might lead to distractions. I would have to experiment and see how well it worked. The other concern was 'incidental damage,' I earned two points of damage when I slapped the beetle away. The beetle itself wasn't the cause of the injury. I did it to myself. It made sense. We could hurt ourselves just as always. Something else in the text was saying something important, something which mattered, but I couldn't see it yet. With a sigh, I gave up, whatever had caught my attention was just out of reach, I would not find it by the focused study of these few lines. As usual, I would realize this hidden idea in some other random time doing some other random thing.

The sound of a beetle crawling through the grass ahead of me had me crouched and on guard. Baring my teeth, I stalked forward until the beetle's carapace became visible. Its mandibles pointed away from me, and that was the only invitation I needed. Silently I leaped forward and brought my sword down in a mighty overhand strike, the edge of the blade slamming down on the beetles back. Just the day before, no such large beetle could exist, let alone around our summer mansion. The day before, a blow like I had just delivered would have turned that non-existant beetle into jam. But today, the strike left a faint mark on its carapace, and the beetle turned to see who had delivered the fifteen points of damage. Before the beetle could spin around entirely, I slammed my blade down on the beetle again and ended its life. The fading corpse had me glancing around then continuing my journey.

The slow trudge through the grasslands to the small forest was oddly idyllic. Ignoring the occasional stops to swat away beetles and the paranoid checking for attackers, it felt like the point at the start of any hike. I was warm, but not sweating, comfortable in my gear, and eager to exercise long unused muscles. What made this experience different, beyond the battles to the death, was that this feeling continued unending. My body never overheated from exertion, I didn't sweat, and my gear never pinched or rubbed. I remained as collected as when I started the trip. The apocalypse had some minor benefits to it, and this was one of them.

Reaching the woods, I ducked under the pine trees, the sudden shade feeling nice after the walk in the sun. The 'forest' was a wooded area with very little underbrush. When I was a child, it was a magical land of fairies and trolls, dragons and elves. When I was older, I realized that the forest was so small and so sparse that a good logging company could have removed it in a couple of years of effort at most. There had been no fairies, no trolls, no dragons, no elves. Now though, I could see that the nature of the woods had changed. What little underbrush existed, it failed to hide the forests newest inhabitants.

Wolves.

Like so much about this new world, wolves being in these woods made little sense. There was not nearly enough prey for animals of their size, the animals themselves failed to act as wolves would having spread out as individuals, and finally, wolves had been extinct in the isles for at least five hundred years! Focusing on one of the near animals, one who seemed to be walking a short patrol (another oddity), I gained its information.

Grey Wolf
Warrior - Lvl 3
This would be a difficult opponent.

It was a warrior, so I didn't have to worry about any odd new abilities like with the beetles and it was only level three. The real question though, was a level three grey wolf too difficult for me to fight on my own? Gnawing on my bottom lip I watched the grey wolves, even though they had more than once looked in my direction, none attacked. There had to be some reason for it in this new world. But did that mean that they wouldn't work together the moment I struck one? I had roughly a mile to go to the east and a short walk into the woods. The cave was marked where the clearing and pond had been before. I could walk in the grasslands and continue killing beetles; they had proven to be a secure source of experience once I had learned not to turn my back on them. But if my courage failed me here, would it fail me when I finished my walk east? What of when I needed to walk through the woods to reach the cave?

Ducking low, though none of the wolves seemed to care, I tightened my grip on my sword and wished I had a shield to go with it. I waited, letting two of the grey wolves pass each other and watched for a straggler to come near by itself. After a few minutes of waiting and watching, I realized that these wolves were walking a patrol, one that endlessly repeated. None of the wolves near me were going to approach close enough, but walking fifteen meters or so would have me just at the far end of one of the paths and nowhere near another wolf. My real concern was if two attacked at once. 'Difficult' was not impossible, but two foes might make it so.

When the wolf reached the end of its path and turned around to repeat its motions, I attacked. I had intended to slice at the back legs of the wolf. Such a wound would make it easier to flee if needed. Unfortunately, I made more noise than necessary, and the wolf spun to meet my attack. I was barely able to redirect my aim and strike the wolf along its muzzle. The canine only yelped once before it raised its head to return the attack. My blow was solid, but for some reason, a red ten flew from its face, far less than with the beetles. Was this because of a higher level? Some better defense? The difference between beetle and wolf? I didn't know, and the lack of knowledge exacerbated my fears.

If asked the day before if I would be crouched opposite an angry wolf, my answer would have been peals of laughter. That I would be doing it in men's work pants, with a sword, and wearing the top half of a metal corset, would have left me apoplectic in disbelief. But now, I couldn't think of a more grand adventure or a place that felt more right.

Lunging forward the wolf tried to bite my ankle. Only a careful step kept my skin unblemished. The miss left the wolf's head near my ankle, and the downward stroke of my sword hit the animal directly across the brow. This was a far more significant blow, and the fifteen damage and the image of the man with rotating stars and a duck made an appearance. Continuing my assault, I brought my weapon up for a stab, the tip entering above the left shoulder of the animal. A shackled limb joined the revolving stars. That is where my uninjured success ended. Being close to the wolf's left side had my left arm near the animal's mouth. Taking advantage of its position, stun notwithstanding, the animal bit down on my left forearm with bone-crushing force. The snap of the arm, along with the red twenty and the bleeding and broken bone images, said that I had made a royal mistake. I should have stood away from the animal and sliced at it as it approached. Without weaponry or armor, it needed to latch on and disable me, which it now had.

My thoughts were oddly coherent for the amount of pain I was experiencing. The cur hanging from my arm was only able to shake intermittently and cause fives and sixes to bloom from my limb. Stabbing my sword, I drove the top into his ribs and flank to a shower of eights and tens. On my third strike, the beast released my forearm and pulled back, its jaw filled with red foam.

My now free arm was held tight to my side as I clenched my belt with my hand. Pain shot through the break at each swing. There were moments of suprise and fear in the rest of the fight, the wolf having some kind of charging lunge attack was a surprise, but nothing like the first bite. The wolf had around fifty hit points at level three, far less than I had at even level one, but also much more than the grass beetles had. The last blow which killed the beast was anti-climatic, I struck it across the nose in a glancing blow, but it was enough to leave its health at zero. The monster collapsed as if it were a puppet which had all its strings cut in a single moment.

I stared at the downed animal, the adrenaline pumping in my body and my breath still forced through my clenched teeth. I leaned on my sword like the Colonel would lean on his cane after climbing the stairs. In my mind's eye, the icon with a broken bone came into focus.

Debuff - Broken Bone (Left Arm)
Increase damage taken to injury.
Movement of limb increases damage taken.
Reduced damage delivered.
Reduced ability to block with a shield.
Duration: 20 minutes

A broken limb in the old world could mean permanent disability or even death. In this world, it meant reduced capabilities for a short period. If it was true that in twenty minutes my arm would no longer be broken, then battle injuries were short-lived affairs and something to avoid but not worry over. My health was hovering around forty points, the bleeding and movement had done almost as much damage as the initial break. I moved away from the patrol area of the wolves and rested against a tree while I watched the timer tick down. My health slowly recovered as I sat and relaxed, the rate of recovery being something like a weeks worth of improvement a minute. When the timer ticked through its final second, a sharp snap sound rang out from my arm but without pain. Holding my hand up and clenching my fist I rotated my arm in different directions in wonder.

Like this, what could stop me?

Chapter 8

While I was dealing with yet another grey wolf, a small blinking icon popped up in the corner of my vision. I focused on the canine and ignored the blinking, the slavering, snapping teeth helping focus my attention. Once I finally killed the wolf, the twenty-five experience pushing me one step closer to leveling, I looked around to check that I wouldn't be disturbed by another enemy.

The icon was odd, it was three people, in outline only, huddled together. When I focused on it a window popped up.

You have been invited to a group by Robert Collingwood.
Do you wish to join this group?
(Y/N)

I knew that I would have to deal with running off to level instead of huddling down, but I didn't think they would be able to do it remotely like this. Wiping my hand down my face, I focused on the 'y' and accepted the 'group' invitation.

"Vick. Where are you?" Robert asked, his voice strained.

I knew that tone of voice. That was Robert's 'trying not to judge my antics while still trying to rein me in' voice. Not this time. I've got ten days to get to level ten, and each level has required more experience than the last. I needed to keep killing and fast. Once I reached level ten, then no one could stop me, they would be stuck here, but I would be free. I just needed to focus on my freedom.

"I'm going to reach level ten. I'm perfectly fine. You can stop worrying about me, tell the Colonel he should stay there, I don't need him," I said, intending for my voice to reach the group and using the group chat feature just like it had been described in the tutorial. The tutorial had only glossed over it, but it was as easy as it had been described. Intend for your voice to go to a specific 'channel,' and it went there. Odd, but useful.

Robert didn't respond for a moment, long enough that I thought the conversation was over before he continued.

"The Colonel isn't coming. It's just us in the group, and we are going to help you with this insane plan," Robert said.

I glanced at the group list, a set of small icons on the left-hand side of my vision, Emma, Annie, Robert, Me. I fully expected Robert, but the lack of the Colonel and the stablemaster had me confused. Emma and Annie would have wanted to help, but I never thought for a moment that they would be *allowed* to come along.

"Why?" I asked, the question slipping out in my confusion.

The next pause had me looking around for another grey wolf, the fights were easy enough, now that I knew to keep them at a distance, that even a conversation shouldn't cause me a problem. Walking along I intercepted another wolf and began the, by now, routine dance of death.

"Do you know why the Colonel retired?"

The odd question had me stumbling for a moment. The Colonel retired because of his injury; he had a limp. My answer to Robert had him sighing in my ear, a curiously disturbing experience when no one but the wolf was near.

"The Colonel has Soldier's Heart."

I almost brained myself with my sword, the large cleaver-like blade sliding past my ear. With an aggressive roar, I kicked the lunging wolf in the snout and slashed the edge of blade against the canine multiple times. I didn't even wait for the regular pauses in the wolf's rhythm. I was bitten on the ankle, but I failed to let it slow me down. I would recover after the fight. I kept hitting the canine until it died with a whimper, then I focused on the chat window which I had left silent.

"The Colonel is one of the bravest men I know! He's no coward!"

I couldn't contain myself. It wasn't ladylike to shout like this, it would be rude for even a gentleman, but such an accusation was worthy of ostracism or a duel as far as I was concerned.

"He isn't. He has just seen too much of combat. He has trouble making decisions. He has been under too great a stress too often. I think that he is afraid that if he changes his mind about what to do, then he won't be able to make up his mind at all. That's why your Father asked him to retire, he was going the way of more than one soldier, and he didn't want him to end up in Colney Hatch," Robert said, his voice rising at the end.

The mention of the new asylum had me frozen in place. More than one young dandy had tried to gain my fancy by telling me tales of their adventure and daring. One that had drawn a sick fascination was a recitation of the tours which had once been popular at Bethlem, a tale so lurid that I was ill in short order. I knew that over the years that reforms had been instituted for asylums, but the shame and the suffering of such a thing would have ruined the Collingwood's.

"Mr. Nye has refused to leave his son, no one can trust Rebecca, and Owen…uncle is barricading the mansion and making it safe."

I slowed at the mention of Owen. I was sure that the disruption of his schedule was a burden to him. Just moving from London to the summer mansion had him confused and upset for days. This confusion would leave him angry but unable to express it because of his training. I felt for him, but the others could care for him. I needed this if I was to be able to travel to father, and if I was going to be free of this place. I refused to be stuck in the countryside unable to leave.

Emma's voice cut across the group chat, she and Annie had let Robert take the lead, but she wouldn't allow his failure to convince me to rest.

"You are acting like a child. You haven't even prepared for this little journey, have you? Did you even pay attention during the tutorial?" she asked.

"I went through the tutorial just like…" I began, but Emma cut me off.

"No, you paid attention to the things which you found exciting and ignored anything else, just like you always do. You don't have a lick of practical sense in your head. I can see your level is two in the group window. Have you even assigned your attribute points?"

Quickly I opened my character window. The 'stats' for my 'character' were displayed in white, all tens, the human normal at level one. Each stat was abbreviated, and I had to focus on them to remember what they were: strength (STR), constitution (CON), agility (AGI), dexterity (DEX), intelligence (INT), wisdom (WIS), charisma (CHA). What I hadn't noticed at first, though I remember the tutorial mentioning it, was the little area below my stats where I would gain attribute points. I had five points there, and each of my stats had a little plus next to them.

"Focus on your class name, and it will say what your primary and secondary stats are, put most off your points in your primary stat and the rest in your secondary stat. Waste them, and it could cause your death," Emma said, her voice cold and sharp.

The tutorial had said something about this, but I had paid little attention to it. I had been filled with adrenaline and excitement from the fight with the rat.

I was reminded of the time I fell from a tree and landed on a sharp rock, the point driving into my side and ripping the tunic that had been part of my early adventuring clothing. Emma had explained to me that she needed me to be safe and that if she caught me doing something dangerous again, she would write to my father herself. While she had coldly talked to me, she had also been white-faced and tense. Her mother, Sophia, had died no more than a few months before that incident. I think the fragility of life and her place in it, was uppermost in her mind.

This was the same voice as that day. Cold, sharp, and suppressing the fear of loss.

As much as I hated being told what to do, she was right. I needed to act within this world's rules. It was far more violent and deadly than the old one. I couldn't just ignore the things that had bored me before. Now they could mean my death. When focusing on the warrior class, the information window told me that my primary stat was constitution and my secondary stat was strength. Point distribution was simple, three to CON, two to STR. I would continue that pattern at each level.

I was secretly thankful that Emma had said something. If I had noticed on my own, I might have been tempted to put points into charisma. I wasn't vain, but like any woman, I had compared myself to others and found myself wanting. Being a little bit prettier sounded nice, but staying alive in my new world seemed better.

Once I assigned my points, my health shot up, the ninety-three becoming a hundred and twenty. Twenty-seven more life would make all the difference. I didn't seem to be any stronger as far as I could tell. My blade was oversized and thick, the weapon looked more like a long cleaver than a sword. Despite its size and mass, I could move it quickly and freely, a pleasing experience for someone who was barred from most types of outside activity.

I stared at the group window for a while, trying to control my conflicting emotions. Anger at the way they were talking down to me, frustration at the lack of control in my life, happiness that my family and friends cared so much for me, sadness that they would want to stop me from being free.

"I'll be safe. Thank's Em," I said, trying to sound appreciative only.

"Don't thank me. If you die, I'll beat you myself. Now come back home."

"No, but I'll stay in chat, and sis, I'll be safe, I promise."

My sister didn't respond, but she had always been timid in stressful situations. She was more likely to accept the consensus than make her own decision. The silence weighed on me; I could feel her disagreement. They remained in the group, but silent. On my minimap, I could see their markers still at the mansion. I wondered if they were trying to convince Markus or Philip to 'rescue' me. This just meant I had a shorter deadline than I had first thought.

I continued my march to the cave marker, the wolves becoming more sparse as I went. The first change I noticed was the increase to the damage my blade and kicks did since my attribute change. It wasn't a significant difference, twelves becoming fifteens and the like, but it was enough to notice. Each wolf went down faster, and my experience grew. In short order, I was level three and distributing my new attribute points.

The new skills were the real benefit.

Level up!

Victoria [Warrior lvl 3] - at level 10 NPC's will no longer be zone locked.
New Skills!
Gained Skill - War Cry - Vigour.
Gained Skill - Taunt.

I didn't know how I knew, but I *knew* that my taunt skill would only work on an opponent. I couldn't practice it without a target. 'War Cry - Vigor' on the other hand could be done at any time. Checking for nearby enemies, of which there were none, I decided to give it a try. Focusing on the skill, an odd feeling inside that was unlike anything I had experienced in my earlier life, I selected the ability.

A roar of violence screamed from my lungs. The sound made me think that my vocal cords had been shredded from the force of my shout, the wave of sound bursting outward. Grasping my throat I prepared for my voice to be hoarse or the pain to suddenly reach me, but I felt fine. A few tests of my voice found it as usual. The new buff in the corner of my eye explained what my new skill did.

Buff - War Cry - Vigor
Increases aggro generation (self)
Increases melee damage output (30 meters, group)
Reduces stamina usage (30 meters, group)
Duration: 1 minute

The frightening sound aside, the 'buffs' effect was useful. It didn't last long, the buff began blinking at the thirty-second mark, but until now my marks of rage had just been sitting there doing nothing. They had filled quickly in each fight, then faded slowly at the end of each battle, this was the first skill that allowed me to use them.

Continuing my walk I noticed that the forest was now empty, no grey wolves were anywhere near. The reason why was soon apparent. Walking along an animal trail was a goblin hunter.

> ***Goblin Hunter***
> ***Ranger - Lvl 3***
> ***This would be an even fight.***

While it said it would be an even fight, I still remembered the goblin raiders and how quickly the Colonel had dispatched them. The grey wolves were level three, just the same as this goblin ranger, which means this should be easy enough. I glanced to my buff, and it was fading out and had only seconds left, so I rushed forward to try and attack the goblin before it faded.

I failed to reach the goblin before the buff disappeared, but my haste caused me other issues. The goblin was using a bow, and when it noticed me, it drew back an arrow and let loose. The shaft burying itself into my shoulder as a red twelve floated free. The sudden pain had me clutching my wound and gasping, the bleeding debuff knocking off another five points. The sound of an arrow leaving the goblins bow brought me out of my stupor, but only long enough to watch the bolt slam into my chest. The second arrow hit me above the bust line. The chain mail was too low cut to block the blow. Despite the non-functional nature of the armor, the arrow still bounced off my bare skin. The impact did ten damage, but the bolt failed to penetrate, and I wasn't suffering from a second bleeding debuff.

The goblin hunter had backed up after each shot. It stood, watching me, it's bow ready and with an arrow nocked, but it didn't fire. With a minor pinch the shaft in my shoulder popped out and the bleeding debuff faded. I was down forty life, and it was barely recovering since I was 'in a battle,' but the goblin just stood and watched me. I could see how our battle would go, I would attack, and it would just retreat, peppering me with arrows as it went. I would probably run the monster down, but it was a question of what condition I would be in when I finally reached him. Worse, if an arrow struck my legs, it might just be able to stay beyond my reach. At that point I wouldn't be able to escape or attack it, my death would be assured.

Grinning, the goblin just waited while I clenched my sword. Gritting my teeth, I made the only smart decision I could make. I turned and ran.

I wasn't able to hear the goblin behind me, though the arrow flying wide of me during my flight told me that I was still being pursued. I knew the terrain in this area, the area around the clearing being the most heavily explored by our group. Angling my escape towards a small ravine, always dry except during the beginning of spring, I slowed to watch for the creek bed. Coming over a short rise, I nearly fell over the stony cliff even as I anticipated it. Hopping down, I ducked under the short overhang. Waiting, I listened for the sound of the pursuing goblin.

My wait was short. The little green man hopped down into the rocky creek bed without slowing. Reaching over his shoulder, he grasped another arrow, but his movement was interrupted by my sword clubbing down on his elbow. The sickening sound of a bone leaving its socket, familiar to anyone who has had to debone a chicken, sounded from his shoulder. His elbow showed only a minor nick from the blade, but the broken bone debuff flashed above the monsters head.

The goblin barely paused as it swung around, whipping his bow out at my head. I wasn't sure how dangerous the stringed tool would be as a melee weapon, but I still wasn't eager to be struck by it. The goblin's left arm flopped as it wielded the bow with its right wildly. The sickening display was making me nauseous even as I batted its useless weapon away. My disgust and the attempt to ward away its weapon, left me dealing little damage to the little green menace.

After a successful blow to my face, I stopped waving my weapon around ineffectively and instead attacked the creature's head in retaliation. The meaty impact of my blade into the monster's neck, as well as the critical hit, returned my confidence. After I focused on fighting instead of dancing away from the worthless attacks, the fight went quickly.

The goblin hunter had little health, but the damage it did with its arrows was still dangerous. The risk of being lamed and unable to advance or retreat made it a far more dangerous opponent than the wolves. I resolved myself, again, to be more careful with each new opponent. Each time I had to fight a new opponent, a new danger had presented itself. If I had been less capable, or a little less quick to respond, in each case, I could have died.

Each time I had told myself to be more careful, and each time I had ignored my own advice. I was starting to think that Emma was right about the amount of sense I had.

Out of combat, my health began to recover quickly. The apocalypse didn't seem as dangerous as I thought it would be. It almost felt like the danger was being kept down to a minimum level and that as long as I was careful, I could handle whatever was thrown at me. That line of thought was dangerous, even if it was true. All it would take would be another young ogre, and I would be in grave danger. I couldn't count on a flurry of lucky strikes and debuffs to save the day. If that situation repeated itself, most times, our group wouldn't have survived. I was more capable now, with a higher level, but I was sure there were things with higher levels still.

The hunter's corpse faded away while I was standing around having my existential crisis.

Scrambling up the rise I started back through the woods. I kept a close eye out for another hunter, but my approach was clear. The clearing where I had spent summers swimming and playing with Emma and Annie was changed. The small pond was still there, but the large grassy area was gone, and instead, a large rock jutted from the ground. The side of the stone was hollowed out. A crude bone gate was lashed together raised above a swirling moving gateway. Whatever it was, it looked dangerous. Focusing gave me its information.

Dungeon - Goblin's Den (suggested level 3-5)

The more I learned about my new world, the less I understood. In what way was that a dungeon? Was it a cell block housing goblins? Considering the two goblin warriors, one on each side of the door, it seemed unlikely. Unless these were the wardens, but wouldn't they be 'goblin wardens' then?

The goblins were both warriors, and level three. I was worried about taking on two at once, but I had done well enough before with the hunter, and I had killed multiple warrior type creatures before. Standing in the trees I looked around, checking carefully to be sure nothing else was about.

Since it appeared clear, I strode forward with confidence.

Both goblins noticed me as I approached, but they stayed at their posts until I had edged around the pond and came within a few paces. One was wielding a spear, but the other had a sword similar to my own: wide, thick, and chipped. The goblin warrior with the sword was the closer of the two, so I attacked him first. I was hoping I could keep the sword wielder between me and the spear goblin. I dodged backward and avoided the first swing, a broad left-to-right movement which left the goblin wide open. Stepping within the goblin's reach I was surprised at a sudden lunge. It's pointy teeth snapping at me as I approached. While I had been surprised, I didn't hesitate to kick the goblin, trying to knock him into his compatriot.

My kick landed, but I failed to tangle the two together.

So began a slow slog. I was trying to strafe around the sword wielder and keep my opponent between me and the spear goblin, while he would try to run around the fight and stab at me with his longer reach. Oddly enough, neither goblin was doing a lot of damage. They would hit for tens and twelves, but they were both slow, and I was dodging most of their blows. My attacks were faster and did slightly more damage, but they also had far more health than the hunter. I was starting to worry about my own health, being at half-life when the sword wielder finally died. The death of his companion had the spear wielder hollering out with a war cry of his own.

I wanted to smack myself in the face when I realized I had failed to use the skill I had just earned. Triggering the throat-ripping scream, I returned to the fight. One on one, and with the spear user doing far less damage now that I could focus on him alone, made the match a quick affair. I was proud of myself with my performance. I had thirty percent of my life left, and I had killed two goblin warriors of equal level. Sometime during my fight, the group chat icon had started to blink, but I had ignored it for the far more important battle. My celebration was cut short when an arrow impacted on my back and another hit my leg.

The shackle icon appeared the moment the second arrow hit. Spinning around I watched as from the tree line two goblin hunters drew and released. Dodging one bolt, the other hit my left arm and produced the dreaded bleeding debuff. My life ticked down to ten percent, and I made the only decision I could. I turned to the dungeon entrance and dived within.

Chapter 9

My dive through the dungeon entrance became a tumble. The floor through the entrance dropped into a ramp into the center of a large cavernous room. The stone floor snapped off the arrows in my back and leg as I began to flop down the slope as damage numbers flew off my body in a scarlet shower. Gritting my teeth and screaming through the agony I spread my body along the slope and slowed my movements.

Lying helpless on the ramp, shuddering in agony, I wondered if I would survive my latest act of stupidity. My health bar was barely there in my vision, the sliver of life left blinking and flashing scarlet along the length of the bar. The pulse of the blood loss debuff would fade away before the bar emptied, but I was only barely able to notice, my vision blurring and shuddering from the pain. The tutorial had mentioned 'adverse debuffs' at low life but failed to say what they were. Apparently one of them was extreme pain. With all my effort I focused on the number on the bar.

Three health.

My health started to refill quickly, indicating I was out of combat, but I couldn't count on that continuing. The hunters would make it around the small pond and into the cavern soon, leaving me a pincushion if I couldn't get up and prepare. My hands scrapped along the stone as I dragged them to my body, the effort of moving my limbs seemed to be like climbing a mountain. Only my approaching death had me stirring at all.

I wasn't tired, my stamina bar was two thirds full, but mentally I was exhausted. The thought of yet another fight, more movement, more pain, had me wanting to curl into a ball and sleep. Father and the Colonel had emphasized that battles were part exhaustion and part terror. For me the terror translated into excitement, I enjoyed it far more than was likely healthy, but only now did I understand the limb shaking fatigue.

When my health hit twenty percent, another debuff ended, and my world snapped into focus. Whatever was weighing down my mind lifted, and I scrambled until I faced towards the entrance, my sword in a wet grip.

Only to face a solid wall.

Clambering to my feet, I lurched over to the stone surface. Only damp rock greeted my questing hands. Feeling around I tried to find a hidden lever, an elusive doorway, or some other explanation for how I moved through solid stone. I also couldn't forget the fact that at any moment the goblin hunters could push through the barricade and attack. My health was recovering, quickly, but I was in no way ready. Worse, I couldn't be sure they wouldn't just fire arrows at me through the stone and kill me without resistance. I hadn't been able to see through the swirly doorway, but who was to say that they couldn't? The name text over our heads had made it clear that what one person perceives may not be what someone else will.

After five minutes of anxious waiting, I stopped crouching in preparation and instead started to lean against the wall. The flashing group channel icon was staring me in my mind. With focused intent I selected it.

"Vick! Talk to me. Vicky. Vick!" screamed my sister, her voice cracking with tears and hysteria.

My first few tries to answer were almost shouted over, and her voice was still filled with fear.

"I'm here. I'm alive. I'm alive," I said. With each answer, my voice dropped in volume as I could hear my friends calm themselves.

"Your life was dropping. You weren't answering. You were almost dead, and then, your health bar went grey," Annie said, her voice hiccupping as her speech started to lose coherence.

"I'm alright. I am. I had to kill two goblin warriors, they were tough but I did it," I said.

I wasn't looking forward to explaining my predicament, but it was obvious that I wasn't getting out of this without help. I had rushed ahead time after time, even as I berated myself not to, and this was the result.

"Why did you're health bar go grey?" Emma asked.

That was a good question. To me, my health bar was fine, recovering nicely in fact. But everyone else in the group had a grey health bar. This was more of the world doing one thing for some people and another thing for others. I was not a fan of this new trend. The only answer I could think of was that I was in the dungeon. A dungeon was where you put people when you didn't want them ever to see the light of day again. I wasn't going to be seeing it from this entrance, that was for sure.

Hitting my fist against the stone wall then standing, I looked around. The walls were grey stone with small chunks of bright blue quartz. Even with the glowing quartz, there shouldn't have been enough light to see by. All the same, while it was dark, it was still possible to see the tunnel around me.

Finally, I was unable to ignore the increasingly angry questions in the group chat. I wasn't intentionally being rude, and it wasn't that I was upset, angry, and embarrassed. I just needed to be sure I was safe before I started talking. The excuse sounded like a lie even in my thoughts, but I pushed that aside for now and focused on my situation.

"The cave icon is for a dungeon. I'm not sure it's a dungeon as we think of it. It might be. I can't tell yet. Things are odd, as usual. When I stepped through the swirly portal, all of your health bars went grey as well. I think it's like the name text; it depends on who is viewing it," I said with my answer barely calming the tirade of questions.

"Leave the dungeon now," Robert's strained voice cut through the discussion and left the other two silent.

Banging the pommel of my sword against the wall, I shrugged even though I knew he couldn't see me.

"A bit of a problem with that. The dungeon entrance is one way, and it's stone on this side. I'm going to look around and see if I can find an exit."

"No! You will stay at the entrance. We are coming to help. You almost died a few minutes ago, and you are already running off to do it again," demanded Annie.

Usually, Annie was very quiet and agreeable. The etiquette lessons I had always shunned and derided, she viewed as useful for manipulating others and controlling the discussion. Annie was not a social butterfly in London, but neither was she avoided or the talk of the town. She managed her social persona perfectly and never had to worry too deeply about the social game. She played it only to be left alone. For Annie to start barking out commands and abandon all social niceties was a shock. One that left me even more ashamed of my previous actions.

I had let the adrenaline and adventure get to me. The excitement of my freedom and what it could mean had thrown what little restraint I had away. To me, this was a new world where I could do anything, become anything. For me, it was like the chains I carried my entire life was ripped free. For Annie and Emma, it was like someone knocked the floor away beneath their feet. Robert, poor Robert, has had to step away from his uncle, the man he has respected for decades, and go against his commands. Worse, it was on the backdrop of the fear of the loss of his family and friends. My family had always worried about a letter from the Queen arriving to talk about our fathers bravery; we had already lost our mother. Emma lost her mom only a few years ago. We knew loss and pain. Robert still had his grand-parents.

"All right. I'll wait until you three arrive," I said, "I'm sorry I've been so erratic, I'll do better. I just feel like I have a chance at freedom and I don't want to miss it."

None of them answered, I continued to wait in silence, the urge to explore overwhelming but I resisted. I just rested against the walls. The blockading stone was cold and gritty against my clothes, but the very fact that I was lounging around on the damp stone and not sitting for tea with a full-length dress made it pleasant. I was sure that my enjoyment of even these difficulties would fade into a disgruntled annoyance, they always had before, but for now, I would enjoy the novelty.

Beyond my boredom was my hunger and thirst. I had failed to prepare as well for this outing as I had believed. Weapons and armor had been my only real thoughts. Now that I considered what an adventure would really take, the list started to grow, the distraction of planning alleviating my boredom. Matches, a nightman's lamp, food, water, spare clothing, a tent, bedding, the list was long. Looking down at my trousers I blushed as I considered that with my current attire, the knickers that I pre-ferred would add too much padding and would not allow for the standard belt and loop for cotton napkins. A problem that was not currently an issue, but would be soon enough. That was one issue with the Clothing Reform Movement I had not given suffi-cient thought.

After a few hours, hours where the group focused on fighting and not talking to me, they finally decided to discuss my predicament. It was likely that Annie had decided my punishment was to be silence, it felt like one of her penalties. Emma would just have told me how much of a nit I was being and would wait until we were alone to pinch me.

"Getting here was not terribly difficult. The wolves were simple to kill, and the one hunter we found died shortly, but you owe Robert for this Vick. He has been run ragged trying to keep these curs away from us," Annie said, her voice suddenly loud in the silence of the stone tunnel.

"Thanks. All of you. Thank you. I know running off was dumb. I'm trying to rein in my excitement. This isn't playtime, and I'm not a child, so I shouldn't act like it," I said.

Robert coughed awkwardly. It was interesting how a cough traveled through group chat since he was trying to 'speak' using it - mainly trying to convey his embarrassment. Robert never could take a compliment or appreciation well. Ducking her head and continuing to work was Emma's solution to praise. Only Annie ever dealt with compliments well, smiling and giving all the right social cues.

"Right, right. Did you really enter that swirling doorway Victoria? Whatever convinced you to do that?" Robert asked his question more about ignoring the appreciation than out of any real interest.

"Oh!" I said, realizing that my silence could have been a cause for danger, "watch out. When I killed the goblin warriors, two hunters attacked me."

That brought up another interesting question though. Why were there two warriors at the cave and where did they come from? Did the two hunters find reinforcements to replace the warriors? Why didn't they enter and attack me? None of this made any sense, and I was starting to fidget in confusion.

"One of the warriors is down. This is much easier than the

beetles. We can see them from far enough away to do some real damage before they arrive," Annie said, her voice very chipper for some reason.

A few seconds later had Annie continuing with her chipper tones, "...and two! Eww, a burnt goblin is much worse than burnt dog hair. Still,"

That 'still' at the end of her statement was deeply disturbing. Annies' voice had almost shone with happiness, and that was not the sound you wanted in your sister's voice as she burned her enemies alive.

Before I could respond to the new disturbing tones, Robert stepped through the tunnel wall, and into my lap. I took a few points of damage as I fell over and scraped my hands on the stone, while Robert nearly tumbled over me. While Robert regained his balance against the wall of the tunnel, I found my-self the focus of both Annie and Emma, both of whom burst into hysterical laughter over my appearance. Flat on my back, legs spread wide, arms over my head, cloak spread under me, with my up-thrust chainmail covered breasts seeming to be dis-played for all to see.

Even Robert was not above a few embarrassed chuckles, though he turned his view away as quickly as he could.

"What are you wearing?" asked Annie, her voice nearly as flabbergasted as she was scandalized.

Scrambling up off the ground I pulled my cloak tight around myself, then shrugged as I pulled the sides around on either side of my bosom, hiding nothing.

"It's AC is thirteen. This new world requires us all to make ad-justments to survive."

With an unladylike snort, Emma responded, "And the fact it makes you look like you added twice your growth doesn't hurt your feelings either."

My face reddened as I tried to remain straight-faced, but I found myself laughing with Annie and Emma, the reduction of tension much needed after the last few hours of silence. Thinking of the time that had passed, I realized that it must be reaching toward night now. I had failed even to consider what it would be like camping out in the woods while fighting ravenous beasts and humanoids. My adventure could have been even shorter-lived than expected given my wild acts.

Eventually, we decided to creep along the tunnel, Robert insisting on taking the point, and trying to find a way free of this 'dungeon.' Our exploration was cut short by the two goblins standing guard at a large stone entranceway. These goblins were very different from the ones outside. The ones outside were short and olive green, their bodies lean and almost emaciated looking. These goblins looked to have been eating plenty of beef and lifting weights. Still short, they were taller than their brethren, reaching to the height of my navel. The most substantial change was the leather armor instead of rags, and the biceps which bulged as they held their weapons.

The two goblins waited and eyed us, unwilling to leave their assigned positions, though they did heft their weapons and look on eagerly. Returning the assessing gaze, I brought out their information.

Shan-Dar Clan
Goblin Warrior - Elite
Warrior - Lvl 3
This would be a difficult opponent.

Shan-Dar Clan
Goblin Warrior - Elite
Warrior - Lvl 3
This would be a difficult opponent.

The inclusion of the clan information was not the only new bit of information. The 'elite' designation was worrying. The name tags above the two goblins were surrounded by a border of copper gears and pipes. It was the first appearance of anything besides text, and it was not a comforting sign. I had learned my lesson, anything new or different should be seen as dangerous first.

"I killed the two level three warriors outside myself. I'm sure we can do this if we all work together," I said, the excitement rising in my voice.

The three looked at each other, the apprehension clear, but then Annie smiled oddly as she eyed the two targets down the hall. Emma stood to the far left, her hands clenched tight while Robert stood close to Annie on the right wall. I stood in the center of the tunnel in a wide stance, sword held in front of me and eager to begin the dance of death.

Annie chuckled as her hands started to glow with an orange light. Lifting her right hand a ball of glowing fire grew until it was the size of an apple. Pointing her hand at the rightmost guard, her ball of flame leaped forward and slammed into the goblin's face. Roaring their anger at the attack, both started straight for Annie. Robert slipped in front of her with his make-shift club held ready to strike. When the goblins had reached half the distance, Emma held one hand forward. From her palm shot a black and purple projectile, dripping blobs of shadow that evaporated, which struck the unharmed goblin.

Emma's projectile seemed to eat at the goblin before a scarlet line returned from the creature and drew itself into Emma. Emma staggered backward from the force of the red line's return but seemed unharmed. The blistered and screaming goblin turned away from Annie, and its eyes drilled into Emma's as he narrowed in on her as his only focus.

This seemed like the perfect time to use my newest skill that I had been neglecting to use. The purpose of it seemed to be to draw the attention of our enemies away from my allies. Keeping my eyes on Emma's warrior, I triggered my taunt skill.

From deep in my mind the perfect words burst forth, my tone and cadence subtly conveying a level of extreme satisfaction.

"I would be upset if I was a goblin also. Look at you, so small. Hell, I bet I've even got a bigger penis than you."

Chapter 10

It's possible that I may have used that term before. If I had, it was said in whispers over tea with a close friend. Even then, it was with a red face and many furtive looks to be sure I was not overheard. Never would I use such a term where others could hear it, let alone in such a context. The very words themselves, about myself, left my face burning like a furnace and stunned speechless.

Unfortunately, this is how the now enraged goblin found me when it drove its fist into my face. The monster's knuckles slammed into my nose and the sound of it breaking was louder even then the grunts and snarling of the beast. Despite the tears blinding me, and the pulsing pain, I was still aware of the debuff that was now afflicting me: Temporary Blindness.

This blindness only lasted seconds, but they were seconds in which the goblin warrior repeatedly pummeled my body. Along with the bare-knuckle blows, the stabbing of a dagger into my stomach played sharp counterpoint to the drumming I was receiving. Fortunately, Emma was also able to attack the goblin while it was enraged and distracted with me. Through my clouded vision, I could see blasts of purple and black splashing onto the monsters back, it's roaring raising in volume after every hit.

After a few seconds, I could see once again, and I returned to the fight. I had only lost a quarter of my life despite the repeated uncontested strikes. Seeing that I had a five full Marks of Rage, I triggered my war cry skill. My yell distracted Robert's goblin as well, long enough that he was able to land a stunning blow, but it soon returned to trying to move around Robert and kill Annie. For all of the violence, I think it was Annie's cheers of joy as she lobbed fireballs at Robert's monster which was the most concerning.

At first, my disquiet was the flying flames that were far too close to Robert. But, once I watched him swing his arm through an oncoming fireball without notice, my worry turned to the unmitigated joy Annie was showing playing with fire. All of us had shown changes from this new world, but none so severe as Annie's. The moment she called upon her magic, her personality seemed to switch. That, or her character was freed from the shackles she willingly bound herself with. I was afraid for my sister and her changes, but also fearful for what it meant for me as well. Were my wild and adventurous antics my own, or some subtle impetus, an enhancement of my wild tendencies, from this new world? What would that mean for Robert or Emma?

Throwing these thoughts to the back of my mind, I blocked a stab from the waist-high monster and kicked it as hard as I could in the chest. The slavering green creature bounced off the wall and fell to its knees before I could kill it, Emma then hit it with her purple attack and finished it off.

Rushing to Robert and Annie's aid, I noticed that his life was down to a quarter; he was taking far more damage than I was. With all four of us attacking the goblin, its already injured body soon gave up and dropped to the ground. Each of us was breathing heavily, trying to adjust to the severe increase in difficulty. Once Robert caught his breath he stood and cast his healing spell on himself and then on me. The ability to instantly heal massive amounts of health was a godsend, though saying so might upset Robert. His earlier silence about his class bespoke his conflict in the potentially blasphemous nature of his new abilities.

Only one of the corpses remained when I went to loot the corpse. I smiled as I pulled out a crude iron club. It was ugly, but it would easily replace Robert's wooden table leg. When I stood to hand it off to Robert, I found the group staring at me with an odd look.

"What? We have to protect ourselves, and they sometimes have gear. Robert should use this," I said.

Annie flapped her mouth in consternation before she responded, "It's not the looting. We understand that. It's your language!"

I ducked my head as Annie's voice rose in anger. In the heat of the fight and the feeling of my nose breaking, my words had slipped my mind. Somehow they just didn't seem that important when compared to the visceral sound of a part of your body being destroyed.

"It's a skill I have. It lets me 'taunt' a creature and make it attack me instead of someone else. Someone like Emma, or you."

Annie backed up at this and shook her head then responded, "No, you can't blame us for this. You shouldn't say such things, and if it's a skill that made you say it, then you shouldn't use that skill."

Throwing the iron club at Robert's feet, I moved towards Annie and started to yell, "No. I'll use it any time it's necessary. We can't pretend the world hasn't changed. We need to adapt, we need to use whatever advantages or skills we have to survive. People are dying, and I refuse to be one of them."

"Whatever skills we have to survive? Anything? Anything at all?" Emma asked, the vitriol in her voice so unlike her normal tones that it left me flinching away in surprise.

Emma's face was scrunched up in disgust, made all the worse

when compared to her usually composed demeanor. If I had been told that Emma was capable of such an expression, I would never have believed it. Even then, watching her mouth pucker in disgust, her hands clench as if she wanted to hit me. Even then, I had trouble recognizing my friend in her features.

"No, some lines can't be crossed, things that shouldn't be done. No," she said.

I wasn't the only one concerned with Emma's words. Even Robert had turned to Emma with a face white in surprise.

"Emma, it was crass and crude, but she doesn't deserve that," he said.

Emma's face scrunched up and then she started to cry. Heart-rending sobbing that I had only heard from her when her mother fell ill and died. This was the sound of heartbreak, and I didn't know why. She rushed to Robert, his arms seeming to envelop her almost against his own will. With her face crushed into Robert's chest, her words were unclear. From group chat appeared the cause of her upset.

Emma [Level 2 Necromancer] - Spell: Create Soul Gem.

With a sinking feeling, I focused on the text.

Necromancer Spell: Level 2
Target: Single
Mana: 10 Mana
Effect: Captures the soul of an enemy upon death and creates a crystallized soul. Used in necromancer summoning spells and the creation of sentient magic items.

The great mage researcher Seldem was the first to extract a soul and force it into a physically contained form. His discovery was soon utilized by necromancers to create durable minions. Beyond deadly skeletons and specters, a crystallized soul is a crucial ingredient in many of the most powerful of magical items. - On the

mysteries of magic, Vol 1.

I just stood there staring at the information window. Disgust and confusion were bouncing around inside my mind. How could something like that spell even exist? It was disgusting, and I now understood Emma's reaction to my insistence that we should use whatever we could. If I needed further proof that our world had changed in ways incomprehensible to me, this was it.

While Emma cried in Robert's arms and Annie hugged her from behind, I looked around without direction trying to understand.

Robert's voice brought me out of my confusion and silenced Emma's tears, "You should use it."

All three of us turned to Robert. Emma was still held in Robert's arms, but she pulled back and looked up at him in confusion.

Looking at the ceiling, Robert closed his eyes while his arms tightened around Emma.

"I'm casting healing spells which are supposedly powered through my belief in the divine and mana. That's a miracle. I'm not the Messiah, and I'm not worthy of that kind of power. I'm not even sure if it *is* divine, it could be some demonic force trying to corrupt me."

Emma's look softened at Robert's words. The clench of Robert's eyes and his frown only underscored the tears and the dead tone to his voice.

Looking down into Emma's upturned face he continued, "But if it's for the people I love, it's worth it."

Both Annie and I turned away from that declaration. We knew it was his love, but not the love for the two of us that was the deciding factor in his actions.

"I agree with Robert," Annie said with a tentative voice, "I feel…something when I use my magic. I don't know if it's right or not, but we can't just give up."

I found myself remembering the words of father and the Colonel. How war drove men to do horrible things and that knowing it was for Queen and country was a poor balm. That it was the men standing beside them that became the real reason to fight.

Chapter 11

"Is that?"

Emma was crouched down next to me looking around the edge of the doorway. When I turned to confirm what I was seeing, she nodded.

In the large stone cave through the door were two goblins. The focused information was similar to the goblin warriors.

Shan-Dar Clan
Goblin Hunter - Elite
Ranger - Lvl 3
This would be an even fight.

The real surprise was the copper and wood rifles they had hoisted over a shoulder. At least they appeared to be rifles. The long copper barrels flared into a wide funnel while the wooden stock had little bronze triggers. They looked like something that a jeweler would make as a joke. Even with the bit of knowledge of weaponry I had, I knew that such thin copper would never be able to handle the force of the gun powder exploding.

Like the goblin warriors, these hunters knew we were here. They had pulled their rifles from a shoulder cocked position and were standing ready, but they were not attacking. They were not even aiming their guns at us. They just stood there guarding the next room's doorway while sneering and baring their fangs. It didn't make any sense. They could have just aimed at the door and picked us off as we tried to enter the room, but they just stood there. Watching.

Something was keeping them from attacking, and given the odd behaviors we had all exhibited lately, I was concerned that it was compelling us as well. The problem was determining if it was actually some outside influence or just the extreme situation we found ourselves in. I've always wanted adventure so when the chance for freedom was presented to me, I jumped for it. Given the way Emma and Robert were standing close ever since their shared decision to bend their morals in the name of survival, they were on the road to having what they wanted as well.

The odd one was my sister Annie, but she might be the clearest indicator of an outside force of all. I had assumed that she supported the restrictive rules and controls of society. Given her pure joy of throwing fire, she might have just been using the rules for what little control of her life she could obtain. While I had rejected societies rules and rebelled, she accepted them to have as much agency as possible. The same root feelings, just different expressions of them.

Shaking my head, I returned to staring at our enemies. While I was concerned, I wasn't as concerned as I felt I should be, yet more evidence for outside influence. All that being the case, it could wait until we were not literally staring enemies in the eyes. Moving through the doorway, I edged myself to the side of the door. Annie followed me out, while Robert and Emma moved opposite of me.

"Let me attack first. I've got better armor and more health. Once they are attacking me, then go ahead. Watch out for the room on our side," I said.

I wasn't sure if we should be going through the guarded doorway or the one on our side of the room. But my guess was the protected room. Guards meant something was important enough to defend. Like, possibly, the exit. We could open the other door and check after combat. Besides, the goblins were watching a stone archway, having that cleared and checked first seemed like a priority.

Moving slightly further to the side I charged the left most goblin. I had pulled to the side so that if the hunters shot at me, Annie wouldn't be in line behind me. Having my sister shot because they missed me would be deeply upsetting.

Both goblins bared their jagged teeth in their grimace smile and brought their rifles on target. I tried to dodge, sidestepping as I approached, but the retort of the two weapons came with two impacts. Surprisingly the weapons were quieter than I had expected, sounding like a loud popping noise instead of the sound of ordinary firearms.

Both rounds impacted on my chest, one above the armor, one on it, yet they did only slightly more damage than the arrows had. Both goblins fiddled with something on the side of their rifles, then raised for another shot. Slamming the broadside of my sword against one barrel, I kicked the other goblin in the stomach. The first weapon miss fired into the wall, but the goblin I kicked was able to shoot me in the hip before my kick landed. Noticing that I had enough Marks of Rage to trigger my yell, I did so. I wouldn't be making that mistake again.

While I was screaming my war cry, I tried swinging at the goblin I had first interrupted. The yelling, combined with the debuff from the leg shot, had me swinging wildly and missing. Distracted from my fumbling attack and the pain in my hip, I missed the moment that Annie decided to join the fight. The explosion of fire that impacted the goblin's face made her assistance known. That goblin turned, and that was when I used my taunt skill. The words that came from my mouth were sophisticated in their overwhelming crudity. While I disliked the sensation of something taking over my mouth, as well as the disgusting taunts which seemed to degrade both me and my target, I did enjoy the fact I could protect my family.

Emma took this as the cue to use her taboo skill. The spell snapped out of her lips, the sounds scratching across my mind. At the finish of her chant, a translucent green cloud flowed into the goblin's mouth and nose. Glancing at Emma, I noticed the look of disgust. Hardening my heart, I turned back to the goblin and continued my assault.

Most of my effort was spent switching between the two goblins and keeping them attacking me. Something about that felt correct. My job wasn't to kill these creatures, my job was to defend my family. When the two goblins lay before us, I tried to brush the sweat from my head and move my hair from my eyes. I felt a moment of disorientation when I realized that I wasn't sweating and my hair was just as I had left it this morning. I wasn't tired, it had to be late in the evening, and I had fought for hours, yet I felt fine. I could feel cold fingers of terror crawling up my spine at the disturbing differences in my world.

Robert had healed me during the fight, but he had remained next to Emma instead of rushing forward to attack. This was just more evidence that something was poking at us, urging us to work in specific ways. It didn't feel like I was being controlled, if I wanted to, I could leave all the fighting to Robert, but it felt like I had new instincts which pulled or pushed me towards success.

Everyone was now level three, which seemed wrong to me since it had taken so much for me to reach the same level. Emma pointed to the logs which mentioned bonus experience for dungeons and working in a group. That left me conflicted. I worked hard to level as far as I had, but I could have leveled faster with help. But then, I wouldn't have leveled at all unless I had pushed forward on my own since they would have just listened to the Colonel and hunkered down. Shaking my head, though my long hair barely moved at the motion, I turned to the loot.

Only one of the corpses remained and when I tried to take

its rifle my hand passed through it like it was a specter. Looting the body, I found a cloth cap. Focusing brought its information forward.

Raiment of the Dark
Non-Tradeable
Armor Type: Cloth
AC: 4
Class: Necromancer

Effect: 5% more health from the spell Lifetap.

"Emma, I think this is for you," I said while looking at the black cloth that was mostly a hood with rips and holes in it.

Watching, I waited for the moment that Emma noticed the condition of the cloth hood. I couldn't contain the giggle when her hand came back holding the ripped item. With her eyes focusing off into the distance, Emma was suddenly wearing the black cloth hood. With a glare at me, she focused into the distance again, and then the hood disappeared.

"Emma, I know it looks ugly, but you should wear it. We need every advantage we can get, and I want you protected," Robert said.

I was glad Robert was the one to say it. With my obvious joy at the silly apparel, I don't think she would have taken my suggestion as well.

"I am wearing it. If you look at your character sheet, there is an option to turn off the appearance of helms and hoods, that and cloaks. Nothing else though, I don't know why," Emma said with a pout.

This new weird world was equal parts beautiful and horrible. Far more than anything though, it was arbitrary. Rules seemed to exist for no sensible reason, they just were, and we had to adapt.

Forming up in our now familiar arrangement, I approached the closed door. Pulling the wooden door open, we found a small closet of shelves. Only a single curled up piece of paper sat on the shelf. The paper was a soft cream and reasonably new. The inked words on the back were in a sharp and precise hand. The letter detailed the layout of the mansion and the people who protected it. As I read the text, a new quest window appeared in front of me.

New Quest - Defend the Mansion.
The Blythe mansion has been targeted by the Shan-Dar Goblin Clan. Someone within the estate has given the goblins detailed defensive information. Discover evidence of the traitor and inform the Colonel of the coming assault.

Objective:
Find evidence of Traitor 0/1.
Inform the Colonel of the coming Assault 0/1.

Accept?
(Y/N)

Accepting the quest, I looked to each of my friends, and they each had the same grim look as I had. None of this made sense, this goblin dungeon hadn't existed even a day ago, but now it was apparently preparing to assault the mansion. Someone was supposedly handing over information to the goblins. For what reason?

We discussed it, but none of it made sense. We agreed that no one was able to do such a thing, let alone would have a *reason* to do it. I had a sinking feeling that I knew who would end up being the traitor in the quest. Despite my dislike of Rebecca, I didn't think she had been capable of betrayal, the timeline just didn't make sense. Besides, who would save such a note or even store it in such an accessible and unguarded place near the entrance? This quest had holes all the way through it, but we couldn't do anything but make our way forward and hope to warn the Colonel when we found an escape.

"One second," Emma said as we prepared to continue.

Stepping away from the group the new necromancer began a chant. The dark words which bubbled forth from Emma's throat scratched and ripped at the world. The hair on the back of my neck stood on end as she spoke. Emma's spells were not like Annie's. Annie would just focus, and a fireball would form at her effort and will. Emma had to talk, and her words were ones that man was not meant to know, never mind speak.

After more than a minute of focus and chants, Emma threw forward a sizeable white gem that contained a swirling fog. At her final pronouncement, the gem burst with a silent flash. Replacing the gem was a hunched over creature formed of bone. Recoiling from the beast, I realized that it was a goblin's skeleton. Its bones were shockingly white and unconnected to anything else. No muscles moved its body, but it turned to watch us all the same. Its form stood between Emma and us. Within the eye sockets was a glowing green flame.

"Follow," Emma said, her voice straining.

The abomination of bone made a ducking bow motion, then stood next to Emma.

With a concerned smile at Emma, we all turned to face the doorway the goblins had guarded.

Chapter 12

Emma's skeleton minion was useful; I'll give it that, but creepy. Then again, no more disturbing than the apparent manipulation of our minds. We talked about it, and we all agreed. We had some outside influence pushing us, making us develop in certain ways. I wanted to push forward, and everyone else wanted to hang back. I wanted to lead the charge and sacrifice my body to protect my friends. They wanted to hurt the monsters, all except for Robert. Robert wanted to heal each of us.

So, whatever was manipulating us, was trying to get us to fulfill our new 'classes.' It's useful, just like Emma's minion, but creepy.

"Oh!"

The sound of Emma's surprise had me looking around like a startled cat trying to see if monsters had attacked from behind. When she noticed my alarm, she gave me an embarrassed look.

"All right, what surprised you?" I asked, a small smile forming on my face.

"Well," she said, "I found a little button on my 'pet' window. It said 'first P.o.V.' and when I selected it…it's…hmm, hard to explain."

Waving her arm at the group she began, "I'm here while I'm also-"

Then the goblin skeleton waved its arm and continued her words, its voice hollow and filled with echoes, "-and also here at the same time."

The group stopped awkwardly and looked between Emma and her skeleton. The voice of the pet had neither been female or male, instead, a strange androgynous mix, but the body language and tone had been entirely Emma.

"Can you see through the skeleton's eye...um...sockets?" I asked.

"It's like I'm in both places at once. It's as if I had another arm...only this arm has eyes and feet and a mouth. It's weird, but this should help me fight a lot better!"

For someone who had been so conflicted over her spell, she was very chipper and excited to be using it now - more evidence of insidious mental manipulation.

For a while, each room we came to was joined with a hallway, and each doorway was guarded by two goblin warriors. We were surprised the first time that we noticed a goblin hunter inside a hall. I had been concerned that the hunter would run to another room and bring more goblins to kill us, but strangely the hunter just stood and took shots with its rifle at us. Charging to attack, I was joined by Emma's goblin skeleton. Her minion would swing around behind our enemies, and she would attack ankles and arms or try to knock them around. Being small and only a collection of bone, it was not very effective at knocking the goblins down. Emma eventually just had it climb on the goblin's back, this distracted them, ruined their attacks, and she managed a few critical hits while biting at their necks.

We moved forward at a plodding pace to let everyone's mana recover before we attacked. It was very odd that these monsters would watch us and let us recover. I tried calling out to them while we waited, hoping to see if one of them would respond. I wanted the experience and to increase my level, but being locked in this 'dungeon' was still a scary prospect. Finding the way out was more important; we could always go back to killing beetles and wolves outside if we had to. Despite my best efforts, the most I could get was for a goblin to hiss and bare its sharp teeth at me.

After finishing and resting up, we moved into a wider hallway, this one with graphic depictions of combat on the walls. At the end of the hall was a raised iron portcullis. The room beyond the gate was large, almost a hundred feet around, with two other gates diagonal from the entrance. Around the edge of the room was bench seating, and directly across from our hall sat a large goblin and throne. The throne was made of stone and bone, crude in its formation and wide. It had to be since the goblin which sat on it was huge, it's body crisscrossed by small white scars. It was slightly larger than the orcs we had fought during the event, but as fat as the young ogre.

Moving into the room, I focused on the seated goblin while it furiously dug a finger into a nostril while staring in disdain at us.

__Shan-Dar Clan__
__Mel'tar, The Arena Master - Boss__
__Warrior - Lvl 4__
__This would be a difficult opponent.__

A boss was something new, and so far, new was terrible. Though from the casual way he was leaning sideways on his throne while digging, he didn't seem that dangerous. He was large, and he showed the signs of many battles, but what did that mean in this new world? I had broken bones and didn't have a scar on me, so how was he so covered in them?

When we finally reached the center of the circular area the portcullis behind us slammed down leaving our retreat blocked. To our horror, the two other gates opened and the room slowly filled with goblins. We huddled together, with Emma's skeleton standing towards the entrance and me facing the throne. When goblins surrounded the arena, the two gates shut. The room wasn't filled, but there were more enemies than we could safely handle at once. The standing goblins thumped their chest and then sat, the large goblin slowly lumbered to his feet before addressing the crowd and us.

"Today we have new contestants! Welcome! Your first opponent is Yal'now!" he bellowed before sitting back on his throne.

Each of us received a new quest the moment the large monster planted his backside on his throne.

New Event - Conquer The Arena!

Objective:
Survive Five Waves 0/5.
Defeat Mel'tar 0/1.

From the back of the room, a small, sickly goblin stood. The little goblin's body was pale, almost albino, his arms weak and spindly, his legs nobby kneed and exposed due to his only garment being a loincloth. A more pathetic monster I could hardly imagine. But appearances had been deceiving before, but when I focused on his information, it confirmed my first assessment.

Shan-Dar Clan
Yal'now the Sickly - Elite
Warrior - Lvl 1
This opponent appears to be beneath you.

I was curious how he could be both sickly and an elite, but it didn't matter, we had to focus on survival. Emma looked to the weak goblin and had her skeleton attack while I watched the surrounding enemies. We had slowly formed into a competent fighting group, the unsaid command being natural after repeated battles. The sound of the skeleton slashing through Yal'now's chest, was drowned out by his squeal of terror and pain. A few seconds later he was dead. The event counter ticked over to one of five, but none of us shifted positions.

"Good! Good, the weakling is done for. Next, are the Dwar Brothers!" said the grotesque blob of a goblin, his voice being distorted with the finger which was now in his mouth.

Stepping forward were two goblins which resembled the ones from outside — though smaller, and lighter green. Screaming with mindless rage, both of the goblins charged. The first few seconds were a scramble. I managed to taunt one. I almost regretted the use of the skill since the cursing involved a comment on their smell, my genitals, and a fish. Despite the danger, I could hear Annie cackle in laughter as she threw a fireball at my enemy, but I doubt it had anything to do with her usual fire happy behaviors. I was worried when the other goblin charged towards Robert, but he just moved behind me and allowed me to attack his opponent. These monsters were very simplistic, and their minds seemed to forget everything around them the moment they were even slightly distracted. A few wacks to the back of the head were more than enough of a distraction.

When both enemies were down, I breathed a sigh of relief. My life was at fifty percent, having both of them attacking me at once had made dodging and blocking far more difficult. While I tried to calm down, Robert healed me to full life. Most of my contribution came from my war cry and holding their attention. Annie and Emma, along with her pet, did most of the actual damage. While I was breathing deeply to calm myself, Mel'tar was rearranging himself on his throne. Scratching his belly, he kicked both legs over one side of his chair and turned to the side, watching us out of only the corner of his eye. While he lounged, the event wave indicator ticked over again, and my confidence rose that we would be able to succeed here.

"Very good, very good!" Mel'tar began, only to interrupt himself with a horrible belch, "yes, now you fight. Hmm…them!"

Mel'tar's negligent hand wave pointed to three new enemies.

One was wearing a necklace made of bone while covering its face with a large reptile skull. His companions though appeared to be much like the previous brothers. This was starting to be a worry. If I taunted one, and Robert directed the other to me, what would we do about the third enemy?

My concerns were short-lived as the first goblin charged forward with his eyes locked on Emma, while the other was focused instead on Annie. When my first opponent tried to run past me, I swung hard at his neck with my sword. My weapon struck him across the throat, the blow which should have decapitated him only knocking him to the ground. I took the opportunity to stomp on his ankle. The kick skill did more than just provide information about kicks. The skill had wormed knowledge into my brain about tripping ankle blows, knockbacks, even odder sorts of related movements like shin strikes. I took advantage of this information while aiming a stomp for the large round bone on his ankle. The sound of the crack a pleasant counterpoint to his screams.

Glancing around I noticed that Robert was being attacked by one goblin while the bone adorned creature was just standing and watching. Ignoring the watcher, I turned to Robert's Goblin and used my taunt skill. This time the insult was mild and only involved the goblins supposed heredity and a dung beetle.

Annie began to scream, and her lowering health broke me out of my focused combat. Writhing in pain on the floor, Annie was curled up in a ball as little yellow and black insects swarmed her in a cloud. Every few seconds she would scream as another insect would stink or bite her and her life would dip a bit further. My distraction cost me as the goblin I was fighting slammed the pommel of his weapon into my temple, the swirling ducks and stars telling me what I already knew; I was stunned. I took multiple blows, and my health dropped.

Robert was casting his healing spell on Annie as fast as possible as her health fluctuated up and down repeatedly as the drain of the insect bites did damage every couple seconds. The metronome-like precision of the attacks was yet another oddity given it was creatures doing the damage. Once I killed the goblin that was giving me so much trouble, I turned to check the one on the ground. It was still crippled, but it was crawling its way towards Robert.

"Robert, keep an eye on the crippled one, I'm going after the other!" I shouted as I charged the watcher.

My choice to attack the bone adorned one came from the information window.

Shan-Dar Clan
Gid'gow, Shaman Apprentice - Elite
Shaman - Lvl 3
This would be an even fight.

I wasn't sure what abilities a shaman had, but the scare stories from the Colonel and father from fighting in Africa suggested this was a caster of spells involving nature. Insects attacking in a swarm seemed just like a shaman.

My first blow was right across the shaman's shoulder. The strike stopped on impact in a rather odd way, a green glow appearing around the shaman. The lack of damage was a concern, but the fact that it caused the shaman to focus on me instead of Annie was a relief. My sister's health quickly returned to normal, so that was even better. The shaman hissing in my face and releasing a gigantic putrid cloud of green gas was a problem though.

Gagging, I stumbled back, the cloud burning my eyes and nose. The green smoke cleared quickly, but the debuffs remained: sight and nose impairment. I didn't care about not being able to smell things, but not being able to see made hitting things difficult. The world was a blurry swirly mess. I was still able to find the shaman, but it was a hit or miss ordeal, mostly miss. The only good thing was that the debuff was short lived and the crawling goblin was slain when both casters focused on killing him. This left the shaman as the only goblin left to fight.

Each blow on the goblin was stopped by a green glowing aura, but that only lasted for a few attacks. After that, the impacts started to harm him if the flinching and hissing was any indication. The scary part was that this was the first creature we had fought that could heal itself. While we had worked to break through its shield spell, it cast some kind of red swirling mist around itself. The damage that had made it through the shield, almost entirely spell damage, was healing at a visible rate.

Even though it was healing, the damage it was taking was too severe. The shaman would occasionally move back and try to get clear to cast a spell in its rasping language, but I was not letting it. My blows, especially my kicks, kept interrupting its incantation. That meant we didn't take much damage once we were all focused on the shaman, but Robert was running low on mana from all the healing.

When the shaman finally died, we huddled up and glanced around at each other. Each of us had a similar look.

Fear.

We knew that with those three it had been a close fight and that at any time the goblins even now surrounding us could have ended our lives. It was likely this would get harder and harder until we started to drop.

"Hmm, I liked how you kept hitting Gid'gow. Served the stupid shaman right, he would never give me stomach medicine after feasts, said I had to eat less instead!" Mel'tar shouted as he rolled his corpulent body around to lean on his throne from the other side.

"Next, next, um…you!" The fat goblin shouted as he pointed at an unusually large goblin near one of the gates.

This goblin approached in a carefully balanced movement. This creature was wearing an outfit made from bits of metal scrap and chains. The metal was all cast-off; horse bits, a pot crudely hammered flat, but despite its makeshift nature, on this large goblin it was still frightening.

Shan-Dar Clan
Mid, The Wild - Elite
Berserker - Lvl 3
This would be an even fight.

When I noticed his class, I had a flashback of the overly large fists and the horrific damage that Philip had done.

"Watch out! He's a berserker. If he starts screaming, don't let him hit you," I shouted.

"I'm low on mana, I'm not sure we are going to make it," Robert said.

Looking at the group window, I saw what he meant. His mana was at around thirty percent. We had discovered earlier that just like low life had a debuff, low mana had one as well. Annie had tested it and described it as the worst headache combined with flu-like symptoms. Our situation was grim, and it was getting worse. We were surrounded, all of us had wounds and were mentally exhausted from the constant fighting as well as the stress, and our healer was now running low on mana.

"I think I've got an idea," Emma said with a wicked smile.

Chapter 13

"How is this possibly working?" I asked.

Emma's idea was simple, but should never have worked. If the goblins had even the slightest bit of intellect, it wouldn't have worked. I watched as the large goblin with makeshift armor slowly trudged around the outside edge of the arena, Emma carefully walking the circumference while Robert rested with us in the middle.

The goblin audience just placidly watched the slow, plodding circles. None seemed to be bored or even upset by the weird foot race. Our opponent should have switched to trying to kill Robert or even Annie but seemed fixated on Emma. Emma's idea had rested on two things. The oddly mechanical nature of our enemies thinking, always attacking whoever annoyed them the most, and her latest spell.

Spell: Creeping Shadows
Necromancer Spell: Level 3
Target: Single
Mana: 10 mana
Effect: Calling forth the shades of the unjustly killed to torment and slow the movements of the living. Reduces movement speed for 3 minutes, does 10 damage per 6 seconds.

Altog the Shade was the mastermind behind the creeping shadows spell series. His refinement of the spell over his many decades of research has produced the definitive work on the use of shades against the living. It is regrettable that his research was cut short because of his lack of experimental rigor. - Necromancy,

the Masterwork. Volume 2, 3rd Edition.

Annie had a spell that also slowed the movement of her target. Both of them could use this strategy, but only Emma's spell caused damage. Annie's spell slowed the creature more, but that was a smaller concern. Emma just kept running in circles and re-applying her Creeping Shadows as needed while Robert sat and recovered mana. His recovery would be faster outside of combat, but it was still better than nothing. Emma being low on mana at the end of the fight wasn't as big a deal as Robert being unable to heal. Each round had left me with lower life, and if one of the other girls were suddenly attacked, they would need healing as fast as he was able.

While this strategy was working -Robert was at eighty-five percent mana and rising quickly- it felt weird to me. My new instincts thought this was perfectly fine, but it hurt my sensibilities. We were supposed to be in a battle arena fighting to the death, not taking a walk around a park. I was happy that we would be able to survive this. It just seemed so very odd.

Finally, the goblin fell over. The corpse faded away quickly like each of the goblins during this event. I was a little concerned that we had found no loot during this quest. We had killed a large number of enemies and found nothing. We had never killed this many before without seeing something, usually something worthless, but something none the less.

While I was fretting, the large goblin rose from his throne and began his usual quip before combat. The pattern was clear, but I didn't know what it meant if it meant anything at all.

"Very strong. Very capable. Now they fight you. Try to live. I'm bored," Mel'tar said as he plopped onto his throne while pointing to two smaller goblins who huddled together and began to chant.

Rushing forward, I was almost able to attack one before he

completed his spell. With a flick of his wrist, a glowing blue shield appeared around the two goblins. The goblin I tried to attack paused and hissed at me through the bubble of magic then gave me a broad smile and returned to his chanting. The cheeky look had distracted me, but not enough to stop me from bashing away at the shield. My focus on the smiling monster in front of me allowed the other goblin to attack me without me being aware and I suffered because of it. The blast of flame looked like a mirror image of the one my sister was casting. The small ball of fire impacted me under my right arm and then expanded into a billow of force that threw me at least four meters.

Crawling back to my feet I charged back to the goblin pair driving an overhead strike into the glowing shield with all my strength. The shield flickered for a brief moment, and I could feel the grin stretching across my face, but it was short lived as the goblin started the chant from before. I swung wildly at the wizard's spell shield but was unable to stop him from recasting the glowing protection.

My stamina was draining quickly, rarely had our battles lasted so long that there hadn't been brief pauses between fights. Even just moving around to reposition myself had been enough to allow some stamina to recover. In this case, I was just standing there and beating against the shield. The goblin pair just chanted and cast at me repeatedly.

Total exhaustion weighed upon me like lead weights. My body felt like I was covered by hot wet blankets, the press and strain of my body aching along every muscle. Swaying in front of the shield, my body almost unable to remain upright, I tried to drag my sword through the dirt to lift it to deliver another strike but failed. The goblin in front of me grinned at my struggles, the smirk flashing to horror as Emma's skeleton tackled him. During my efforts, I had failed to notice that the spell shield had faded due to the bombardment from Annie and Emma. Struggling to breathe, I waited until my stamina had returned some before I waded into battle.

The two goblin wizards died seconds after the shield went down. The high damage output but low health was a concern. If Annie followed in the same vein as these goblins, I would need always to keep myself between her and any melee opponents. Each time they had tried to enact a spell, a kick or blow to the head had stopped their casting. Spells were powerful, but in close combat, they could be negated with a strike to the mouth. For most, if you can't speak, you can't cast.

The different debuffs were starting to take on an importance in my mind. Snares to control enemies, stuns to stop casting, and I'm sure a myriad of others. Each had a use, and each could turn the tide of battle. It wasn't always about the amount of damage or health you had. I needed to keep that in mind since my instincts screamed that I just needed to attack every foe head-on. More importantly, these debuffs could affect me as well. A snare could stop me from saving my family, or a stun could leave me standing around while enemies slaughter them. I needed to do better, be better, then just heading straight in and attacking. Before, I wanted to level to be free, now I had a new reason. I was going to keep my family safe.

Clapping his hands Mel'tar climbed to his feet.

"Yes, yes, you won. Now you fight me!" the boss yelled to the excitement of the few goblins left around the arena.

The event list flashed in the corner of my vision. All we needed to do was beat Mel'tar, and we would win the event. I wasn't sure if we would have to fight the last of the goblins, but compared to their leader, they shouldn't be that hard.

Roaring like a lion, Mel'tar started to lumber forward, the fat of his belly swinging back and forth as he strode forth. His sight was locked onto Annie, so I pulled his attention to me with my taunt skill. This time I made every effort to contain my voice. If

I could stay silent, then I could have the benefits of the ability without the embarrassment. To my chagrin, I remained silent, but I still performed a rude gesture. My gesture was successful in turning the goblins charge in my direction, but to my surprise, his steps kept accelerating. By the time the goblin arena master had crossed half of the field of battle, he was moving so fast his legs were a blur beneath him. Clipping me across my left side, I was flung away in a twirl, my health dipping dangerously.

I was trying to climb to my feet when I heard Emma scream. Some instinct took hold, and I rolled across the ground, the dirt on the stone floor rubbing across my face. My instincts saved me from being flattened by Mel'tar's flying fat. His body was laying across the ground with arms and legs spread with ducks and stars floating around his head.

Rolling further away from the downed goblin I stood and rushed to the now recovering boss monster. My kick hit the goblin across his jaw but failed to induce the stun debuff as I had hoped. Unfortunately, my blow left me unbalanced, and Mel'tar took advantage of this by grabbing me by my ankle and throwing me away as he stood. It shouldn't have been possible for the fat goblin to throw me five meters with a single hand, but little in this world seemed to make sense. I managed to land on my feet though I did stumble to my knees from the impact.

While I had been thrown through the air, Emma had been casting her life draining purple bolt as Annie continued to use her favored fireball spell. Robert's heals caught me whenever I dropped below fifty percent life. I spent most of the fight flipping through the air mostly when the goblin used his charge attack. Even so, the fight itself was not particularly dangerous. We were steadily beating him down, Emma's skeleton doing almost as much damage as I was. Most of my effort was just spent in using my body as a shield for my friends. I used war cry as it was fading and taunted the goblin any time it looked like he was turning to one of the others. At seventy-five percent of his life, things changed.

Slamming me into one of the walls, Mel'Tar raised his arms and shouted, "I need a timeout, you fight him!"

Pointing at one of the goblins around the edge, he jumped backward, his body flying through the air until he landed before his throne. The jump was more than ten meters, it shouldn't have been possible, but he did it in an almost casual way. I had just used my taunt skill, so I was caught without it. This was a problem since the goblin who was taking Mel'tar's place was running directly for Robert.

"Watch out Rob!" I shouted.

With a panicked look, Robert turned and hefted his mace in preparation for the new goblin's attack. Annie demonstrated her version of the snare spell with a pulsing golden glow. The golden lights surrounded the goblin's legs, his movements seeming normal above the hips but below them, his legs slowed as if he was running through syrup. In the group window, Annie's mana plummeted. Her spell might slow the monster to a greater degree, but it was also far more expensive. The tradeoff was worth it. With the goblin slowed to nearly a standstill I was able to rush past Robert and intercept the goblin. This monster was a warrior, and we were able to kill him quickly once we had him restricted and only aiming for me.

"Good now. Time in!" Mel'tar shouted before his flying body tackled me to the ground.

The next few minutes were filled with yelling as my head swam under the effects of the stun. The only thing in the room I could see was the duck quacking in a circle past my head, the light of the stars hurting my eyes too much to see. When I returned to myself, Robert was being pummeled by the boss, his life all ready below a quarter. Using my taunt failed to drag the goblin off him, but my running tackle seemed to work. While it left me on the ground next to the goblin, a fact he took advantage of by slamming his fists into me, it also let Robert move away.

Scrambling upright I used my war cry since its effect had faded. To my horror, the goblin had only lost five percent from when the boss had called for a time out while the rest of us were suffering from low mana or health. Robert used up some of his precious mana to recover his own health, the act of healing drawing the goblin's attention once again. Crawling up onto his hands and knees the goblin lunged into a staggered run towards Robert which turned into his full speed sprint attack. Unlike me, Robert was able to dodge out of the way. To my surprise, Mel'tar ran past Robert and into the wall at full speed. The stun timer over his head was double the duration of any stun I had seen before.

"Lay into him while he is stunned!" I shouted as I rushed to the boss.

Emma's skeleton reached the goblin before I did; her minion's bony hands clamped onto the boss. The skeletons weird glowing eyes met mine and Emma's words came from its skull.

"Be careful, use your taunt only when you need it. He could try and pull more goblins into the fight," the skull said in its disturbing tones.

I agreed with Emma. If he were willing to cheat once, he would do it again. Though we had fought less than fairly with Emma's snare, we had at least battled instead of calling a timeout!

When the stun effect faded, the goblin stood and turned to Annie. Her fireballs had done the most amount of damage out of all of us. Every few fireballs had exploded with a more massive explosion and had twice induced a burning debuff on the boss. Leaning forward the boss began his windup run, his legs starting to pump faster as he charged. I couldn't see Annie being able to dodge out of the goblins way as Robert had. Trying to keep the goblin from stampeding my sister I kicked the side of his knee, and the results were spectacular. Flopping forward, his face sliding across the ground, I watched a broken leg debuff appear over the goblin.

I couldn't contain my excitement at this development, with the goblin's leg broken, he wouldn't be able to flee, and we could kill him with little effort!

"No. Time for timeout, need water. You play with them!" Mel'tar said, his debuffs instantly disappearing as he jumped into the air.

Landing next to his throne he pointed to another goblin who obligingly strode forward only to be snared by Emma. My taunt flew moments later. The crude guttersnipe language coming from my mouth was partly the skill and partly the fact that Mel'tar was suddenly free of debilitating injury. There was nothing fair about this battle, and the entire thing was beyond acceptable. We were running a gauntlet of an arena battle, and he was taking timeouts!

Roaring my rage, I slammed my weapon with a two-handed grip into the goblins head. I was focusing on his bulbous noggin in the hopes of stunning him, but also to release some of my anger. These weaker goblins were not that difficult to fight. They were slightly more fragile than the ones we had fought on the way here. The real issue is that we shouldn't have to fight them at all. Before the goblin died, I looked around and realized that besides Mel'tar, there was only one goblin left. I had a feeling that sometime before the end of the battle, another timeout would be called.

When the last goblin died, Mel'tar spat some water on the ground and screamed, "Time in now!"

The last time he had done this I had been unprepared. This time I was ready for the jumping green menace. Watching his overweight body flying through the air, I sidestepped and swatted him with my sword as he passed. The impact on the ground left him with another stun debuff, though this was far shorter than his run and slam version.

With him laying there stunned, those of us beating on him were able to deal significant damage. There was a difference between the damage done when a monster could move and when they couldn't, and the difference was substantial. Beyond being unable to dodge attacks while lying helpless, the damage the boss received was increased as well.

When the bosses' stun faded, his eyes focused on Annie again, and he started his stomp-run routine. It had worked so well before that I decided to see if I could break his knee again. I was unsuccessful, but my follow up taunt had him trying to swing around in a wide turn, his body already halfway to full speed. In a weird display of athleticism and buffoonery, the goblin launched himself into his high-speed sprint, only to slam into the wall.

His life was around twenty-five percent, and when Annie's fireball knocked him down to twenty-five exactly, he launched himself to his throne again.

"Again?!" Emma shouted, just as frustrated as the rest of us.

Wobbling near his throne Mel'tar pointed at the last goblin and gestured him into the fight.

"Um...fight...yeah...um," he said, his body swaying uncertainly.

The last goblin was snared by Annie using up the rest of her mana. She started running around the arena, though she stepped wide around Mel'tar. After a few minutes of Emma's skeleton beating on it, the goblin turned to attack the calcified minion. I jumped in at that point and attacked as Emma pulled her skeleton back. We couldn't let her pet die. We would need every bit of damage to finish off Mel'tar. Once the goblin was focused on me, I started to walk backward keeping it at range.

"I've got as much mana back as I'm going to, let's do this," Robert said.

Slamming my sword into the goblin, I attacked while Emma's goblin paired up with me.

"Watch out for the boss jumping in when this guy dies!" Emma shouted.

Emma's warning was timely since a particularly precise strike from my sword killed the goblin, forcing Mel'tar back into the fight.

While airborne the boss shouted, "now time in!"

Robert was the target of this particular impact, and he dodged the blubbery goblin handily. Letting lose my war cry and then my taunt I walked forward, trying to conserve as much stamina as possible. We were all on edge as we slowly chipped away at the bosses' health. Without other goblins to call on for help, we were concerned with what Mel'tar would do instead. His running charge was easy enough to handle when I was able to use my taunt to pull him away from my friends. When he slammed into the wall at ten percent life, and the stun appeared, we attacked with every last bit of our stamina and mana.

At two percent health, he recovered from the stun and stood up, but was unable to stop us from finally ending him.

The event text flashed, and a vast amount of experience flashed into each of us. By the end, each of us had leveled twice. Our event log showed us with a bonus for the first time finishing

'Conquer The Arena!', a bonus for being 'NPCs,' a bonus for having a partial group, and another bonus for completing an event that no one had finished before.

I was left staring at the log trying to make sense of the message. How would anyone have had a chance to 'finish the event before us'? How would anyone be able to finish it again? Mel'tar was dead! None of it made sense. But it didn't matter. We lived, we were all stressed even if we were not tired in body. I needed a moment to rest and collect myself before we did anything else. Closing my eyes, I started to weep silently. I turned away to keep my pain and stress from spreading to my friends.

Chapter 14

"Vick? You need to see this hun," Annie called, her voice subdued and gentle.

While rubbing my tears away with my forearms, I chuckled when I noticed that my eyes weren't puffy and irritated from crying. Even when upset, I was still looking for the oddness in my new world. This change was a welcome one. I never liked how anyone could tell I was upset for hours after a cry. My pale skin and dislike of cosmetics made the red puffy eye bags obvious.

With a pause, I considered, was I getting too comfortable with my new world? It had only been a single day, and yet I was already enjoying the freedom and power of my world. Yes, I had just cried from the release of tension and worry from the recent fight, but I had also enjoyed the battle and the contest of wills. Biting my bottom lip, I shook my head and turned to Annie to see what she was worried about.

"I'm good, what is it?" I asked.

Annie gave me a look that said she wasn't convinced but that she would let it go if that was what I wanted. With a small smile, I gave her a slight nod, which she returned then turned to point to the throne. I already knew I would have to talk to her about how I felt later, her and Emma both. I felt for Robert being unable to share his feelings, but maybe in this new world, he could talk to Emma?

In front of the throne sat a large chest with golden straps

bolted into white polished wood. In the front was a giant keyhole, a keyhole far too expansive to actually be useful in hindering thieves. Lifting the heavy lid, Robert moved the items inside the chest while his eyes lost focus as he tried to read the information for our 'loot.'

"Oh…this is going to be useful," Robert said as he passed a large metal shield to me.

Mel'tars Bulwark
Non-Tradeable
Armor Type: Plate
AC: 18
Class: Warrior, Paladin, Cleric, Death Knight

Effect: Once every 2 hours, surround each party member with a mobile shield which will attempt to block physical attacks automatically.

My grin spread across my face as I hoisted my new shield onto my forearm. The front of the shield had a red circle emblem with a yellow lightning bolt crashing through it. It was a large slab of metal, longer even then my sword, and slightly curved along its width. The forearm strap was a simple loop of leather bolted to the metal, but the grip was a handle of metal with a wood and leather wrap. Equipping the shield, I started to shift it around checking to see how it felt. The shield moved almost effortlessly and how to use the protection was floating around inside my mind ready to be used.

While I played with my new shield, Annie was holding up a pair of slippers. They were light blue with tiny sparkles floating around them and had upturned toes, and they reminded me of something out of Edward Lane's 'The One Thousand and One Nights.' Annie flipped through her menu, the vacant far away stare giving it away before her shoes suddenly appeared on her feet. Her new footwear contrasted oddly with her summer style dress, but fashion was the least of our worries now.

"What are they, Annie?" I asked.

With a mischievous look, Annie sent the title of her shoes to party chat.

Annie [Level 5 Wizard] - Slippers of the Sorcerous Concubine

The name had me blushing and giggling, but the information for the item had me confused.

Slippers of the Sorcerous Concubine
Non-Tradeable
Armor Type: Cloth
AC: 5
Class: Wizard

Effect: Reduces cooldown of Spell: Blink by 1 second.

"Blink?" Robert asked.

Annie started to hop around in her new shoes, a level of joy I hadn't seen from her since father had left for India.

"It's a new spell I just got," she said before she barked out a word in a tongue-twisting language.

Once the word snapped out, a white flash appeared and surrounded her. A moment later there was a small popping sound and Annie was gone! Spinning around I noticed Annie standing at the edge of the arena smiling at us and waving!

"Useful, right? It's quick to cast, and it teleports me in a random direction a short distance while also making everything around my last location slightly less angry with me. It's expensive on my mana though," Annie said with a small pout.

I could only shake my head at her display. We needed to let each other know about our new spells and abilities, one of them could be the difference between life and death, just as Emma's Creeping Shadows spell had almost been.

"I know I earned some skills from leveling. What did each of you gain?" I asked.

Emma stepped closer and shared a slight smile with Robert before speaking up, "I have a spell called Root which ties an enemy to the ground for a time and a spell called Envenomed Bolt. It does a bit of damage at first, and then every few seconds it does a little more damage. It's really cheap so it should be better than just casting my lifetap spell all the time."

I nodded at that. I had noticed that Annie was able to cast very damaging spells very quickly, while Emma's spells didn't do nearly as much damage. On the other hand, Emma's spells were able to heal her as it hurt the enemy, a significant benefit.

"Robert?" Annie asked as she turned to face him.

Robert had a strange look on his face before he began to cast a spell. After a few seconds with his hand outstretched in front of him, he clenched his fist and ended his chanting. Around each of us, a transparent white shield appeared then soaked into our skin. In my mind, I could see a new buff protecting each party member. Focusing on the spell's effect, I asked for its description.

Spell: Protection of the Righteous.
Cleric Spell: Level 4
Target: Party
Mana: 35 mana
Effect: Increases AC for each party member by 20, reduces spell damage by 2%.

Edward the Righteous spent many years perfecting his spell of protection. After decades of effort, his spell was finally completed with a whisper of divine power. - Words of Warding.

"That should help, though I don't know how much. I also gained a group heal spell that is very expensive but fast casting.

I probably won't use it much if I can avoid it," Robert said.

Nodding, I turned to Annie, "We know about blink, anything else?"

"I also got the root spell," she said.

I grinned while looking through my log windows to see what I gained.

Level up!
Victoria [Warrior lvl 4] - at level 10 NPC's will no longer be zone locked.
New Skills!
Gained Skill - Block.
Gained Skill - Parry.
Level up!
Victoria [Warrior lvl 5] - at level 10 NPC's will no longer be zone locked.
New Skills!
Gained Skill - Riposte.

"Oh…I know how to Block using my new shield, and I also gained Parry and Riposte…hmm," I started to hum to myself as I let the information for my new skills float through my head. It was odd how I just suddenly was able to do things that I hadn't been capable of a moment before. What was stranger was the idea of using my sizeable cleaver-like sword to parry and riposte. But my new skills insisted that it should be possible even if the concept was ludicrous. Given the insanity that was my world, I didn't doubt that it would work just as the new information in my mind said it would.

"I think we should rest here," Robert began, "We can slip into one of the earlier side rooms and barricade the door. Emma planned ahead and brought food. We might not need sleep, but after that fight, I'm a bit tense, and some rest would help."

I was worried about the time we spent resting when we

didn't really need it. If we didn't get to level ten, then we would be stuck. Everything said the next five levels would be harder than the previous five. Yes, we had made it halfway in a day, but I didn't want to leave it up to the end. Looking at Annie and Emma, I noticed the weary looks that they had and reluctantly agreed to rest.

Chapter 15

Not needing sleep is not the same thing as not being *able* to sleep. The difference was apparent when Emma's screams and tears woke me. Somewhere in the night, I had slipped into slumber while resting on my makeshift bed. Robert had been laying near the barricaded door, and he woke and flopped around before rushing over to hold Emma through her tears. Annie and I had tried to calm Emma down, but in her distress, she had been inconsolable. Only once Robert wrapped her in a hug and shushed her while rocking did she seem to get through her suffering. Over Emma's head, Robert gave me a haunted look before he closed his eyes and continued to rock her tightly.

The pain was so raw that I had to look away. Annie I noticed, had a look of wistful yearning before her face cleared into her usual polite neutral. But I had seen behind the mask. I knew she didn't want to marry Robert, but there was something there just the same. The marriage plans had provided a direction for her life, and protection, and the safety of the rigid structure of society. Even if she rejected it, having that support had been a comfort of a sort. Now we were all, literally and figuratively, on our own.

After Robert had calmed Emma, a process involving gentle hugs and whispers -something we all pretended was not happening- we prepared for another day of fighting. We had only rested for a few hours, but it had been a needed respite from the high pressures of constant battles. We may eventually become resistant to the strain of daily fighting and near death, but for now, we had adapted surprisingly well but were still needful of rest.

Gathering the dresses I had used for a pillow, I passed them back to Annie, and she returned them to her inventory. She hadn't explained why she had stored her entire wardrobe of dresses in her inventory, but our lack of sleeping gear had turned it into a surprising advantage. This outing was showing that even those who had planned and prepared had been underestimating the requirements. Blankets, bedrolls, pillows, tents, food, water, even firewood for when we were in places like this dungeon, would need to go onto our future lists for things to take in our inventory. Luckily, with Annie's pyrotechnic ways, a lighter or matches wouldn't be required.

Once we had gathered all our wayward supplies, Robert and I moved to the shelf we had used to barricade the door. We had picked a room that had been a few hallways before the arena. The side hall we chose had a six by six meter room that had shelves all around it. After we cleared off the dusty junk from one shelf, we moved it together in front of the door. It wouldn't have stopped a persistent opponent, but it would have woken us with enough time to equip ourselves and prepare.

One of our initial concerns had been what to do with our waste. An issue that Robert had reluctantly brought up, but it was a serious concern. Father and the Colonel had told more than one story of how failure to properly prepare a campsite had lead to an enemies defeat through disease and disorganization. As we had discussed the logistics, the truth had slowly dawned on us. Just like we no longer sweated, or how our stamina bar determined the difficulty (or lack) of an action, or how our hair always seemed to fall perfectly coifed, so too did we no longer need to use the facilities. It's amazing how even when something is objectively an improvement, it can still be disconcerting when you no longer are required to do it if you have been doing it all your life. This fundamental law of the universe, what goes in must come out, no longer being iron clad shook me more than seemingly all the other inconsistencies.

With the door free, Robert was about to open it to check and see if the coast was clear. Tapping him on the shoulder, I gestured him to step behind me. I could see the moment of hesitation, but in the end, he stepped back. I was honestly impressed with Roberts adaptability. Few men would be willing to step back in this situation, and I felt a warmth in my heart knowing that he trusted me to do my part in keeping everyone safe.

There were two potential ways to handle the closed door. Either I could slowly open it and peek around the edge checking to see if any enemies were close, or I could whip the door open quickly and prepare to defend with my shield up and blocking the way. Both had benefits, but I decided to go with the second option. I hoped that none of the goblins had moved from further in the dungeon into the areas we had already cleared of enemies. If the goblins acted the way the grey wolves had outside, walking a specific path and only reacting to close enemies or aggression, then there would be no enemies to fight. The fact that we had rested uninterrupted supported this hypothesis. Either way, I would be prepared to use the doorway as a chokepoint against any opponents.

Grabbing the handle, I slowly turned it listening for any disturbance beyond the door. When the handle turned far enough that I could feel the latch slip past, I yanked the door open. I took care not to slam the door into the wall, not being sure if a loud noise would draw in enemies or not, but my efforts to tuck behind my shield was a klutzy mess. The arm holding the shield was also the one used to turn the doorknob. In my effort to keep from slamming the door as well as return my guard to a protective position, I almost slammed the door closed instead of resetting my shield. Luckily there were no enemies to defend against, but I would remember this foible and try and improve in the future. Somehow I thought that opening doors while trying to protect my group was going to be an ongoing issue.

Listening to the empty hallway I signaled Emma that she should summon her new minion. Last night she had had the foresight to capture another goblin soul to have one in reserve in case her pet was killed. When we bedded down for the night, she had not needed to poll the group to know that no one wanted it watching over us. We couldn't be sure it wouldn't attack the moment Emma went to sleep. In truth, it had just been unsettling with it standing there, gently bobbing, its joints clicking and its eyes glowing. I had instructed Emma to wait before summoning her skeleton because of the loud and extended period it took for her to create it. This way if the pathway was clear we could watch for approaching enemies, if the sound caught their attention.

Fully buffed with Robert's new spell and Emma's new pet following along, we ventured forth. As we moved forward in formation, it became apparent that our first hypothesis had been correct. None of the previous locations with goblins had been re-manned. Even the arena was empty. We had two ways to proceed from the arena, a door to the left or right. After a short discussion, we decided to go through the right door. We were not sure it was the correct way, but we needed to make some progress, and so we used one of the coins we had been collecting to make the final decision.

Through the doorway, we again started to see goblins, though far fewer hunters. At first, we had found it difficult to get into the routine of fighting, our teamwork not as well practiced as it had been the day before. But after three rooms worth of enemies, we had restored our performance. The fourth room though was different. Instead of a pair of goblins guarding the doorway and a third goblin walking through the hallway -the most common arrangement- this room had only one goblin barring the way. There was a goblin standing on the left-hand side of the door, but the right side was without a goblin. We could see a goblin walking a pathway through the door from the middle of this room and into the next, but with only one guard it looked odd and lopsided.

"This doesn't feel right," I said, to which the others nodded in agreement.

We had returned to whispering when uncertain, even as none of the goblins seemed to care.

"Should we wait until the patrolling goblin is walking away before we attack this goblin, like usual, or should we grab both of them?" I asked.

Robert hesitated to answer, probably not wanting to look weak, but Annie had no such compunction, "Something is wrong, let's play it safe."

Emma nodded her agreement, so it was decided. Once the patroling goblin warrior moved out of range into the far hallway, I stepped forward and attacked the goblin guarding the door. My usual routine here was to attack and taunt, then immediately move back so that we could fight the goblins at the doorway we entered. It had taken some practice and Annie resisting the urge to burn everything, to let me pull the duo back without one of the others getting attacked. But with our recent practice, it was almost second nature.

When I had finally positioned the goblin warrior I was just starting into my fighting routine of War Cry - Vigor when I noticed Annie's life plummet. Spinning around, ignoring the goblin beating on me, I watched Annie fall to her knees as a dagger was ripped from her back. The goblin behind her was short and covered in blackened leather armor. Annie's life was at fifty percent, and I tried to charge her attacker, but I wasn't quick enough to stop him from slamming his dagger into her again. Her life only dropped by ten percent this time, but that was little comfort. A particularly nasty attack from the goblin warrior I had been ignoring struck my head and I returned to seeing the world through stars and floating duckies. Snapping out her blink spell, Annie disappeared from her prone position. She reappeared near Robert and the spell that he had been casting during this fight finally completed and healed Annie to full life again. This sudden shift in position, along with the heal, left Robert as the primary target of the second attacker.

All I could do was stand there and be beaten senseless while Robert faced down the short black-clad goblin. After a few hits by the small goblin and his feeble attempts to return the blows, he risked casting his fast but expensive group healing spell. This helped restore his health, as well as my own, but it caused the monster beating on me to turn to Robert instead. My stun faded just in time for me to see the backside of the goblin warrior running at Robert to join the short goblin's onslaught. Oddly, before the Goblin warrior reached Robert, it stopped to try and attack the goblin skeleton that was riding on its back. I wasn't going to waste such a distraction. Sidestepping the skeleton and his goblin mount, I taunted Robert's enemy. For once this was not enough to change an enemies target. After slicing into the short goblin's back a couple times, I gained his ire enough that he turned from Robert. Focusing on the smaller enemy, I requested his information.

Shan-Dar Clan
Goblin Stalker - Elite
Rogue - Lvl 3
This opponent appears to be beneath you.

A rogue!

I now knew what had happened. Somehow this rogue had gotten behind us and attacked using a backstab just like the beetle. Rogues had less life than warriors and took more damage, but from behind they could perform one single massive attack with their backstab. Luckily they couldn't repeatedly use that attack. Otherwise, Annie would have died in seconds. With the thought of my sister bleeding out on the ground, I attacked with greater ferocity. It wasn't long before my attacks ended the rogue and I turned to attack the warrior. It was a good thing as well since the goblin warrior had just finished the skeleton that had been clawing at its back and was turning to Emma.

Contemptuously, Emma cast creeping shadows on the warrior and then her soul capturing spell. The warrior was slowly moving towards Emma while drooling and slavering. Attacking the goblin from behind, I had free rein to beat on the enraged warrior as it ponderously chased after Emma. When it was finally dead, Emma began recreating her skeleton while Robert sat and panted trying to recover his mana.

"We should probably go back and clear out some of the other goblins to keep another rogue from coming up behind us," I said.

Emma shook her head, but we had to wait for her to finish her casting before she explained further.

"That won't help. That goblin was invisible. He just appeared behind Annie. I think he was standing next to the other goblin guarding the doorway, but we couldn't see him," she said.

My stomach knotted at the new problem. Invisible enemies could mean suddenly fighting a large number of foes at any time with no warning.

Chapter 16

Once I detailed my experience of the beetle backstabbing me when I wasn't paying attention, everyone grouped up in an awkward circle facing outward. It seemed like the obvious solution to a potentially invisible enemy. The rogue we killed never disappeared after he ambushed Annie, so it was likely their invisibility was like their backstab: limited. Once they were visible, they would have to remain visible. It wasn't a certainty, but it was likely, and it was our only plan. As long as they didn't ambush anyone with a backstab, they would be limited to being just a weaker warrior.

The next room clearings were awkward in an entirely new way. Maintaining such a tight formation meant slowly walking along while trying to keep shoulder to shoulder. Fighting was a nightmare. After a hidden rogue appeared next to Robert, who was right behind me, I had to use my taunt to pull the rogue away from him. This meant a delay where the rogue stabbed him multiple times before my taunt was available. This, in turn, had me only maintaining the aggression of my warrior enemy through damage, something my sister was able to overpower in short order.

After the third room, Emma called a halt to our progress.

"I think the rogues are just standing in the spots the warriors would be, just invisible. If we don't see a goblin in the hallway beyond the room, it might be an invisible rogue. That's the only real risk that we would get all three at once," she said.

Robert voiced my frustration before I could, "That doesn't

make any sense, why would they act like that? Even the mentally deficient would be able to see that as a poor plan!"

"I think they are limited in the ways they can think," I said.

At that, everyone focused on me.

Straightening up I continued, "Remember the first message? These are the forces of the 'Old Ones,' I think these creatures are being mind controlled to only act in certain ways. These are the ground troops. Their thinking has been restricted like a clockwork automaton. They act stupid, but there are many of them, and they will never rebel. As long as these 'Old Ones' have enough troops, they could march across the earth."

My proposition was a sobering one and left everyone thinking silently. While we were handily defeating these goblins, these might be the weakest enemies in the Old Ones' army and the most mindless. More than once we had almost died, if the later enemies were more capable, more intelligent, then we were in trouble, the world was in trouble.

Emma shook her head slightly before speaking up, "It doesn't matter, we have to get through this dungeon before we can do anything else. We don't even know how the Colonel and the rest of the household are doing, let alone the world."

I frowned at that. I had left everyone alone and had set out on my own to gain my freedom, and if I was honest, the power to control my own life. Everyone else had been left in my wake without a second thought in my drive to be free. It was only because my family and friends cared so deeply for me that I was still alive. They had aligned themselves with my goals without even needing to be asked, and I would have to repay that loyalty in kind from now on. A fierce wish to do better, and a bitter pit of guilt sat in my stomach from my thoughts, but all I could do was press forward and keep it in mind.

"All right, let's keep moving forward," I said before turning to the two casters, "You two stand back to back while we fight. I want you two protected from any backstabbing rogues. Robert and I can survive an ambush but a lucky backstab while I'm stunned could be the end of one of you."

Our new formation was more straightforward and allowed us to continue the long march through the enemy-infested stronghold. The length of these tunnels was mind-blowing. Both caves and stone block rooms, each had to be carved from the earth and would have taken humans hundreds of years to build. Yet, here it was, all of it in a day. Whoever these 'Old Ones' were, they had power.

The next room looked clear, and that had us bunching up in concern. This was the very issue we had been worried about. Was it clear? Were there two or three rogues there? Was the room packed full? It could house a horde of the invisible enemies, and we wouldn't know.

"Annie, I'll stand at the entrance here. I want you to throw a fireball at the other door. If Emma is right, there should be two goblins there. If the fire makes them visible, so be it. Otherwise, I hope they attack me as they come through the doorway. After you throw your fire, get back to back with Emma. Robert, you should stand back to back with me as well," I said, trying taking charge of the situation.

Biting her lower lip, Annie stepped forward with a glowing orb in her right hand and aimed for the empty doorway.

When the fireball exploded on the ground of the stone arch, two rogues suddenly appeared. Their skin burnt, both goblins focused on Annie and screaming, they attacked. With a feral grin, I bent my knees in a wide stance preparing to take the focus of the two enemies. I used taunt on the rightmost goblin, its bloodshot eyes shifted to me, and I knew it was no longer planning to attack Annie. The goblin on the right though was going to try and run around me and attack her. I left slightly more room on my left side to entice the goblin in, and he stepped into the trap. When the goblin was in front of me and moving to step around, I bashed with my shield trying to knock the oblivious goblin to the ground. I failed to knock him down, but the top edge of my shield caught the goblin across the bottom of his nose at the bridge of his lip. The swirling stars and duckies told me he was no danger to my sister for now.

The rogue that I had taunted tried to stab under my sword arm, and I noticed that unlike the goblin warriors, it was trying to move around behind me on my right side. With the left-most goblin stunned, I had room to step around the goblin on my right, keeping both enemies in my sight. My movements and shield bash had caused my left arm to be open to a slash on the inner wrist. Three debuffs appeared in my mind's eye from that slash: crippled left arm, bleeding, and poison.

"Their daggers are poisoned, watch out," I said while trying to defend while my suddenly limp arm dragged my tower shield beside me.

The dangers of having such a large shield were now apparent. If I were using a smaller shield like one of the bucklers or kite shields on the wall of the mansion, then I wouldn't be as hindered. Still, the ability to duck down and be covered entirely might be as useful in the future as this was a hindrance now. While I clumsily attempted to attack the rogue, Emma used her darkness spell and poison bolt on the stunned rogue then attacked with her skeleton minion. I was tempted to turn to try and keep it in sight as she dragged it behind me, but I had to trust that she could handle things for herself. Besides, I was having enough difficulties with this goblin alone. The multiple debuffs had significantly reduced my combat effectiveness, the shield hindering me severely.

After almost tripping and falling over the edge of my shield, I mentally pulled up my character window. Selecting my shield with my mind, I willed it to be removed and placed in my inventory. The sudden loss of the weight on my arm and the flopping bleeding hand threw my rhythm off. Now that I wasn't dragging the dead weight around, I was in a far better position to fight. My ineffective combat, and Robert healing me from the poison, suddenly had the rogue turning to attack him.

I smiled as the rogue tried to go around me to attack Robert. Ignoring one opponent to attack another, leaving your defense open, seemed to be another idiotic thing these monsters were prone too. Swinging my cleaver of a sword down on the goblin's shoulder, returned his focus to me. A few seconds of attacking and powering through the goblin's attacks had the monster dead on the ground. A few seconds after it was down the cripple and poison debuffs faded. Emma's target was slowly following her as she pelted it with poison bolts, so I paused to try and re-equip my shield. In my vision, a new blue box appeared.

Equipping items disallowed during combat.

Growling, I charged after Emma's trailing goblin and joined her minion in striking against its head and shoulders.

When the second rogue was dead, I explained my discovery about equipment in combat, a restriction not mentioned in the 'tutorial.' Being able to unequip an item had been useful, but not being able to equip my shield until out of combat could have been a severe problem.

"Victoria, I think you should have this," said Robert after looting what the goblin left behind.

Robert had been looting and storing the items from the goblins. He had a decent strength stat, required for the weight which was not reduced even when in the inventory. Annie had a mostly filled inventory, while Emma and I were close to empty. Still, by unspoken agreement we let Robert handle it.

Passing me a small silver ring with intricate knotwork on the band, I focused on its information.

Band of the Recovered Warrior
Tradeable
AC: -1
Class: All
Slot: Ring

Worn Effect: 2 health per second regeneration while worn.
Trigger Effect: Once an hour, increase regeneration by 20 health per second for 12 seconds.

The fact that the ring could reduce my AC was upsetting, but the two effects would be helpful. I wasn't sure how useful the worn effect would be, but the triggered effect was terrific. I wanted to experiment with it, but I wasn't willing to waste the effect just to see if 'willing' it to work was how it was used. My instincts said it was, but I would wait until I was in combat and had a bit of health gone before using it.

After resting up, I asked Annie to cast another fireball into the hallway. Her fireball was useful for grabbing an enemies attention since it exploded into a ball of flame and damaged all monsters in the area. Emma's spells only affected the enemy she was directly targeting. Each of these spells, while seeming to have the same use, had slightly different effects. It was subtle, but I was betting that there would be other issues like these. Annie and Emma had spent a while last night discussing the possible problems.

The explosion of the fireball revealed the single rogue that had been patrolling the hallway. With only a single enemy to focus on, the fight was over shortly. With three people attacking a single enemy, the rogue died so quickly I was unable even to use my Warcry - Vigor ability. The feeling of so dominating an enemy was a nice one.

The end of this hallway had a small bend in it, unlike the rest.

Approaching the doorway, I was listening for any movement. It was possible that a rogue was hiding anywhere in the area and my first knowledge of them would be a dagger to my back. The arch of stone appeared empty, and when I reached it, I peeked around the corner to see if any goblins were around. Finding none, I gestured for my family to follow along. The hallway had an odd z like structure, first turning left from the doorway, then right. Approaching the right turn, I found another doorway, but this door opened into a large room. In the center of the ample space stood a goblin cloaked in black leather with a mask and hood.

The only part of the goblin not covered by black leather or cloth was his mouth and eyes. Yellow teeth were displayed in a sharp grin while the green eyes stared at me. Focusing on the goblin, I felt my stomach drop at the information.

Shan-Dar Clan
Den'tah - Clan Rogue Trainer - Boss
Rogue - Lvl 4
This opponent appears to be beneath you.

Chapter 17

Pulling back from the doorway I huddled down next to my group and thought about what this meant. A rogue boss was a serious problem. The last boss was a warrior, and that is about as straightforward a class as possible. Even then, we had severe issues fighting him and all his minions. If this boss has minions, they would probably be rogues. For all we know, the whole room will be full of rogues hiding invisibly and waiting to attack the moment we step into the room. Even if there are no other rogues in the room, the previous boss had struck hard and had more health than his minions. If the rogue could hit harder than a normal rogue goblin, then a single backstab would be able to kill anyone but me in one hit.

Glancing around at each of my friends, I bit my bottom lip before outlining my thinking.

Emma and Annie were silent, both looking away from me as they considered the coming fight. Of all of us, they had the worst chances. If the rogue even once managed to get behind them, they were looking at a short, sharp end to our adventure. Robert might or might not survive a single hit, he had mentioned he had more constitution and better AC than the girls, but it was by no means certain.

"I think we should go back," Robert said before Annie cut him off.

"No," she said with a brave look.

Looking around at each of us she said, "No. We should move

forward. I think we can do this. We should use our original circle formation."

Robert looked away; I could see he wanted to argue but wouldn't allow himself that kind of petulant behavior. I could understand it though; I wanted out of this dungeon as much as everyone else. But we had to fight smart to get out of here with all of us alive. Annie's idea had merit though. If the rogue couldn't get behind anyone, he couldn't backstab them. Then we would have to worry about any minions, and if they were invisible then staying back to back would protect us even there. It wasn't foolproof, but it looked like it would work.

Emma's minion joined our huddle, and she had it speak, "I'll have my skeleton outside the circle. It might draw in an attacker," the voice was still creepy even after hearing it multiple times.

Shuffling into our circle position, we moved into the room. Walking like this was just as awkward as I remember it, but it was necessary. Robert faced the door we exited while I confronted the rogue trainer. As we approached the goblin opened his mouth, the sharp jagged teeth bared to the air before he held up his hands. The rogue spread his fingers wide, the index finger and palm lightly gripping two daggers while between each of his fingertips was a small black ball. Pulling his hands back down he took a firmer grip on his blades and raced forward only to fade into invisibility during his charge.

"He's invisible! Be ready!" I shouted.

The sudden appearance of a dagger inches away from my left eye announced the arrival of the rogue. The feeling of the blade sliding into my eye socket and the wet feel of my eye bursting on my face was a white-hot ember of pain inside my skull. Screaming I swung my sword back and forth while flailing my shield to shove the goblin away. When my shield felt a momentary resistance, I pushed with all my might. I only managed to catch the rogue with the edge of my guard, but the pull on my skull as the dagger was removed made the experience excruciating. If I survive this, the feeling of my skull being moved from within by a handle of metal would haunt me.

In my mind's eye, I could see an eye patch covered head on the debuff. The timer read one hour and counting. The lack of vision on my left side would seriously hinder me in this fight, but I had little choice but to continue. The black-clad monster was directly in front of me when he regained his balance from my shove, his mouth open in a grin until I tried to shove my blade into it. I failed, the goblin was far too agile, but he didn't come away unscathed. The left side of his face from lip to his ear was torn open through the cloth wrappings. A debuff of 'disfigurement' was floating around his head, but it didn't seem to hinder his combat effectiveness as my debuff did.

Robert applied a heal to me as my life dropped while Annie and Emma cast spells in an awkward over the shoulder casting pose. Once Robert threw his first heal on me, I taunted the goblin. The crudity of the newest taunt was even more than I was comfortable hearing.

My fresh eye wound should not be referred to in such a way.

I had gotten into the habit of waiting for after Robert's heal to taunt since these creatures seemed to dislike nothing more than healing. Once I was sure the goblin had shifted his focus to me, I started my Warcry - Vigor. Unfortunately for me, the moment I triggered the skill and began to scream the goblin stepped into my guard and slammed the pommel of his dagger into my throat. My ability deactivated mid-use, and I gained the silenced debuff, though this debuff was only for a few seconds. My skill would take longer to recover before I could use it again, effectively wasting its use.

When the goblin reached the seventy-five percent health mark, he backflipped off my shield and over Emma's skeleton, then threw down one of his black pellets. From the dark bead, a large cloud of black smoke billowed out and covered the room. My voice was rough from the strike to the throat but still understandable.

"Stay close, don't break formation," I shouted in scratchy tones.

From my left, Emma cried out as her life dropped by a few percent. Before I could turn to attack the rogue, Annie next called out. Whipping my head around I was just able to see the goblin fade into the blackness before Robert also grunted in pain and had his life dip a small amount. The pattern was clear, and I was ready, so when the goblin reached for me, he practically had to run up my blade to attack. He still managed to nick me lightly on the arm, but he took a cut to his middle before he could escape.

After his round of attacks, he faded back into the blackness, and the dark cloud faded away. Looking around desperately I failed to find the rogue. Each of us had minor damage. My health was lower than anyone else's, but that was because it had been lower before the cloud had formed. Emma's suggestion of using her minion as a rogue target showed its merit. The goblin faded into view as it drove both daggers into the skeleton's spine. The minion's life dipped to less than ten percent in that single blow as he staggered towards me.

To my surprise, Robert had been prepared for this possibility and cast his quick group healing spell the moment the goblin's daggers drove the skeleton's life low. This fast casting saved the skeletal minion but gained Robert, the ire of the boss. Luckily, the skeleton was directly between the boss and me, and I was between the boss and Robert. A vigorous finger gesture and the use of my taunt skill which had just recovered had the goblin irate at my rudeness instead.

Either I had become complacent and fallen into a pattern, or the rogue trainer was just that good, but the shield bash I tried to use to meet the goblin's charge was a failure. Instead of the sweet sound of crunching nose cartilage, the monster slid under the rising outward swing of my shield and popped up under my arm with both daggers driving into my hip and left leg. The lamed debuff wasn't as severe as the crippled debuff, I could still use the leg, and I wasn't walking or running so its snare portion was of little concern, but the lack of stability in my stance made my damage far less decisive for the next minute.

My injured leg and weak swings left Emma and Annie providing a more significant portion of the damage, which both were more than willing to deliver. I could see a couple of times where my enemy had glanced at my sister or friend in consideration of switching opponents. While they both could probably survive a few blows from the boss, it would still be something to avoid. I tried to increase the anger I generated with a few well-placed strikes, but my excessive movements caused me to suffer a few extra return strikes. I didn't gain any debuffs in that period, but it was still a drain on Robert's mana.

At fifty percent life, the goblin boss jumped back again as he had before. The pattern was starting to be clear, for some reason bosses had health percentages where they would perform dangerous maneuvers. For this boss, it was seventy-five percent and fifty percent, if the pattern held, we could expect it again at twenty-five percent.

While the goblin held up his little black balls and prepared to produce his cloud, I shouted my conclusion that this would happen again when the goblin was near twenty-five percent life. Annie screamed her agreement but the other two remained focused on the fight, the most the two love-birds did was a grunt in agreement while staring out into the billowing cloud.

Robert was the first to be attacked by the goblin from the smoke. Robert's life dipped slightly from the attack, but less than it had from the first round of smoke. Annie and Emma were next to be assaulted, while I was treated to the goblin climbing over my shield and slicing across my forehead. While the smoke dissipated and I watched for the invisible enemy, I noticed my life dropping from a new poisoned debuff that flashed in my mind.

"Robert, use your group heals, I've been poisoned, but I'm going to try and use my ring to save you some mana," I shouted, and Robert yelled something that sounded like agreement.

With Robert starting his group heal, I mentally triggered my new ring. The spells landed almost in tandem with mine occurring just before Robert's. Robert had been watching the skeleton's health, and the moment it dipped down he cast his spell. The boss' attention bounced from the minion to Robert, to me in short order. A more perfect arrangement would be harder to plan.

The second pattern for the fight was the unwelcome discovery of the goblin bosses ability to circumvent any defense and deliver a debuff after leaving its invisibility — this time I was hit with a bleeding debuff from a slice along my sword arm. The regeneration effect from my ring was still pulsing health into me and counteracting both the poison and the bleeding. While the ring's triggered effect worked to counter the long term damage effects, it didn't work as well to heal me. In the end, Robert had to use another large heal focused on me. Those were his more efficient heals, but I would have his mana instead be saved for the emergency heal right after the smoke cloud.

This round of combat, Emma tried to use her Clinging Darkness spell as well as the Root spell. Annie's root spell would cause small clumps of wood to burst out of the ground and grab onto her enemy. Emma's version had a bone white and gnarled root doing the same. The sudden pause of the goblin as its limbs refused to move was all that I needed to deliver an overhead strike onto the goblins noggin. The stun was surprisingly short-lived, but it left the goblin reeling past his twenty-five percent health trigger. My excitement was short lived since the moment the stun debuff faded the boss jumped backward ripping clear of the wooden root shackles.

"I think this will be the last time. We are doing well, stay focused," I shouted while lowering my center of gravity.

This time when the goblin flashed his hands up to show his smoke generating balls, some of them were red instead of black. With a sinking sensation, I prepared for the new onslaught.

This time when the smoke billowed out, small puddles of burning liquid splashed onto the ground, one such puddle was just short of Emma's feet. This time when the rogue trainer attacked, he did so with a glowing green dagger. Each of us suffered from a poison debuff while the timer on mine was renewed. Robert ignored the minion's health this time and only used his group healing spell as our life dropped. I had more difficulty staying the target of the rogue's aggression this time, but a few well-placed insults about the size of his smoke balls worked wonders.

When the rogue was at five percent life, Emma's skeleton minion died in a clatter of bones. All of us were at fifty percent life at this point, and our health was fluctuating up and down as the poison, or Robert's heal, would apply. I was worried that at any moment the goblin would turn to one of my family and strike out and end them, but my worries were unnecessary. When the goblin sliced along my arm in one last act of viciousness, I retaliated with a shield bash and a kick to the knee.

The goblin rogue boss crumpled from my kick and the fight was enough to ensure we all leveled.

After the fight I had to calm the party and convince them that my eye would recover from the injury. The fact that they could check the debuff timer themselves reduced their worries, though Robert did stare at the flesh covered socket for longer than I was confortable with.

Checking my character sheet, I noticed that the battle had almost been enough, with all the bonuses, to bring me to level seven. I was slightly ahead of everyone else in experience, but not by a significant amount. While I had been focusing on my character sheet, Robert was casting his group heal spell repeatedly until the poison debuff faded. Giving me a surly look for my spacing out, and accepting my sheepish grin back, he sat to let his mana recover. Annie squealed in joy when she noticed the gold treasure chest in the center of the room, twin to the one from the previous boss.

"Women and their presents," Robert said with a small grin and a shake of his head.

I wanted to rebuke him for the comment, but I couldn't. I was barely resisting the urge to rush to the chest with the other two who had failed to hold themselves back. Giving him a loud sniff, and raising my nose, I turned to see if we gained anything useful for our survival. Survival was my only concern!

Chapter 18

From the chest, Annie pulled out a billowing silk scarf that she proceeded to wrap around her shoulders. The information window for the scarf was in line with her slippers.

Silk Wraps of the Sorcerous Concubine
Non-Tradeable
Armor Type: Cloth
AC: 2
Class: Wizard
Slot: Wrist or Neck

Trigger Effect: Once an hour double the damage and mana cost of a single target spell. Reduces hate from the spell by 80%.
Set Effect (2): 1% less hate from fire spells.

"It says which slots it can be used in, but only if it can be used in two slots?" I questioned in a mutter.

Annie's excitement from her new scarf turned to disgust when the item resting below was revealed. Her disgusted face and recoil had me leaning over the box to see it for myself. A shiny necklace was lying in the box, but it was the skeletal fist mounted on a wooden handle which had caused her reaction. Emma looked at it with a quirked smile before she reached in and picked the item which was apparently for her. Emma had never been easily grossed out. When we were younger, all of us would gladly tromp through the woods or the city park exploring, but Emma and Robert would take it further and hunt for snails or frogs. I had more fun climbing trees and hopping across logs, which in my imagination were cliffs and chasms.

Annie was quieter and spent most of her time reading a book in the shade while watching the rest of us destroy our clothing. Emma's relaxation around creepy and crawling things held her in good stead as she lifted her find from the chest. I was focusing in on the fist of bone to see its information when the fist opened and then clenched. My surprise unbalanced me and I fell backward while the information screen filled my view.

The Creeping Grasp
Non-Tradeable
One Handed Blunt / Wand
Class: Necromancer
Slot: Primary-Hand
+15 HP
+25 Mana

Effect: The shadows of the spell line of Creeping Shadows gain temporary physicality in the form of skeletal hands which adds a small damage over time effect.

Altog the Shade was never happy with his creation of the Creeping Shadows spell series. He always felt that with the appropriate foci the spell could be enhanced with further effects. After five years of effort, he demonstrated his magnum opus in the form of a wand that added acidic wounds to the shadows grip. Shortly after, many other necromancers created their own version of his foci, it even became a minor fashion trend. - Necromancy, the Masterwork. Volume 1, 3rd Edition.

Emma's new wand/fist was held at a distance as she turned it around and inspected it. Every few second the hand would relax and then tighten into a fist again. The entire thing was genuinely creepy, but that seemed to be the way Emma's class worked. Creepy, and dangerous, but as her snare and damage spells showed, useful. I just worried that the unholy nature of her class would corrupt her mind and soul. Annie had shown signs of this, but to be honest, we all had. Annie was just the most extreme of a switch from calm and silent to giggling and throwing fire. How much was just her sudden freedom from expectation and how much was some insidious infection? It was also possible we were all losing our minds from the stress and fights, but as I looked around at the calm of my party members, I doubted that last possibility.

The necklace at the bottom of the chest was passed to Robert and seemed like a bit of a let down from my point of view. He lacked any neck slot item, so it filled a slot he was missing, but it failed to compare to the other things we had gained.

Amulet of the Sun
Non-Tradeable
AC: 5
Class: All
+25 Mana

Effect: +3 mana regen per six seconds while in direct sunlight.

The mana regeneration would be useful for Robert in the future, but the limitation of having to be in direct sunlight meant he wouldn't gain the effect in these tunnels. Still, a small boost to his mana and AC is better than not having an item in a slot at all.

Emma waited until Robert had looped the necklace over his head before she used her motherly 'do as you are told' tone.

"Everyone, use your stat points and look at your new skills," Emma said.

Ducking my head in remembered shame, I distributed my stats as I had been instructed. When I looked at my log for my new skills, I was confused.

Level up!
Victoria [Warrior lvl 6] - at level 10 NPC's will no longer be zone locked.

New Skills!
Gained Skill - Defensive Stance.
Gained Skill - Offensive Stance.
Gained Skill - Balanced Stance.

Pulling my sword from my inventory, I moved to the center of the room away from my family and triggered my defensive stance skill. Almost without thought my knees bent slightly and my sword raised so that it was held angled across my body. In my head, I could see how this position allowed me to block attacks, riposte, parry, and deflect even ranged attacks. Held as it was, my sword could be used as a poor warriors version of a shield while said shield was locked tight and behind my sword, acting as another line of defense. Even the nick in the blades could be used to disarm enemies with a deft twist of the wrist. Moving forward in small mincing steps I could feel the solidity of the ground beneath me and how to use it for protection. After a few seconds of my new stance, I could feel that I could change into one of the other available stance options.

At random, I decided to try the Offensive Stance next. Unfolding inside my mind were blazing lines of possibilities for death and pain. I could see potential movements which would let me flash out and slice, drive my shield into faces, necks, and even slamming the edge into toes. My shield could be used as a weighted pivot to throw myself around obstacles as well as for damage. My movements were free and flowing, unlike in my Defensive Stance, but I could feel a lack of protection in my movements. My sword, on the other hand, was a blazing web of death spreading out even beyond my direct reach. The tip could be used surgically to slice into blood vessels close to the surface or deep into gushing fountains of death. The pommel of my blade was a hammer that I could use to distract as well as break through defenses. The edge was the queen of destruction: it could slice, cut, or even be used to bludgeon through armor.

My body shuddered at the sudden change in perspective, my

thoughts now revolved around the maximum way to deliver death and destruction. Then I switched to my final new stance.

I had been prepared for a new disturbance in my view of the world when I shifted out of my Offensive Stance and into my Balanced Stance, but oddly, I felt normal. I didn't see the world in terms of defense or offense, and I had no restrictions on my movements. Tilting my head to the side, I moved forward and back, swinging my sword and dodging and blocking an imaginary enemy, but nothing felt different from before. With a shrug, I turned and realized I was the focus of everyone's attention.

"Um," I said in surprise, "I gained three skills, but it's actually more like two?" I said, the end coming out a confused question.

At the questioning looks, I explained the different effects of the three skills and how they seemed to come with trade-offs. Balanced was the neutral stance, neither good or bad. Offense Stance helped me deliver death but left me more vulnerable to attacks. Finally, Defensive Stance seemed to be as the name described, all about defense but it came with a reduced movement and hampered attack.

"You will probably use Defensive Stance more than anything," said Robert though he seemed preoccupied with his character window.

"Annie? What did you get?"

The almost manic smile of my sister was disconcerting. Facing away from us she swished her hand a few times through the air then muttered a command before pointing her finger. From the end of her digit, a large spiral of flames formed then condensed into an incandescent bar of light and heat that flashed across the room and into the wall. Spinning around Annie was almost bouncing and clapping in excitement over her new spell.

"It's called flame lance. I also got a Cold Burst spell and…

well…this."

At her last word, she cupped her hand and a shimmer formed and a ball of water, resembling a large raindrop, was wobbling in her cupped hands.

"The spell says we can drink it, and it's safe, but it only lasts for thirty minutes before dissipating if it's not consumed. Useful though," Annie said while flicking the ball of water away from herself, leaving it to splash against the ground.

"Annie, I'm sure we are all thirsty and could do with a bit of cleaning up. Could you make more?" Robert asked.

For a moment, Annie seemed ready to yell at Robert, but then the look passed, and she glanced down and then quickly at Emma. Nodding she proceeded to conjure water bubbles for all of us. After providing each of us a globe of water, my sister moved over to the corner of the room and conjured another. Using her new water source, she wet her face and hands. None of us were dirty -it didn't even appear we could become dirty any longer- but scrubbing up felt nice, it would also give me a moment to talk to my sister. Annie was focused on her cleaning, but she had noticed my approach since she summoned another globe of water and held it out in invitation.

Rubbing my wet hands together I stared at Annie's back while I tried to figure out how to phrase my concern. I had never been as capable at the social games, that was always Annie's arena, so I did what I was good at. I made a frontal charge and hoped I could beat through the problem.

"You need to talk to Robert and Emma. Get it out in the open. It's going to happen, and if you talk to them first then it might not hurt you as much," I said, then watched for my sister's reaction.

I had started rushed and louder than necessary but ended slowly and almost mumbling. Annie nodded silently and returned to summoning water globes.

"I'll...um...go get Robert so he can get clean also," I said then quickly retreated.

Pointing Robert to Annie, I turned to Emma who had been watching the interplay the entire time.

Smiling at me, Emma started a different conversation entirely, "I gained a fear-inducing spell, and a buff for my skeleton as well as a spell which increases my AC but it only works on me."

Taking her cue to avoid the larger subject I asked, "What did Robert get?"

"He said he gained a heal that pulses out over time, a group AC spell, and a spell which increases physical damage output," she said while her eyes avoided the corner where the whispers were coming from.

"We will get out soon Emma, things will get better, you will see," I said to which she nodded, but we both knew I was trying to convince myself as much as her.

<h1 style="text-align:center">Chapter 19</h1>

About an hour after we had defeated the last boss, we were pushing through a group of goblins in a large room with multiple hallways. We had entered similar large rooms before, most of the corridors just reconnected together further on. Some of the time they only lead to dead ends. As always, the goblins were stationed as guards on either side of the doorways. Our first clue that something was different was when I moved forward to attack the patroling goblin, and I came face-to-snout with a goblin and his wolf. His massive, very upset, foaming at the mouth, wolf.

Hollering in surprise, I tried to return to my team who were just on the other side of the doorway. This was a mistake. From behind me the wolf gave a deep-chested growl and launched itself into my back, its jaws biting into the back of my head. Luckily the wolf got more hair than he did neck. Unfortunately, the wolf was followed by the goblin who led with an ax strike to my legs while the wolf tried to maul me. The impact of a fireball in the goblin's face pulled his attention away from me, and the tackle of Emma's skeleton into the wolf left me to recover from my belated retreat.

Rolling over I stumbled as I tried to stand up, still woozy from the sudden attack and limping from the near hamstringing the goblin gave me. The wolf was distracted by the skeletal minion, but the goblin was already on his way to Annie. Before I could taunt the goblin away from Annie, Robert stepped in and took the brunt of the charge. Almost dragging my leg behind me, I limped over to my now closer team and attacked the goblin from behind. My taunt skill pulled the goblin's attention away from Robert, and our healer took the chance to step back. Seeing that neither Annie or Emma were injured, and I was only suffering a few debuffs more than lost health, Robert started the movements for his large heal on himself while I 'tanked' the goblin. A term I learned from the tutorial.

I don't know if it was the surprise of the attack or the unusual circumstances, but I failed to consider what would happen when the wolf finished off the skeleton. I never even thought about it; I had become focused on attacking the goblin. My defensive stance helped me take as little damage as possible, but my movement debuff from the goblin's first strike and the stance skill had me nearly immobilized.

Despite my single-minded focus on the goblin, when Emma shouted in surprise, I responded. Turning to the wolf, I barely clipped it with my sword as it bounded past. My taunt skill recovered and so I used it to gain the last bit of aggression from the wolf I needed to divert its attention to me. Even as I was spitting out a growl and a bark, apparently a serviceable taunt for wolves, I regarded in horror the fireball that Annie had just released...

...into the goblin.

The first fireball had been to the goblin's face, sensitive areas like that did more damage and consequently caused more anger. Annie's second fireball had been cast after I had managed to pull the goblin off of Robert. This one landed while I had moved slightly away to intercept the wolf and after I had used my taunt skill.

While the wolf instantly shifted its gaze to me, the goblin turned and lunged for Annie who had crept forward in the heat of combat. Before I could change my tactics, the goblin was out of reach and heading towards my sister! My stance, combined with my debuff, left me shuffling after the goblin even as the wolf tried to rip into me. I barely had the presence of mind to keep my shield between the wolf and me as I watched the goblin charge Annie.

Annie let out a loud 'Eep!' as the goblin charged at her. Before I could scream for her to run she used her blink spell. The white light flashed from her stomach and covered her body in a moment, but the spell's nature was our downfall in this instance. While the spell teleported her a short distance, where it teleported her was random. This time the teleport moved her to within arms reach of the goblin. Grunting while attacking, the goblin kicked Annie in the stomach, the impact causing her to vomit almost on the goblin's leg.

With a burst of will, I triggered my shield's effect. Each of us now had a small glowing shield the size of a dinner plate that shifted to be directly between them and the closest attacker. Annie knelt at the goblin's feet while the monster raised his ax high and brought it down in a two-handed chop that was slightly deflected as it passed through her shield. The glowing shield shattered from the force of the ax but it lasted long enough to divert the weapon's pathway from her head and instead into her shoulder and then into the ground, severing her left arm.

The sound of my sister screaming was heart-wrenching as she fell on her side and clutched at the stump of her shoulder. Robert was grim-faced as he cast fast heal after fast heal as I charged the brute who was winding up for another overhead strike. Instinctively, I switched to my offensive stance, tucked my shield in close to my body, and drew my blade in tight. Before the goblin could bring down the ax on my sister's head and kill her, I drove the edge of my shield into his armpit and lifted with my entire body. Without Offensive Stance, I would never have gotten the balance right. The shield lifted the goblin off one foot and disrupted his attack causing him to spread his arms out to catch himself from his stagger. Arching his back and throwing his arms out left his neck exposed. Continuing my motion, I drew back my shield and thrust forward with the tip of my blade, driving it through his neck and leaving him to blow bubbles of blood.

Shifting on my feet, I used the weight of my shield to turn and line up for a thrust at the wolf I was sure was chasing me. Instead, I found a wolf covered in shadows and skeletal arms, whimpering as it was dragged to the ground. Emma's Root and Creeping Shadows spells had torn away from the wolf the last of its life while I had handled the goblin. Dropping my shield, I reached for my sister.

Robert's heals quickly stopped the bleeding, and my sister's health read as full in the group window, but still, she clutched at the now sealed wound of her shoulder. I grabbed my sister and tried to hold her, but she just continued to scream that 'it was gone' as she reached for her now missing arm. Above her head were multiple debuff icons.

Debuff - Amputation - Left Arm
Reduced Dexterity - 50%
Reduced ability to dodge - 5%
Reduced ability to block - 50%
Reduced ability to parry - 70%
Reduced maximum health - 10%
Reduced crafting success chance - 15%
Reduced Charisma - 5
Duration: 36 hours, 14 minutes.

Debuff - Shock
Reduced Intellect - 8
Reduced spell resistance - 80%
Reduced spell power - 40%
Reduced mental focus - 20%
Duration: 5 minutes.

The second debuff was the apparent cause of her hysteria.

All I could do was hold her and rock as she cried and clutched at her arm. This was the worst injury any of us had suffered. From the white-faced look of Emma and Robert, they didn't seem to understood it was a long debuff, but of a temporary nature. Once the shock debuff faded, Annie began to calm down. The sniffles and crying reduced in volume and her screaming stopped entirely.

"Annie, it's all right. It's a debuff, in thirty-six hours you can get your arm back. Check your debuff's, it has a duration," I said while rocking my sister.

Eventually, she calmed enough to check for herself.

"What if...what if the debuff is gone, but I'm still missing an arm?" she asked, her voice sounding like a little girl instead of the confident woman I knew.

My heart twisted at her question. I couldn't know for sure that her arm would regrow. Just because my broken arm healed didn't mean her lost arm would return. There was a distinct difference between a broken arm and a missing one. The evidence of that was the severed limb that was laying beside us, which I was careful to keep my sister facing away from.

"I'm level seven now. The wolf was the last I needed, I gained a cure disease and a cure poison spell, next time I might get a regrow limb spell. Whatever it takes, we will help you get your arm back Annie," Robert said. His voice was shaky but resolute.

"If we had just stayed in the mansion, we would all be fine. This is all your fault," Annie said as she pulled away from me.

My guts roiled as Annie staggered to her feet. She was right. If we had stayed in the mansion, we would have been safe. But I didn't want safe, I wanted adventure and freedom, and it almost cost my sister her life. It still could cost any one of us our life.

While I turned away from Annie, Robert moved in to comfort her. Turning to the goblin, I pulled up his information.

> ***Shan-Dar Clan***
> ***Goblin Beast Tamer - Elite***
> ***Beast Tamer - Lvl 6***
> ***This opponent is beneath you.***

Level Six! The dungeon information said it was level three to five!

Feeling betrayed, I checked the wolf's information next.

> ***Shan-Dar Clan***
> ***Worg - Pet - Elite***
> ***Warrior - Lvl 6***
> ***This opponent is beneath you.***

The 'Worg' was also level six!

"She is just upset, and in pain, she didn't mean it," Emma said as I looted the Worg's corpse.

"Doesn't matter if she meant it, she's right," I said while watching the corpse fade away.

Emma always worked to take care of us, she had tried to take the place of her mother who had been an unofficial mother figure for all of us. This time though, it couldn't be solved by a hot cup of tea and a good cry over the horrible things the society ladies had said about me. This time my sister's arm was laying on the ground because I had pulled them into my mess. She was hurt, possibly maimed for life, because I wasn't paying attention during combat. I had rushed forward without checking where the patrol goblin was, convinced it would only be the one enemy. I was playing with my abilities and left myself unable to move and do my job. I was supposed to protect my family.

We had been in these tunnels for at least a day and a night, and we had seen no hint of an exit. We might end up tromping through these tunnels for the rest of our short lives, all because of me.

Hugging me from behind Emma leaned her head onto my shoulder.

"It will be all right. I think we all wanted freedom, to change our situation, the apocalypse just gave us an excuse. We came to save you, but we did it as much for ourselves as because we are family," she whispered while holding me.

"If it's your fault for us being in here, then it's also your fault when we reach level ten. That Robert will be able to check on his family, and that you two can find your father," she said as she pulled away and held me at arms length, "now enough of the whining, straighten up and march soldier!" she said trying to imitate my father's favorite instruction. She even put a single finger beneath her nose to simulate the mustache wiggle at the end which forced a chuckle through my tears.

"Good, now you need to stay focused. We are all counting on you," Emma said before she turned to see how my sister and Robert were doing.

Nodding to Emma's back, I tried to keep my mind clear and focused on the goal. Three more levels and freedom from the dungeon.

<h1 style="text-align:center">Chapter 20</h1>

After the multiple scoldings for failing to assign my stats, I made sure to assign them for this level without being told. The first step to correcting a mistake is being aware of them, and I was well aware of my issues now. Next, I turned to my log file to see what I had gained for this level.

Level up!
Victoria [Warrior lvl 7] - at level 10 NPC's will no longer be zone locked.

That was it?

Seeing that Robert was comforting Annie, something I wouldn't interrupt for multiple reasons, I asked Emma what she had earned from her level. Glancing into the distance with the vacant look I had come to recognize as checking one of the windows, Emma made a humming noise before her focus returned to me.

"I've got two new spells, and I gained the skill 'dodge,' but it's not like how you described it. It's a bit more bare bones. It only helps with leading an enemies attack and timing. The spells are useful though, here see," she said while pushing the spell descriptions to group chat.

Spell: Aura of Death
Necromancer Spell: Level 7
Target: Self
Mana: 15 mana
Effect: Surrounds the caster in an aura of the dead. Every six

seconds converts 5 health into 3 mana.

Telchor, who later became known as Telchor the Lich, created the first spell in what is now considered the defining spell series of Necromancy. Aura of Death is a rather minor spell with very low efficiency, but its brilliance is in what it does. Slowly infusing death into the necromancer's body allows the conversion of the natural force that all life produces into death aligned mana. - Necromancy, the Masterwork. Volume 2, 3rd Edition.

I was a little uncomfortable with the idea of Emma eating away at her health to regain mana, but the truth was this spell barely did any damage to her and would significantly increase her mana regeneration. With her lifetap spell, she would be able to heal whatever damage was done, and it would allow her to do even more damage then she had been. Between the two of them, Annie was able to do a lot of damage in a very short period, but her mana drained quickly. Emma, on the other hand, was able to create a lot of damage over an extended period very efficiently. Necromancers also seemed to get a large number of utility spells while Annie's class didn't seem to have as many. Emma's next spell linked in chat was a good example of this.

Spell: Breath of the Dead
Necromancer Spell: Level 7
Target: Self
Mana: 55 mana
Reagent: 1 Fish Scale (Consumed)
Effect: Removes the necromancer's need to breathe for 30 minutes.

Not all necromancy spells were created to assist in the destruction of enemies or the conquering of mortality. No. Some were merely created on a whim but were found to be so useful that they became common in almost all necromancy spell books. Such is the case of the spell Breath of the Dead. Rumor has it that this spell was created to allow a young apprentice to catch fish for his master. - Necromancy, the Masterwork. Volume 1, 3rd Edition.

I couldn't help but giggle at the description of the Breath of the Dead spell.

"What did you get?" asked Emma.

The reminder that I had been denied any benefit from my level up, except for my increased health and damage output, returned the frown to my face.

"Nothing, I'm not sure why," I said.

Emma looked surprised but then shrugged. Turning back to Robert and Annie, Emma voiced the question I had been wondering but was to afraid to interrupt the comforting of my sister in order to ask. Maybe she thought that reminding Annie that she had power would help her peace of mind?

"Annie, what spells did you get from your level up?" she asked as I strapped on my shield and prepared to defend us from more enemies.

When Annie answered, I found myself hunching at the return of the soft tones I thought my sister had forever abandoned.

"I...um," Annie started then continued after a delay, "I linked them in chat, they should be useful," she said.

Spell: Wall of Fire
Wizard Spell: Level 7
Target: Single, Area (Modified)
Mana: 185 mana
Effect: Creates a wall of flame which burns intensely for 30 seconds.

"Burn! Burn! MWAHAHAHA!" - Fredrick Nashe, 'The Pyromancer'

The description was somewhat disconcerting and given Annie's recent...exuberance...with her fire spells, upsetting.

Though, with her injury causing a return to reticence, I would rather see her happy and fire manic again instead of silent.

Spell: Lightning Storm
Wizard Spell: Level 7
Target: Single, Area
Mana: 165 mana
Effect: Produces a storm cloud over a location which continually releases lightning bolts into enemies. Lasts for 1 minute.

The storm is one of nature's most devastating phenomena. Lightning can damage enemies, runic constructs, and even fortifications. Learning to harness the intensity of the storm should be every wizard's goal. - Arch-Wizard Joseph 'Old Sparky' Merin.

Both of Annie's new spells were large area affecting spells. The wall spell could be useful to control the movements of monsters by blocking off hallways with flames.

"Vick?" Annie said while looking at her feet, "I'm sorry. I was just hurting and upset. I didn't mean it,"

I was trying not to cry while I fiddled with the leather strap on my shield, my eyes never leaving the rough wrapping as I answered her.

"I know sis. I'm sorry, I'll do better from now on. I promise," I said before facing away from the party and back up the tunnel.

Raising my voice, I said, "Everyone ready to continue?" at the sound of assent; I stepped forward and said, "Then let's get out of here!"

I tried to sound strong and confident, I wasn't sure how well I managed, but we continued up the tunnel we had been trooping through. These new tunnels seemed to narrow and didn't open into large rooms as they had before. Odder still, these tunnels were starting to edge upwards while until now they had been slowly dipping further into the earth. The walls had been a mix of rough-cut stone, and stone slabs crudely formed together into dark grey and grungy tunnels. Now, they were being replaced almost entirely by well-formed grey tiles.

While I took note of the change in the tunnel, most of my attention was for our enemies. No longer was I considering a battle at face value. Each goblin we approached I would first inspect to see if they were higher level or of a kind we hadn't seen before. So far we were only seeing Beast Lords and Worgs, and their level's remained the same at six.

It was getting towards the end of the day, and I was starting to worry that it was getting close to the time to find a place to hole up for the night when the cavern we entered opened up into a large area lined with wooden stalls filled with animals. Some of the pens had Worgs which stared through the loose fitting wooden gates, while other stalls had small bunnies with red glowing eyes and blood caked faces. Standing in the center of the room was a fat goblin, his bulk even greater than the Arena Master. Unlike the Arena Master, who showed the signs of battle, this goblin looked like he had never done a day of work in his life. His leather armor was stained and bulging where his fat pressed around the straps. The only part of his gear which appeared to be well cared for was the whip he carried coiled in his right hand.

When he noticed us at the entrance, he grinned a rotten and gapped tooth smile and stood proudly with his gut hanging forward, and both hands pressed to his hips. His thin, gangly arms and legs were an odd contrast to the almost round body that flowed into a wide layered neck and bulbous head. The only delicate looking part of his body was his ears which formed a sharp point on either side of his head.

Behind the goblin was a swirling portal of darkness like the one we had entered the dungeon through. Focusing on the tunnel, I tried to bring up the window describing the portal, but it failed. We might have been too far away, or exits might not provide similar information that entrances did. Either way, we would need to kill the goblin before we could reach the portal as I doubted he would just let us through.

Focusing on the goblin, I tried to inspect the ugly green brute.

Shan-Dar Clan
Muck, the Stable Keeper - Boss
Beastlord - Lvl 6
This opponent appears to be beneath you.

Right, 'appears to be beneath you,' which of course doesn't actually mean he was easy to kill. The logic for the new world still escaped me, but it always seemed to make some kind of consistent sense if you looked at it sideways. That could have been the efforts of these 'Old Ones' which had brought so much death and destruction.

Looking around the cavern, I checked to see if there were other goblins in hiding or traps which could surprise us. Muck, the goblin 'Stable Keeper' didn't seem to have a Worg pet like the rest of the Beastlords we had fought on the way here, but given the pens were full of animals, I would be surprised if he didn't call on them during the fight.

"I think this will be like the Arena Master fight. Lots of additional enemies at set percentages of the bosses' health. I don't see any other hints at what could go wrong. Any other clues?" I asked.

Annie smiled at me before she answered, "The whip; They are weapons designed to cause pain, not death. We should watch out for it."

Nodding in agreement, I turned to Robert, "Robert, after you provide your buffs we will rest until full mana, then I will start by gaining his focus. Everyone wait a bit before jumping in. If you see anything, call out. All right?"

Chapter 21

"Maybe we should think about resting for the night," Robert said.

Robert's suggestion caused me to stutter in confusion for a moment. We were right in front of a boss and the exit. We had only been awake for what had felt like half a day. While we never got physically tired, we could still suffer from the mental strain from fighting and being active. None of us were at that limit, and even Annie gave Robert a confused look at his suggestion.

Seeing the looks, Robert became flustered.

"I just mean, it has been a difficult day, we should be fully prepared for this fight," he said before looking away.

I could see it on his face: strain, and guilt, and when he looked to Annie, I understood.

"Robert, are you all right?" I asked.

The moment the words left my mouth I knew that I had made a mistake. I had gotten used to thinking that the world had changed and that the old social rules were gone, but they were as much there as we let them, and Robert did not take kindly to an insinuation of weakness. An implication of weakness from a woman was even worse. It didn't matter that we had been friends since childhood, it might have made it worse since he had suffered teasing for his bookish ways and willingness to be friends with women. Robert became stone-faced and reserved, he pulled up his walls that only Emma seemed able to surpass.

The others noticed Robert's retreat into silence, though I think he thought they were fooled, and Annie sent me a look of recrimination. Emma gave me a half smile and a shake of the head. She would talk to him later and help him recover. I had only seen this same reaction once before when he had discussed the potential of being required to work for the military as a doctor. His uncle's stories had not skimped on the horrors of wartime medical practice and how a tincture of laudanum and the bone saw were the most common solution for severe ailments.

Robert was a gentle soul, and these were not gentle times.

"No, you're right. We should push on," Robert said while looking at his mace.

Biting my lip, I looked to the others, but Emma gave a small head shake to let me know to let it go. She would talk to him later and see how he was handling things.

"Very well, we are in agreement. Robert, lead off with the buffs and tell us when you have recovered your mana, then wait for me to grab the bosses attention," I said.

While Robert used his group buffs, I made sure to be in my neutral stance. I needed to keep the different trade-offs in mind when it came to the stances. Forgetting the mobility limitation of the defensive stance had been the main cause of Annie's injury, the rest had been bad timing. When Robert signaled that his mana had recovered, we moved in formation into the room and towards the grinning goblin boss. I was leading with Robert behind me and Annie and Emma to either side, Emma's newly summoned minion standing slightly behind me and to my left.

Once we had moved towards the center of the room, the goblin pulled his right arm back letting the coiled whip unwind behind him. Before I could taunt the boss, a massive clang sound came from a grate closing over the entranceway. This was becoming another repeating pattern in our new world, boss fights had locked in areas that couldn't be escaped from.

The goblin stable master snorted and spat a green phlegmy mess in front of himself and then hollered at us and snapped his whip to the side.

The leftmost stall opened at the sound of the whip, and the largest worg yet stepped forward from his pen. Light blue eyes and grey-furred the beast stepped forward menacingly before its scruff raised in a deep-throated growl. The monster's lips pulling back along yellowed teeth as it eyed us. Yanking back its head it howled in a ferocious roar and a buff appeared above both the goblin and worg's head. The buff over the worg was of two people connected by a chain while the goblin had a picture of a person with a shield over them. Before I could work out what the buffs meant the worg was rushing forward into my own taunting growl.

The worg's head was at the same height as my shoulder, and when it tried to bite at my face, I was only barely able to move my shield between us. When the worg pulled its head back to attempt another bite, I clipped it on the side of the jaw with a forehand swing of my sword. It was an awkward swing, a stab or overhand slice would have been better, but the speed of the animal had left me with only instinctive reactions. To my surprise the goblin was just standing at the back of the room and watching the fight with his hands resting on his hips.

Why the goblin was just watching I couldn't guess, but it made the fight a great deal simpler. Our party excelled at fighting single targets. With me 'tanking' and Robert healing, it left Emma and Annie to decimate the target. With multiple foes, I had found it difficult to pull the various enemies attention to me, though the difficulty had increased when Emma or Annie had attacked the wrong opponent.

The worg was quick, and it attacked in ways I was not comfortable with. When you thought of a giant wolf, the thought of being scratched wasn't the first concern. The wolf's yellow teeth and its agile assault was a slightly more prominent worry. That being the case, a wolf -or in this case a worg- was more suitable to pack hunting. Pack tactics dictated attacking from multiple angles until a pack member was able to slice an ankle, break a limb, or latch onto a neck. Cripple then kill was the preferred strategy for pack animals. A single wolf-like creature, even a large and fast one, was far less effective against a prepared shield, a sword, and a well-placed kick.

After a few seconds of battle, I used my warcry skill, and this was the signal for Annie and Emma to begin casting at the well-angered worg.

Annie and Emma were extremely effective with their spell damage, the worg's health quickly chipping away. Annie would cast a spell, and a large red number would appear above the worg's head while Emma's spells were clicking away with a small amounts every few seconds. Emma's minion and I were doing small but steady damage. While I was having difficulties hitting the worg, it was having problems hitting me in turn. The skeleton was trying to attack the worg, but mostly it was hanging off the worg's back and annoying it. Emma once explained that it was easy to control her minion but she felt strangely disconnected from reality while doing so. She had only the dimmest sense of touch through her minion, and she didn't experience any pain from it being injured. I had been worried that continually throwing herself at enemies while controlling her pet would lead to her forgetting and attacking as herself, but she found that almost laughable. Her response had been 'do you confuse your feet for your hands?' which didn't completely remove my fears but did reduce them.

Only Robert had little to do in this fight. He spent most of it just spot healing me for the rare few times the worg managed to avoid my shield.

This fight was going well and paradoxically, that was concerning me. I was waiting for the goblin to do something. Its casual stance, and watching of the fight was worrying.

Eventually, we managed to end the worg's life. Before we could turn our aggression to the goblin, he snapped his whip out, and another pen door opened.

Instead of the first pen which contained the worg, this time the third pen opened. From within a wild boar like animal stepped out. This wasn't a boar despite its superficial appearance. Boars didn't usually have three pairs of legs and bright green moss-like hair. The double set of tusks were also a concern. Ducking its head and focusing its small black eyes on me the pig-like creature snorted three times. Above the beast and the stable master the pair of buffs from before appeared, the goblin boss resumed his normal arrogant stance, and the pig decided to aim for me. His preference for me might have had something to do with me using my taunt skill and screaming out 'come here breakfast bacon!'

When the pig glowed with a yellow halo for a moment, I should have dodged. My mistake was to duck behind my shield and brace for the charge. A pig that large, so large its head was even with my chin, was a lot of ham moving at high speed. The pig contemptuously used its tusks to shove my shield aside at the same time it began to stomp my lower body before it passed over me. One of its piggy feet stomped down on my shin bone as I fell to the side and snapped it with a horrific sound. The oinker slowed as it reached the far wall near the entrance then ponderously turned and lined up with me again. By the time it had managed to turn around, I was on one knee and trying to get back to my feet even though I knew that my trailing leg wouldn't support my weight. In the lull, I focused and asked for the information on the tusked beast.

Shan-Dar Clan

Sir Oinker - Pet - Elite
Warrior - Lvl 6
This opponent is beneath you.

Sir Oinker!

I was almost apoplectic at this. Attacking our world was bad enough, but to mock our empire by claiming *knighthood* for a *pig*? Roaring my anger at the disrespect, I held my shield and sword out, widening my stance and trying to make myself look as big as possible. The mutated pig snorted at my display and pawed at the ground before charging. At this point I didn't care about an injury, I cared about causing pain. When the pig reached me, I didn't try to dodge or to block with the shield. Instead, I aimed the sword tip for the beady little eyes and drove forward with the entire weight of my body. My sword drove into the pig's bulbous skull through the eye socket causing a sickening sound of squealing and pain. Unfortunately, moments afterward the sword was twisted out of my hands and a pig was stomping over my body, its hooves impacting on my chest and legs as it passed over me. I could taste blood in my lungs, and my health was blinking in my vision before Robert's large heal hit me and returned me to almost half of my health. While my health was half full, I was still suffering from a bleeding debuff and two debuffs for my broken leg bones.

Rolling over onto my stomach I shifted to watch the pig who was shaking its head around trying to dislodge the sword from its face. While it was suffering from a blinded debuff, its life was still far higher than my own. Before I raised myself up into a crawling position -what I was planning to do from there I didn't know- I heard the sound of a whip snap out and another pen door opening.

Chapter 22

The pig was injured, not fatally, but it was mostly out of the fight while trying to remove my sword from its eye. The just-opened pen would release a new enemy, one that would focus on my family, and that would be the end of them. Triggering my ring I used its healing effect. The initial burst of healing brought my health up nicely and the regeneration that would land every few seconds would get me closer to full life and reduce Robert's need to heal me. I still needed my sword in order to draw the attention of the new enemy.

"I've got this, kill the pig!" screamed Annie behind me.

Before I could question her, I heard the sound of expanding gasses and a burst of heat washed over my back. Glancing over my shoulder, I watched the goblin stable master scramble away from a wall of flame that sat in front of the pen's opening. From within the fire, white rabbits with faces red with gore tried to jump through the flames. Focusing on a burning rabbit, I grabbed its information and turned back to the pig.

Shan-Dar Clan
Vorpal Bunny - Pet - Elite
Warrior - Lvl 1
This opponent is beneath you.

With them being level one, Annie should be able to destroy those bunnies as long as the fire lasts. Somehow, I had a sense that we had been very fortunate. I needed to keep my ego and anger in check, the naming of the pig was almost a taunt for me all on its own. The stable master was again standing with his hands on hips and looking around proudly, but the appearance was somewhat marred when the leather armor he was wearing was charred and smoking. What concerned me was that his health was still full, his walk through the flames had been painful but hadn't damaged him.

With a crunching noise my leg healed, the bone violently rearranging itself inside my leg and leaving me gasping. Robert's heal and my ring had been enough to fix the broken bone debuff. With a wobble, I stood. I strode up to the pig, which was still violently whipping itself around while blood sprayed from its thrashing head. I waited until the sword was near and then yanked it free. The resulting piggy squeal was upsetting in multiple ways, from the fact I was causing it pain, to the idea that I was going to cause even more. Without the distraction of the impromptu sword-horn, the pig was now focused on getting revenge on me.

The bleeding debuff had done a lot of damage, but Emma's poison debuff had taken the bulk of the pig's life. I seemed to have angered the six-legged creature enough that it wasn't worrying about the others, but I used my taunt just in case. With my sword hand pulling my nostril up and a loud oinking sound, the pig's attention was solidly locked onto me.

The pig squinted its ruined eye, the lid barely closing around the gaping hole before it started to paw at the ground again in preparation to charge. Giving the pig another chance to stomp my body into the ground seemed ill-advised, so I charged towards the pig. Instead of aiming for the thick-boned skull, a spot which was usually an easy critical strike, I went for the dainty piggy hoofs.

Switching to the offensive stance, I rolled to the side of the pig and sliced at the three legs as they stampeded by. The front leg collapsed as my sword cleaved through it, but the middle and back leg took up the weight. The middle leg was deeply gashed, but the hind limb was only lightly injured from my swipe. My roll had reminded me of doing cartwheels as a little girl and had me laughing over the sounds of Annie's firewall. I was starting to understand Annie's enjoyment of her new abilities. Being able to do amazing things, physically perform actions I never could have done before, was freeing. I had always lacked strength. I had always been small and dainty, though I played rough and tried to be like the boys, now I felt like I was a burly strongman swinging a slab of metal through the air to defeat my foes.

"I've got you *Sir* Oinker! I'm going to knight you!" I hollered as I reversed direction after coming out of my roll.

The banter was silly, and I knew it even as I said it, but I just couldn't resist my whimsy while slamming my blade down into the pig's shoulder between his front leg and neck. Instead of pulling the sword back out and in for another slice, I followed my offensive stance's instincts and continued my motion. Turning away from the sliced pig, I stepped to the side of the downed hog as I pulled my blade free and returned the blood-drenched weapon into the side of the monster. While defensive stance had me huddling up and holding the line against attacks, offensive stance had me swinging, whirling, and chaining attacks together. Sometimes this more aggressive style was able to reduce the damage I took merely by ending the enemy faster or by causing so many debuffs in such a short time that the enemy was laid out too quickly to retaliate.

Learning the details of these abilities was where the real skill lay. When I was fighting another weapon user, and especially a skilled and armored one, then defensive stance was likely to be more useful. On the other hand, brute damage dealing enemies with little defense or skill could be quickly ended with an offensive stance as long as I managed to avoid a major blow which disrupted my rhythm.

When the pig finally died, the battle taking only a few more blows while in his downed and crippled state, I turned back to the primary fight. Annie's flame wall was still burning strong, but her mana in the party menu said this was likely not the first one she had used. The other two were just watching as the bunnies would throw themselves through the flames and die shortly after. A few managed to make it through the conflagration, but even Emma's minion was able to end the severely burned animals quickly.

"When these are done, I'm going to have to regain some mana. These walls of fire take a lot of me," Annie said.

Another thirty seconds was all we had to wait for the swarm of bunnies to end their attack, though Annie's flames continued to burn. With no further pets attacking, we moved towards the stable master. Before I could attack the boss, he snapped his whip out again and opened another pen. This stable was next to Annie's fire, and the four-foot tall mantis which exited the pen was not amused. It rushed towards Annie in a flurry of green leg blades and flapping wings.

The sight of a goblin-sized insect caused Annie to scream and flail her arm as she tried to run behind Robert. Annie had never liked bugs and a large one, mouthparts slavering and poking around, as it rushed towards her was sure to worsen her fears. Triggering my taunt skill induced a new way to annoy an enemy. This time I scraped my blade along my shield setting out a screech of metal, but somehow I could internally tell that my skill was not a full success. I had never had a skill fail before, but its failure was as evident to me as when it succeeded.

The lessons learned from fighting the pig and how it related to my stance now came back to confuse me. This creature was probably like a bug in most ways, its armored form was most likely strong against cuts and slicing, but would take extra damage from any type of crushing attack. My weapon was heavy enough that it would probably count as a crushing weapon. But it was also a bladed opponent with agile movements. A more defensive approach would perhaps allow me to defend against its attacks while still dealing some damage. Ultimately I decided to switch to my defensive stance. If I were able to protect against the mantis easily, then I would switch to my neutral stance or offensive stance. It would be easier to build up an attack and reduce defense as needed rather then starting with a strong attack and realizing too late that the monster's offense was overwhelming.

Before the mantis reached me, I pulled up its information to see what I was fighting.

Shan-Dar Clan
Snicker-Snack - Elite
Rogue - Lvl 5
This opponent is beneath you.

"It's a rogue! Don't let it get behind you!" I shouted the moment I saw the monster's class.

Snicker-Snack was a level less than Sir Oinker, but I wasn't going to underestimate this creature, and it was good that I didn't. The mantis drew back it's left claw in a telegraphed overhead swipe while it seemed to be too far away to attack. The swipe seemed to explode out of nowhere as its bladed forearm snapped out and extended its reach by at least half a meter, the bladed arm screeching as it dragged down my shield. Before I could counter-attack the mantis hopped back and spread its limbs as if welcoming me into a hug.

There was no way I would enter into the range of those bladed arms. Stepping forward would just leave me open to a scissor-like attack from both sides. Instead of stepping directly into the middle of the pincer attack, I stepped diagonally to keep my family further away from the mantis and to leave it only one real attack direction. I was worried the beast would ignore the obvious attack vector of my shieldless side, but it understood the protection a large slab of metal would provide. The beast's forearms were bladed, but the upper arms were not. I needed to get in closer and leaving my sword side apparently unprotected was what would get me within reach.

Abandoning the attack on the shield side the mantis reared up and swung in an overhead attack at my right side. The mantis was trying to cleave down on my shoulder like I had Sir Oinker. Blocking with my blade, I stepped inside the creatures reach and pulled my sword in close, attacking its arm on that same side. The attack worked, the bug spewed green and black blood from its almost cleaved shoulder joint, but it didn't save me from the mantises' retaliation with a bite to my cheek. I screamed shrilly as the mantis drove its bladed face pincers into my cheek and lip, the tugging on my face still less disturbing than the feeling of my eye bursting.

I was saved when Emma's minion began beating on the mantis from behind using Robert's mace. I don't know when Robert gave Emma's minion his mace, but the skeleton was swinging it like a mad machine, raising the weapon and slamming it down into the limbs of the mantis in a drumbeat of damage. The insect's life plummeted after every strike, and it was doing far more damage then my attack had. When the mantis released my face and tried to turn to the skeleton, I decided to switch to the role the minion had so often played before. Screaming at the insect, I looped my arms around its neck and tucked my skull in under the monsters angular head. My shield and sword made it hard to hold on, but the bug's neck and shoulders were thin, and all I was doing was trying to become a weight around its neck.

At the ten percent mark, the insect went into a wild flailing, its arms almost whistling as they cut through the air behind my back. The insect was unable to turn to attack Emma's minion, and it was unable to slice me or even bite me with my close in position, though it tried desperately to chew through what tiny bit of the back of my chain mail tunic it could reach. Emma's minion made a rattling cackle sound as it brought the mace down on the insects back, a spot that I could barely feel through the insect as a dull thump in my own chest.

"Oh...my minion can't laugh," Emma said in a very calm voice as I tried to untangle myself from the insect corpse.

Robert's intermittent healing had landed during my body tackle and had removed the 'disfigured' debuff that I had been suffering under, something I was grateful for. I may have acted like a boy from time to time, but that didn't mean I was opposed to remaining pretty. A hole in the cheek was not attractive.

"Was that what your minion was doing when it made that weird sound?" I asked, while never taking my eye of the stable master who was looking distinctly uncomfortable now that he was out of pens.

"Yeah, I was trying to think of something witty like you did, but I just ended up yelling as I kept hitting it," she said with an embarrassed look.

Robert took back his mace from the skeleton and said, "focus girls, the boss is still alive."

I was a bit annoyed by Robert's tone, but only a bit. We could banter and discuss after the fight. He was right that we still had the stable master to kill.

Chapter 23

Robert's rebuke had me spinning to face the expected onslaught of the stablekeeper but instead he was just standing where he had been, imperiously with hands on hip and whip laying behind him. His small body puffed up in pride and arrogance, his jagged teeth leering in a lopsided grin.

The blood pulsed through my body. The sound of my heart thumping so loudly it should have drowned out everything in the room, but I could still hear my family breathing quickly. We were paused in a nearly silent tableau. My family behind me, prepared to cast spells or heal, me in front with weapon and shield held ready, and the goblin stablekeeper was standing there seeming unconcerned with the force arrayed against him.

All my new instincts screamed to rush forward and attack, and everything told me that I needed to place my body between the enemy and my party. My anger, pain, and frustration agreed, saying that this was a wall I could drive myself against and so burn away my frustrations with the flames of violence. But I held myself back. I resisted my urges. I mastered my instincts and my anger, and I looked.

I looked for traps. I looked for new surprises, and I looked at my opponent. I watched for the twitch of muscle that said he was preparing to strike. I scanned over his form for the subtle shift of stance that said he was cradling an injury, I stared him in the eyes and watched for the sign of an opening.

And I found it.

When it came to me, all the anger I had been holding in, at the world and my own mistakes, urged me to scream forward and cleave the goblin in two. I had never tasted bile in anger before, but I did then. It made no sense, it shouldn't have triggered such rage, but it did.

The goblin was sweating. He was afraid and bluffing.

I couldn't sweat. It was refused to me in this new world. I would assume that in a similar situation I might be able to sweat as well, but under the normal circumstances of exercise, it wouldn't come. Sweating wasn't even a good thing; it was unpleasant, smelly, and only tolerated as the price of the freedom of movement and adventure. But it had been denied to me in this world, and now this goblin had it, and I raged in my heart because of it. The illogic of it never even occurred to me, but it told me what I could do about it. I could kill this creature. I could hurt it, and so, provide some relief to the injustice the world had done to me.

"It's sweating in fear," I growled.

Two beats of my heart. One. Two. That was the entire delay between my words before we collectively lunged at the stable keeper.

I had done more than speak at that moment. I had used my taunt skill to force the disdain I felt into my words. The goblin cracked his arm forward driving the whip towards me as I charged, my shield catching the side of the whip before the tip at the end could crack. To my surprise, the end of the whip was impregnated with fish hooks. Only a couple of pinpricks of metal penetrated, the red threes and fours barely registering to my new understanding on the scale of pain. Heaving backward the goblin tore the hooks free and induced a new debuff.

Debuff - Muck's Draining Bleed

Bleed damage increases over time.

10% of Bleed damage heals Muck.

Specials:

Effect Stacks.

May only affect one target.

If anyone should be the target of this debuff, it should be me. But this meant we had a deadline. The longer the fight took, the worse the damage would be and the more it would heal Muck. The whip's initial damage was almost insignificant, even Emma or Annie would be able to weather its blow, but the debuff was another story.

The goblin's heave caused me to lurch to the side for a moment, but it hadn't broken my charge. While the boss was off balance from its attack, I slammed my oversized blade down on the goblin's head aiming for a stun.

"We have to kill him as fast as possible. Use everything!" I screamed, hoping my family had noticed my debuff and its danger.

Triggering my offensive stance, I began to follow the bold lines of violence in my mind.

I had no time to focus on making my reasoning clear. It took all I could to dodge the stable keeper's blows as I pushed my attacks. He never used his whip in close range, except in using his exper use of the handle like a bobbies' billy club. Contrary to what I had expected of a whip user, he refused to let me attack with the full length of my weapon. Each time I stepped aside or moved to bring my weapon closer, he would step in and strike at my forearm or even block with his arms directly.

Each of my blows was cutting into the leather arm guards the goblin wore, the thin bar of metal hidden under the cover nicking and pinging at each of my blows. After a few strikes, the goblin started taking minor damage from each of his blocks. Though he took damage, each blocked blow opened me up to his counter-attack; a kick, or a strike to the wrist, and even once my hip. My shield mitigated most of his attacks, the left side of my body effectively a plate of metal that he couldn't strike through, but he tried to counter this by continually turning to my right side leaving me almost spinning around him as he steadily advanced.

His life was plummeting, and his damage was minimal, but his whip debuff and the corresponding life transfered to him was growing. Soon we would see the tide shift. Just as I felt small pricks of sweat form on my brow, the irony bright and shining in my mind even through the haze of combat, the goblin stable keeper was drilled through by a white-hot ribbon of fire.

The flash of the fire was not bright enough to disrupt my vision, thanks to the limits one human could do to another, but the fist-sized hole drilled through the shoulder of the goblin dropped his life to below twenty percent. Crippled, burning, and blinded debuffs all flashed up above the goblin bosses head, though the blinded debuff lasted for only moments before it faded.

"I used my scarves' effect, but I missed his head," Annie said.

Somehow Annie was able to make the pout audible in her voice. The sound of my sister pouting because she failed to drill a white-hot flame through a monster's head and only managing to hit his shoulder suddenly rung out in my mind. This sentence drilled home for me that just as I had changed, so had everyone else. The world was new, the rules had changed, and we were not as we were and never would be again.

I let my existential thoughts flicker past. My motions never hesitating even as the epiphany rode my mind I continued to follow the brilliant lines and the blows that my offensive stance offered. When the bosses eyes flickered to my sister and his arm bunched in preparation to strike Annie with his whip I took a note from the stable keeper and prepared to strike.

As the monster's arm drew back and he shifted his stance to aim for my sister I dropped my arm down and then raised my blade in time with his movements. At the apex of his arm's retreat to begin his swing, the edge of my blade met his armpit, and the critical strike drove it through, up, and out.

With his weapon arm gone and his other crippled from my sister's lance of flame, the stablekeeper more resembled a practice dummy than an enemy. Almost every strike became a critical and his dodging was clumsy and off balance. Only the fact that he was a boss and had a large amount of health had him lasting for even a few minutes more. Soon though, it was over, the stable keeper was dead.

Glancing at my log, I frowned upon seeing that I was still level seven, though my status screen said I was but a breath from level eight. Since everyone else trailed me in experience, none of them had leveled either. Just like the copper rifle's before this, I was unable to grasp the whip of the goblin boss. Frowning I shrugged. I had expected it, but I had hoped otherwise. Such a weapon while distasteful would have been immensely useful against slow enemies with large amounts of life. I couldn't imagine there would be many such creatures, but I wouldn't pass up such an advantage even if I found it unseemly.

After everyone had healed up, Robert having spent much of his mana keeping me healed towards the end of the fight, I rushed to the newly appeared treasure chest. Even as I tried to get to it first, Annie, giggling, reached it before me. When she reached for the chest, and only one arm won the race to touch it, her giggles faded. The lack of pain from her amputation was a mixed blessing; seeing her realize her amputation after forgetting caused a different pain entirely. But her quickly straightening shoulders said that she would carry through.

The skin on the back of my neck crawled at the sight of her actions. Not because they seemed disingenuous, but because they didn't. Annie had never had this kind of resilience before. She had never been able to recover from the blows of the world this easily. My sister had inner strength, but she bent with the winds of the world and endured yet remained miserable inside. Now she was like a reed that bent and rebounded, refusing to conform to the shape pressed upon her. This was more of the new world's subtle mind control, and it was both useful and sickening.

When Annie opened the chest a new window appeared with two options and by the movement and distant gaze of my family, they had a similar window.

Select Final Boss Reward.
Four Rare items or one Heroic item?

Vote Tally: 0 / 4

The word Rare was in a dark red script while Heroic was in a shimmering gold. It seemed reasonable to assume that the Heroic item was better than the four Rare items, but four items together would do more for us as a team than any one item alone could offer. When I voiced my opinion, I was surprised to find that Emma agreed with me, but Robert and Annie opposed!

"With my scarf, I was able to make a huge contribution to that fight, with your ring you were able to take on that Worg, a single Heroic item will make a bigger difference than anything else," Annie argued.

Robert mostly agreed, a single major item could have a considerable effect. My ring without the effect, with its stats spread over four items wouldn't be nearly as effective as just the one item with the effect.

"The same goes with your shield and Emma's stick thing, the effects matter. It's like a debuff during a battle, they can turn the tide more than just the damage alone," Robert said as he paced around.

During our discussion, he had remained standing, and now pacing, even as the rest of us had decided to lounge in a circle to debate. The shift in our behaviors, less aggressive for me and more so for Robert stood out to me at this moment. We weren't in combat, my class instincts didn't push me one way or another, and I assumed the same for Robert, leaving him to return to his normal leadership position in our group. The shift was jarring to me only because I had been watching for further mind control effects, and this appeared to be the cessation of one. Our classes didn't apply to this situation, and so we could do as we liked, no hints and subtle nudges enforced. As such, Robert returned to his normal mode and the rest of us to ours. Robert was by no means overbearing in our group, but by the nature of society, even our lovable and sensitive Robert was more domineering of the group's direction and focus in discussions than any of the ladies.

I straightened from my slight slump and rolled petulant shoulders. I was a part of this group, and if I wanted to argue my position, I could, the world had changed, and I would embrace the parts of it I liked. I wasn't the only one to hold this view.

Emma dropped her polite smile and looked Robert in the eye as she responded, her voice only wobbling slightly as she spoke, "We should be fair, everyone should get an item, we all did this together."

Robert opened his mouth to reply as he turned to pace across in the other direction.

"Emma, I think they are right. A single better item really will help more. It might be different with a group random people, but for us, it will help us to have one much stronger item then four weaker ones," I said.

Robert's mouth closed, but he had a slightly bewildered look as if he was happy that he had won the argument but not how he had won it. I stifled a grin at his confusion and made sure he saw none of it, but the twinkle in Emma's eye said she had seen Robert's look.

"Good, so, it's decided. The single Heroic item then," Robert said, though not as confidently as he had before.

Emma shrugged and voted in agreement with the majority making it unanimous.

From the chest, we could hear a thump as a new item dropped into the bottom, though there was nowhere from which the item could appear. Another impossibility in a world full of impossibilities. Emma rose gracefully and passed Robert with a hand trailing along his chest and a smile, while Annie and I passed giggling. By Robert's confused look he had no clue why we were laughing, but he knew we were laughing at him.

When Emma reached into the chest, she pulled free what appeared to be an exact duplicate of my own blade, down to the nicks and scratches, the only difference was that it had a subtle glow and tiny sparks that occasionally drifted along the edge of the blade. With difficulty, she levered up the sword and passed it over to me where I gripped it by my left hand and pulled the blade out of hers. Unequipping my old blade to free up my hands I looked at its apparently improved doppelganger.

Goblin Straight Razor - Heroic
Non-Tradeable
One-Handed Slashing
Dmg: 15-35

Speed: 33

Effect: Has a chance to induce Goblin Straight Razor Bleed effect (Stacking 3) on strike.
Trigger Effect: Once every 15 minutes, all Goblin Straight Razor Bleed effects exchanged for Goblin's Infected Wound Effect (stack 3).

With a squeal I spun around while holding my new weapon like a doll, cuddling the large blade against my cheek. Both Annie and Emma smiled, but Robert rolled his eyes at my display, though his lip curled just a little as he turned away.

Chapter 24

After I equipped my awarded sword I placed my old weapon into my inventory next to the numerous looted rusty weapons. Turning to the swirling exit portal we stood and watched it pulse. There was an awkward pause as everyone turned to me to lead. I had been leading the charge throughout the dungeon, but mostly because it left me taking the brunt of the damage. By nature I was not much of a leader. An instigator of trouble, as my father would put it, but not much of a leader. Usually Robert would have fulfilled that role, though he was more naturally reticent in social situations, his training normally trumped such concerns. I was too direct and forward for the politicking that leadership required. Politics and subtle social manipulation was more my sister's arena.

I stepped towards the swirling portal while trying to suppress my apprehension. The unnatural disturbance was silent though it appeared like it should have caused a great roaring of sound. My first passage through the portal to enter the dungeon was taken at a run and without much time to consider the sensation, but in my memory, it had no texture and failed to cling to the skin. If anything, passing through the portal was like moving from a bright sunny day through a door into a darkened room, a moment of darkness and then one was in a new place.

Turning to the party, I said, "I will see you on the other side. We will go to the Colonel and tell him of the quest we received. There is no evidence of a traitor, but he will know what to do about...what to do."

I received a group of nods, though Robert looked unsure and uncomfortable. How badly had the Colonel broken down after I had left?

A quick breath and I stepped through the portal.

Unlike the last time, where the movement through the portal was instantaneous, this time a swirling tunnel of black and grey appeared to extend into infinity as I flew down the tunnel at an unimaginable speed. I appeared to travel at an incredible rate that is, except that I felt no wind, and I seemed to lack a form. I couldn't feel my hands, my limbs, and I couldn't turn or look away. All I could see was a swirling tunnel and a semi-transparent window which appeared in front of me.

Goblin's Den Completed!

Team members: 4
Bonus XP for completion without a full team!
Bonus XP for completion without a death!

Number of Bosses Defeated: 3
Total Bosses: 3/9

Time to complete: 3 Days, 11 Hours, 12 Minutes, 13 Seconds.
Bonus XP for first completion!
Bonus XP for record completion time!

Heroic Goblin's Den Unlocked!

The window just floated there with no context as to what to do with it or how to exit the tunnel. I ignored it for now, just staring at the time to complete line in the window. Three days and eleven hours! If I had been pressed to predict the time, I would have guessed a day and a half had passed at worst!

With a sinking feeling, I started to work out what had happened. No natural light, Robert had failed to bring his pocket watch, hunger and thirst only mildly irritating and easy to ignore when fighting, a lack of fatigue, all of it added up to a perfect way to lose sense of the passage of time. Even with a day-night cycle, the lack of physical fatigue would work to disrupt the natural rhythms of a working man.

Counting back I tried to determine how much time was left and how many days we had to reach level ten. First was the initial day. Then entering the goblin den in the late afternoon near dusk -and oh how I should have turned around right then just from the approaching darkness alone- then three more days and eleven hours. It should be near the morning on the fifth day. Five days to reach level ten, more than enough time. We had blasted through level after level within the Goblin's Den, and we could continue the process in the forest and hills fighting easier monsters.

With my time concerns assuaged I turned my mind to how to exit the tunnel. With a nudge of mental effort, similar to how inspecting a creature worked, I tried to 'inspect' the window. Doing so closed it and ended the flying through the tunnel effect, dropping me upright on the grass. With my sword in my hand, I turned around to assess the situation. Where I landed became blindingly apparent in short order. I was at the back side of the giant rock that was the entrance of the Goblin Den dungeon.

A few moments after I emerged, so did the rest of my team: Robert, then Emma, then Annie. Their appearance was like the rest of this world, odd. It was like they were slipping from two sheets hanging on a clothesline. Only this was as if the hanging sheets moved and were made out of the world itself. Silent, fast, and profoundly unnatural, but it left them standing and looking around with no idea how disturbing their arrival appeared.

Carefully I looked around prepared to defend against any attacking goblins. If I had known that my den had an exit in this location, I would hold a defensive position here to ambush any escapees. Despite the fresh air, the gentle sunlight, and the sweet smell of grass and the pond, I was prepared for a slavering group of goblins to attack at any time. The obvious ambush point was left ambush free, and another expectation of reasonableness was abandoned. I wouldn't always trust that a dungeons exit was safe, but it was looking to be the case. After asking Emma to watch for goblins, I turned to assign the gains from my leveling.

With all the bonus experience, and being so close to leveling, we had skipped right past level eight and on to level nine. My actions had been risky, but it looked like they had been beneficial overall. With a guilty look at Annie's maimed arm, I thought to myself: *mostly.*

> **Level up!**
> **Victoria [Warrior lvl 8] - at level 10 NPC's will no longer be zone locked.**
> **Level up!**
> **Victoria [Warrior lvl 9] - at level 10 NPC's will no longer be zone locked.**

Again! I tried not to grit my teeth and throw a tantrum, but the lack of abilities when leveling was becoming frustrating. I could see some of the reason for it, or at least if there was a reason it seemed to be a balance of my abilities versus my survivability. I was getting an AC bonus on level up, and my health was almost five times Robert's and his was nearly double that of either of the others. During the last few fights I was able to take attacks head on that would have crushed any of the others in short order. All of that was amazing, but it was just not as flashy as being able to throw balls of fire or summon an undead creature of terror to rip into my foes!

While I assigned my stat points, an almost perfunctory step since it was so mindlessly simple, I noticed the experience required for the next level. To go from level nine to level ten we needed the same amount of experience as all of the levels from one to nine combined! With a sinking feeling, I considered that with the lower level enemies, and the amount required, we might have to kill stray forest enemies all day to make it to level ten within the deadline.

Emma interrupted my thoughts to link the spells she gained in to party chat. A cloud of disease spell that affected an area, an area snare, a light globe spell, and the ability to pull from her health and send it to another. The last spell had a description that physically made me ill.

Spell: Empathy from the Dead
Necromancer Spell: Level 9
Target: Single Other
Mana: 25 mana
Effect: Drawing 300 health from the caster, heals the target for 300 health.

No necromancer has admitted to the creation of this unique spell line. What is known is that the spell's original use was that of healing torture victims. The drawing of health as well as the direct infusion of life allows for the precise application of pain with little to no chance of death from shock. - Necromancy, the Masterwork. Volume 2, 3rd Edition.

That was wrong in so many ways. Emma would never do such a thing, so it was fine for her to use the spell to heal in emergencies, but I would be keeping a careful eye on any other necromancers we find. Having one of the darker classes didn't necessarily make someone evil, Emma was proof of this, but there were probably many like Rebecca as well.

Emma having linked her spells to chat started the others into sending links to their new spells as well. Robert's spells were just more of his usual fare: a heal, a new self only shield spell, a maximum health increasing spell, and a heal over time. Annie's spells, on the other hand, were more unique. She gained an ice storm, a chain lightning spell which jumped from monster to monster, and a spell to summon stone spikes which she could fling at enemies. I wasn't sure exactly why she had so many spells which seemed to do relatively similar amounts of damage but used different elements, but it seemed to be the way wizard spells worked.

When the flurry of links ended, I looked away to watch the forest and avoided the questioning looks. The awkward silence ended when Robert suggested we should head towards the mansion and check in with everyone and let them know we were fine. It would be nice to get a full day of fighting in before retiring, but we couldn't be so selfish that we failed to inform them of our survival. Letting them know that we were alive and healthy seemed like the minimum we could do.

Skirting around the large rock, we approached the front of the den where the goblin guards were stationed. Leading the charge, I whipped out my new blade, my shield ready for a counter attack. My new blade cutting through the goblin warrior with almost no resistance, the blade slicing through and continuing forward to the second goblin's attacking arm. The injured goblin fell to Emma's lifetap spell moments later.

My attention was still on the two corpses when a goblin hunter hit me in the back of the leg, the return of the bleeding and lamed debuffs had me gritting my teeth in anger and recrimination. I should have been keeping my eyes out for additional enemies, but the ease of killing these previously deadly foes had lulled me into fearlessness. This was a valuable lesson. I might have been far more powerful than I was, but debuffs can still cause severe issues, and all it would take is a spot of inattention to turn a moment of dominance into one of danger. I could just imagine a hunter keeping me crippled as I chased him and being peppered with arrows. A recreation of our strategy with the Arena Master -with me on the receiving end- would be a disaster.

While I was unable to charge the hunter, Emma's pet had no such restriction and reached him while I limped along. I needn't have bothered. Annie decided to play with her new ice storm spell. Again, overkill perhaps, seeing as there was a single enemy so far below us in level, but it was a chance to experiment with her new abilities. I could see the appeal. I tried not to let my jealousy get the better of me. I may not have acquired a new skill, but every new spell my family had, was a power we would need if we were to make it through this new world.

Turning to the mansion, we started the hike back to our summer home.

Chapter 25

The hike started enjoyably. Annie and Emma allowed me to experiment with the use of my new sword instead of killing the goblins and wolves before I could attack. I admit I took a perverse amount of joy in backhanding a goblin hunter with the flat of my blade so hard that his body essentially pulped. These enemies were so low level in comparison to ourselves that it would take extreme negligence on our part before we would suffer from it. Then again, father always talked about the random slings and arrows of battle and how they could strike anyone, even those who had prepared and were diligent.

So while I enjoyed the chance to experience my new found power, as well as the joy of having Emma and Annie both give me a disapproving look over splitting a goblin in two, it quickly became repetitive and boring. Each of these goblins, and later the wolves, were low level and worth almost nothing in experience. When we reached the beetles, they actually *were* worth nothing for experience points. This raised my concerns over our future leveling speed. We should be able to kill goblins and level, but would there be enough of them?

My thoughts were interrupted by Robert's change in pace. At first, I hadn't noticed that he began to drift in front of us, he had always been the defacto leader of our troop as the only man, but in this new world, his role was to be protected rather than to defend. It wasn't until I had to slow or walk around him did I realize that we had outpaced him. When I looked up to see what had caused him to slow, I failed to notice an enemy, but I did see Robert's serious face. Shoulders hunched, bottom lip held by his teeth, brow furrowed. He looked to be a man marching to a court-martial rather than a man returning from a victorious battle.

Watching Robert's hunched form, his stride slowing to almost a shuffle walk as we neared the mansion, I realized that he was still seeing the world as it had been and not as it was.

The old rules were gone! I thought with a giddy smile. *I can be anything I want to be and so can you Robert!*

My smile was wiped clean when we entered the foyer of the mansion, and the Colonel stormed through. Above his head floated a debuff: *Severe mental strain.* I had never seen the Colonel as anything but put together and well prepared. The man in front of us now had wild, unkempt hair, his clothing was disheveled, and he looked to have lost five pounds or more in the time we had been gone. The deep puffiness under his eyes underlined his lack of sleep, but despite this, his movements were fast and powerful. Without a word he grabbed Robert by his shoulder and shoved him through the foyer into the tea room, his forceful march was silent, and Robert took the rough treatment as if it was just as he had expected.

Detouring through the tea room Robert and the Colonel finally ended their dragging march at the game room where the Colonel threw open the thick oaken door and shoved Robert through before following after, closing the door without a second look at the rest of us. Beyond the door, I could hear the beginnings of a hollering match between the two men, the subject was that of failing to follow orders and endangering women for his own gain. I would not let that kind of accusation stand, *I* had instigated the trip to the dungeon, *I* had stormed ahead of everyone else, *I* had decided to push forward while everyone else followed the Colonel's instructions. Me, not Robert.

Robert only did that which any man in this modern day would do, he acted to rescue a young woman in need. The fact that I wouldn't have needed saving if I had planned and thought ahead was a different issue entirely. I would not let Robert suffer for my mistakes.

Throwing open the oak door I marched into the dark-toned room and straight up to the Colonel who was standing over a sitting Robert and yelling, his voice far clearer without the thick wood door blocking his diatribe.

"Colonel! Robert did nothing wrong, he was only rescuing me! If-" I said, the surprise of the interruption only allowing so much to escape before the Colonel responded.

"This doesn't concern you. Robert disobeyed, he risked everyone's life for the sake of only your own," the Colonel began while Robert looked up from his bent sitting position. The look Robert directed my way begged me to let the fight continue without my input, but I was going to have to refuse him in this instance.

"No! Listen. It was my fault. I rushed ahead, I pushed forward, and it wasn't-" I began.

Without waiting for my argument, the Colonel stood and grabbed my upper arm and started to drag me from the room! I was stunned for only the shortest of time, the Colonel had never been so rude as to grab me like that. The sudden change of demeanor was alarming, but I wouldn't let him direct me from the room. Stopping, I planted myself in a stance used for stability, a stance I had become deeply familiar with over the many hours of combat. The Colonel was brought up short when I went from an easily moved young woman to an unmovable rock. His look of annoyance turned to one of befuddlement when I refused to budge even when he started to press against me.

Using the now routine request for the Colonel's information told the tale.

The Colonel

Markus Collingwood
Warrior - Lvl 3
This opponent is beneath you.

The Colonel hadn't leveled in all the time we had been gone! Did he just huddle in the mansion without venturing out at all? Even only a few of the Grass Beetles would have increased his level in short order.

"Have you just been hiding in here the whole time?" I asked in confusion.

I knew the moment I said it that it was a mistake. I didn't mean to imply that the Colonel was a coward, but it was clear he took it that way. His suddenly flushed red face and then darkening countenance was nearly as bad as Robert's white-faced pallor as the Colonel gripped me.

"How dare you! You spoiled child! I've been defending your father's property and the people here while you have been galavanting off like a little twit!" he shouted while his facial hair bristled with every word.

His words had Emma and Annie rushing through the partially closed door, a door they had obviously been hiding behind during the short-lived argument.

"And you!" the Colonel said as he noticed Emma, "I will have you thrown out on your ear! You abandoned your post to go… to…go running off after this twit!"

Uncurling from my hunched position I stood tall. I had made mistakes. I had rushed forward, but Emma? Annie? Robert? They had only done what was right. What was brave. It was possible to argue the Colonel had made the right decision to defend the mansion and those living in it, women and children, but to claim that they had made the wrong decision was false.

When Annie moved around Emma's now flinching form,

standing slightly in front of her to defend her, the Colonel's jaw dropped open in surprise at her maimed arm.

Turning on Robert, the Colonel continued, "Look what you have done! Your fiancée is now scarred for life because of your actions! You should have followed orders!"

That was the last straw. Of everyone, I was the most responsible for Annie's injury, not Robert. Robert had more than once been the reason we had survived a blow. He had been there each time, a healing spell ready to protect each of us. He had decided to risk the dungeon and rescue me, and he did it knowing the reception he was likely to receive from the Colonel.

No more.

Striding forward I grabbed the Colonel's towering form, one hand on his jacket overcoat and the other on his belt, and then I lifted. I didn't have offensive stance enabled, but I didn't need it to understand the best way to throw the raging blowhard. Ducking my shoulder slightly I pulled the now screaming Colonel into the air and threw him as best I could at the overstuffed furniture.

"Vick!"

"Markus!"

The Colonel bounced off of one of the sitting chairs and landed on the ground, no red numbers raising from his body telling me that he was uninjured, but the look he gave said he was wounded in more than physical form.

"Annie will heal shortly. Robert rescued us. It was my fault, not his. The world has changed! Get used to it!" I shouted before petulantly stomping from the room and leaving silence behind.

Chapter 26

My dramatic exit was ruined halfway down the hallway when I burst into tears and ran upstairs to my room. Owen tried to stop me in the hall to see if I was alright, but I dodged him and continued past. Throwing myself onto my four post bed, I began to cry as I tried to block out the world. I had power, strength, and the capability to demand my point of view be taken seriously, by the Colonel or any other man, but doing so could cost me my relationships just the same. Would Robert hate me for attacking the Colonel? Would the Colonel hate me? I sniffled into my goose down pillows as I thought of how many times as a little girl the Colonel had lifted me over his head and spun me around. As I had grown those lifts had become hugs instead, but he had always been a substitute father figure. His friendship with our father, as well as the Collingwood families traditional association with the Blythe family, had led him to spend almost as much time around the mansion or London home as Robert. The death of Robert's mother and the Colonel's perpetual bachelor-hood had him overseeing Robert's upbringing and by extension, Annie and I.

Mother's death pushed father into further military postings, an effort to escape his pain as much as the demands of duty. This left me isolated and refusing to conform while Annie decided to take control of London's social scene. I dreaded the thought of losing yet another parental figure, yet another person I depended on leaving. Was my pride and demand for freedom worth the loss of my friends and family?

"So, you came crawling back. The world is scary out there

isn't it. Dangerous. Frightening."

Rebecca Northrop was standing in the doorway to my room, her arms crossed while a frightful scowl puckered her lips. Her words should have driven me into further tears, but oddly they didn't. It might have been that I no longer considered her an authority ever since her thefts had been uncovered. It could have been that if it came to blows, I would be able to defeat anyone in the house, with her likely being only stronger then young Rufus. All of that was in my mind as I turned over on my bed and wiped my tearless eyes, but in truth, it was the sound of her voice and the fear in it, the hunched shoulders and the way her eyes darted around the room as she tried to avoid my gaze.

She was afraid, and she was trying to garner strength from dominating me with words. This world was one in which words would always take second place to action.

Reflexively wiping my eyes again, I slowly stood from my bed, my approach moving Rebecca back a few steps from the door before she squared her shoulders and calmed herself.

"What are you wearing? You look like a streetwalker! Nearly your entire bosom is exposed. Aren't you ashamed of yourself? What would your father think if he saw you now?" she said, her question ending with a sneer.

I was brought up short, but only for a moment. What *would* father say? Father would say that manners are the glue which holds society together, that we must always act well mannered since a community is fragile. That the loss of society results in a quick descent into barbarism and violence and that it must be avoided at all costs.

But he would also say that barbarism is here and that once society has failed, pragmatism becomes the watchword.

I knew this was what he would say. I could remember every lecture on battle and society he had ever opined. I remembered every long-winded diatribe on hygiene on the battlefield and how it related to societies niceties and etiquette. Father had little-enough he could teach his daughters, fully admitting his failings on raising the fairer sex, but he meant well, and he passed on what stories and knowledge he had. This was a subject he held dear and was clear on. Treasure culture, society, and manners for they are easily lost and what remains is nature; brutal in tooth and nail.

Stepping close to Rebecca, my face inches away from hers, I replied, "I'm wearing the newest fashion trend. It's survival, and you look underdressed."

I was so close to Rebecca that I could watch her pupils dilate in fear and her breath accelerate. My satisfaction was short lived as Rebecca turned and rushed from the room; her soft crying still easily discerned as she left. I felt terrible for my outburst and threatening demeanor but not my bullying of the ex-governess. Strangely enough, I felt guilty that I *didn't* feel guilty for threatening her. Shaking my head, I sat on the edge of my bed and looked out my windows at the slowly darkening night.

My plans hadn't changed, and I knew that the others agreed, we had discussed it on the walk home. We would go out and fight and level, if we failed to reach level ten before the time limit, then all our work till now was virtually without a point. Our suffering, pain, and the risks to our lives in the dungeon would be meaningless. I was worried that the Colonel would convince Robert to forgo our outing, the Colonel being a role model and father figure, but he had seemed adamant to push forward, almost more than even I. His glances at Emma spoke his reasoning.

I suspected that if the damage to the world was as bad as I thought, then Robert's concerns were moot. If his family was mostly dead, a likelihood given that no one had arrived at the mansion, and if London had been exposed to similar waves of monster attacks as we had, then his family fortune was likely gone. As was ours. Refusing to follow the family demand's of who to marry had little weight when only his uncle remained, and there was no fortune to be excluded from -a poor silver lining to that cloud, but still a real one. Likely Emma and Robert would be able to marry and live out their lives in this mansion with the rest of the household, locked to this zone as the tutorial claimed, and they could live a happy life together for as long as it was possible. But I knew the look in Emma's eyes, it was the same as mine, and I thought that Robert had seen it as well.

Emma had gained power, the ability to control forces that had for so long been the realm of God alone, and she had gone from a powerless maid to a deadly and destructive force. She may have been less vocal of her demands for power and control than I had been, but her want of control was clear to see. I wasn't as sure what was driving Annie, but it was likely a similar wish for power and control. Certainly, her enjoyment of her spells was evident if her cackling laugh as she lobbed fireballs was any indication.

My rambling thoughts were brought back to the mansion when a new window appeared in my mind.

Event - Defend the Mansion.
The Blythe mansion has been targeted by the Shan-Dar Goblin Clan. Someone within the estate has given the goblins detailed defensive information. Discover evidence of the traitor and inform the Colonel of the coming assault.

Objectives:
Find evidence of Traitor 0/1.
Inform the Colonel of the coming Assault 1/1.

With an unladylike snort, I realized that the quest had been updated. Robert must have explained to the Colonel about the quest we received while spelunking through the goblin caverns. I could just imagine the Colonel breaking down why the 'traitor' couldn't possibly exist and why the idea was ludicrous at best. My gentle laughter was short-lived however as the quest objectives updated once again.

Event - Defend the Mansion.
The Blythe mansion has been targeted by the Shan-Dar Goblin Clan. Someone within the estate has given the goblins detailed defensive information. Discover evidence of the traitor and inform the Colonel of the coming assault.

Objectives:
Find evidence of Traitor 1/1.
Inform the Colonel of the coming Assault 1/1.

My befuddlement was interrupted by the quest awarding experience. This pushed my experience meter to nearly halfway to level ten, but the real concern was the new window that appeared upon completion of the quest.

New Zone Event - Siege of the Mansion!
The Blythe mansion has been targeted by the Shan-Dar Goblin Clan. The goblins are amassing to attack the only near human settlement, the Blythe mansion. Gathering their horde outside their Den the Shan-Dar Goblin Clan prepares to march for war! Survive the goblin horde waves and defeat the Goblin champions and Chief!

Objectives:
Waves survived 0/10.
Champions defeated 0/5.
Chief defeated 0/1.

Time until the horde attacks:
2 days, 11 hours, 29 minutes, 43 seconds.

The timer in the window slowly ticked down as I read over the new event description in growing horror. Rising from my bed I rushed from my chamber and to the game room, I had to find out what Robert had done and what we needed to do in order to survive.

Chapter 27

"What's going-" Rebecca asked as I passed her in the hall.

I never even slowed as I rushed by her, throwing up a bare hand to block her forward movement and reject discussion. Annie and Emma were standing at the end of the hall near the kitchen when I reached the hallway to the game room. Between us, the door to the game room opened and Robert glanced both ways at us then gestured us to join him.

I was brought up short when I entered, seeing the Colonel almost swallowed by one of the cushioned chairs, his head down and held by one hand. Emma and Annie pushed me to enter the game room, my pause in the doorway having blocked their entrance behind me. The Colonel didn't shift though he had to know we were here. In my mind, the Colonel was a large man, strong, capable, loud, and boisterous, his limp only underlining the image of a man who could walk through withering enemy fire and come out the other side still shouting for action. Now though, my girlhood view was being replaced by the image of the man who sat before me.

The Colonel was tired.

I kept trying to see the Colonel as young, healthy, and boisterous. Sadly, this man had thinning hair, and his waistline had started to expand though he was yet still fit. The tide though was turning, the shape of things to come could be seen in the changing cut of his clothing. Even as he pulled his head from his hand and looked up, straightening to show signs of confidence, I could see that his conviction was a sham. His left hand held his cane in a white-knuckled grip, and his mouth was locked in a stoic granite façade.

"Well, we know who the traitor is now. I should have seen this, it's unnatural, but the signs were there if we had only known," The Colonel said while looking to Robert.

Robert frowned before he nodded to the Colonel.

"It was Buttons," he said with a disgusted look.

Emma asked the question before I could, "The barn cat? What?"

Robert nodded then gestured us to a seat at the nearby card table. Instead of sitting to the side at the table while Robert and the Colonel discussed the situation, I grabbed one of the thickly cushioned chairs and dragged it to the circle of the fireplace and next to the smoking chairs that the pair had been using. Emma followed my lead and then assisted Annie in pulling a chair over for her as well. The Colonel watched our actions with a frown but failed to mention our rude response. I did notice that when the Colonel turned to Robert that our cleric's face slipped back into a neutral look instead of the slight smile that he had been wearing during our moving of the furniture.

"A while after you left to rescue Victoria, Rufus came to me and asked if he could make one of the horses his pet. I told him no, and that they were the Blythe families animals. I thought nothing more of this. We were dealing with more important issues," the Colonel said while running a hand through his hair.

Looking around at us as he talked he continued, "Later that night he told me that he had made the barn cat his pet since the animal didn't belong to anyone."

"The next day Rufus was upset because the cat rejected him after he had refused to give it food from the house. I ignored his complaints about this. I thought he was acting out because he was not allowed to go outside to play."

Stomping his cane on the ground Markus stared at Robert for a moment then sighed before explaining, "Later I noticed that the cat was spending a lot of time in the mansion instead of the barn, and it seemed to return each time it was thrown out, but I just figured it was trying to find a safe place. Rufus kept saying the cat was muttering about helping 'the small people,' how was I supposed to know that his Beast Tamer Class allowed him to speak with animals. I thought he was just an imaginative child!"

Bowing his head, the Colonel was silent while he stared at the ground.

Robert leaned back before he responded to his uncle, "Sir, you couldn't have known. The moment we told you of the quest you realized what was going on and the quest updated. We know now, and with this information, we can start taking steps to defend ourselves instead of being attacked without warning."

The Colonel seemed to take strength from this, straightening in his chair he nodded then looked to Robert again, "Agreed. Very well. We will have to defend the mansion. We will gather furniture, barricade the windows, and leave only the back door from the kitchen as an entry point. This should allow us to funnel the attackers through our defenses and whittle them down! This will let us keep the women and the boy safe upstairs and away from the fighting."

Throughout the Colonel's speech, I sat silently waiting for when he would suggest what we could do in defense. I was surprised by his final sentence, but I wasn't going to allow that idea to stand.

"No," I said while looking the Colonel directly in the eye.

"Your actions have gotten your sister maimed and risked

everyone's life; you will wait with everyone else and leave this danger to the men. You will not interfere and risk anyone else's life!" the Colonel said, his voice rising as I refused to back down.

"No," I said again while staring at the Colonel. My blatant rejection of his instruction had him trying to rise from his seat. I had expected this though, his actions before had surprised me, but now I would not let him try and *protect* me in the name of civility and social standing.

Grabbing the Colonel's shoulder, I used the full measure of my new strength to hold him seated. The strain was real, I was holding him to his seat with my arm held out straight and from a sitting position myself, but it wasn't something he could overcome with direct force. The fact that I could hold a fit man to his seat in such an overwhelming way put clearly my argument.

"No Colonel. Women in this world are not weak. Any of the three of us could defeat you in direct action. Women can defend themselves in this world far more ably than in the last. We have fought in this new world, and we should help in the defense," I said as I held Markus until he calmed himself.

When he finally stopped straining against my hand, I gentled the pressure and tapped my fingers on his shoulder. From the chair beside me, Annie held up her hand and formed a swirling ball of fire, the crackling heat radiating out even as her upturned hand rested directly below it. Annie's display of danger was eye-opening, but it was Emma's that drew the Colonel back in his chair. Emma gently muttered while the room darkened then pointed over her shoulder where a puddle of darkness coalesced into a skeletal form that stepped from the shadows. The goblin skeleton's jagged teeth clicked as it snapped its mouth open and closed for a moment then it settled behind Emma's chair with both hands gently resting on her arms, its glowing eye sockets just barely peeking over her left shoulder.

"We are more than capable of handling ourselves. The mansion needs to be barricaded and protected. You are right; you need to be the last line of defense against the horde. But we should venture forth and attack these camps. Unlike the last event where the creatures appeared out of thin air, this event says they are gathering at the Den and preparing to attack. We should move through the darkness, get close, and attack these creatures," I said.

The Colonel was still staring at Emma's skeleton as I described my plan, but at the idea of us venturing out into the night he shook his head.

Before he could reject my plan, I interrupted him, "No, Colonel. We will be doing this. It's the best plan, and we know how these creatures react. If it is anything like in the dungeon, we can safely thin our enemies. Sir, I don't mean to be rude, but you can't stop us. We need to do this, and you need to defend the mansion so that we can fall back if needed."

When he saw that Robert supported me and that Annie and Emma seemed confident in the plan, he looked away before nodding. I had hoped that pressing upon him the need for his protection of our fallback point would convince him that I didn't see him as cowardly, but I wasn't sure if that would come through clearly. I loved the Colonel, but I wouldn't let him shove me back in the social box when we were so close to freedom, and this was a matter of life and death, and his plan would lead to death.

"Fine. In the morning you will find this horde and attack the camps. Be careful, if your father returns and I have to tell him that any of you died, I don't think I would survive the discussion," he said with a self-deprecating smile.

I hated to push like this after he had capitulated, but we had little time, "Actually, I suggest that we go now. We can attack under cover of darkness and escape if need be. We discovered in the dungeon that sleep is no longer a necessity for survival but only for mental recovery."

The Colonel glanced at Robert who nodded in agreement. Once he received approval from Robert, another male, he reluctantly agreed. I was annoyed that it took confirmation from Robert to get the Colonel to admit the validity of our plan, but I won agreement for our actions so being upset about the process seemed silly. Annoying, but I was sure to meet other disagreeable and difficult men in our journeys so I should become used to it now.

Rising in concert, we set out on our duties — Markus to prepare the mansion and us to defeat the horde.

Chapter 28

Laying full length in the grass, I stared at the goblins surrounding the campfire. The fire I was near had nothing but level three goblin warriors. Beyond the fact that it was on the edge of the camp, its lack of higher level monsters was why it was chosen for our first attempt at this deception. I could smell the wet grass and dirt that was inches from my nose, with my head tucked down only the top of my hair was visible if a monster looked my way. All I could do now was wait for the signal.

Far across the collection of campfires, I watched an eerie green light suddenly appear and float away from the camps. The goblins on the far side of the camps stood and started a hooting call and then rushed out into the darkness. When the goblins closest to me failed to attack, I jumped up and struck the nearest one from the rear with a sideways slice across the back of the neck. The heavy blow combined with offensive stance and surprise, easily removed the monsters head, the red critical damage number flying away with more than double the little creature's health. Without slowing, I leaped and delivered a two-handed attack on another of the goblins at this camp. By this point, the rest were aware they were under attack, and they charged me together. This was when my sister's fireball impacted at my feet and slaughtered most of the gathering monsters.

The fireball was also the signal that Annie could see the enemies returning from the minion's distraction. Using the skeleton with a cold light as a disposable distraction was perhaps a bit heartless, but seeing that the skeleton was without a heart and was a puppet for Emma, it seemed appropriate. Annie's second fireball quickly ended the few goblins which had survived the first blast and together we escaped, ignoring the dropped loot. The point of this was to end the threat, and maybe gain some experience, not gather more rusty swords.

Our escape was a bit skewed, and we ran across a group of approaching goblins. Most of the goblins chased us into the fields beyond the forest. We chose this camp specifically as it was closest to the edge of the trees. After running about fifty feet into the field of grass, the goblins stopped and just looked out into the darkness for many long minutes and then returned to the camp fires. We were lucky it was a new moon and that it was so dark out, on a full moon we would have been plain to see for miles. The grass was not high enough to hide us if there had been more light.

Annie was holding her side when the goblins finally returned, and we rose to retry our attack.

"You all right?" I asked.

With gritted teeth, she yanked a bloody arrow from her side then held it up with a blood-flecked grin. In a sane world that sight would have convinced me that my sister was soon to be meeting her maker. In this new world of insanity, the sight brought me comfort. The debuff was going to fade, and her health was recovering. Robert's hand on her shoulder and the gentle golden glow of his most efficient heal said that she would be well handled.

Creeping back to the campfires took almost half an hour of our slow movements. Most of our time was spent waiting and checking to see if a sentry had been placed at the most prominent approaches. Strangely, the behavior of the creatures within the Den continued outside in their camps. They were uninterested in what happened at other camps unless roused to act. Even if they noticed our movements in the darkness, they didn't attack. At worse, the monsters snarled and returned to looking at the fires.

Ducked down low behind a tree stump I sent a message into chat to keep my instructions silent.

Victoria [Warrior lvl 9] - Emma, you handling things where you are?
Emma [Necromancer lvl 9] - I'm fine. I had to hide while a goblin peed near me.

I could hear Annie snort next to me, to which I threw a dirty look. I wasn't sure if she noticed it because of the dark, but she settled into silence so I would let it go.

Victoria [Warrior lvl 9] - They behave like we predicted. I want you to group up with us and we will start clearing the camps.
Emma [Necromancer lvl 9] - Moving.

I had noticed a weird phenomenon with the chat window. The easier it was to send text, the less formal our mode of speech became. Posting a single word response in a message would have never have passed Emma's mind before the apocalypse. I had read Emma's writing when we had been growing up, her mother had ruthlessly trained her handwriting to match the upper crust. I liked to think Emma's mother was preparing her to marry some merchant's son or someone else of a high station that needed a good wife. But the idea of a single word message would have been anathema to all of us. Control of the written word was essential, and a letter was one of the few ways you could completely control an introduction or interaction, to blatantly throw that away with a single word would be tragic. Now though, it was possible to send a single word of a message to anyone in our party with but a flick of a thought. It made more 'off-the-cuff' conversations possible.

My musings were broken up when Emma's form slunk out of the darkness at the edge of the trees and joined the rest of us as we huddled and watched a camp. I say 'joined,' but it was more like Emma 'stumbled over,' Robert. I heard some stifled giggles from Emma as she cuddled up against Robert's prone form. The accident was allowing Emma to snuggle next to Robert unobtrusively. Given the giggles from Emma, I wasn't sure if she had been a 'stumble' or more of an 'intentionally tackled.'

Victoria [Warrior lvl 9] - Professionalism people, we are at war, and these creatures want us dead.

I hated to break up the canoodling, but I could hear my father chastising me to focus on the mission. Odd, since father had never said such a thing to me before, but I was confident that would be what he would say in this situation. Emma's white toothed grin flashed across the darkness at me before the sounds of the movement grew silent.

I loved both of them, but Emma could become distracted by Robert's tight pants at the worst of times. Robert was always a gentleman, so I never had to worry about his hands straying to Emma while something important was being dealt with. But, if Emma happened to have a chance for roaming hands, well, Robert was perfectly willing to accept that call to action. Troublesome, but cute in its own way. Robert had a normally reticent nature, confounded by society's take charge demanding behavior, while Emma -sweet, sweet, Emma- was required to stifle her naturally exuberant actions. In this new world, they were both free to act as they would naturally, and that meant a much shyer Robert and a far more direct Emma.

With my goofy happy grin and daydreaming of Emma and Robert's love story, I almost missed Robert's signal to advance into the westmost camp. The west camp was slightly further away from the rest of the campfires, its closest neighbor had been the one we just cleared out during our testing of the goblin's behavior.

Pulling myself over a stump, my movements as silent as I

could make them, I crept forward. I might as well not have bothered given that the goblins turned to me as I approached. With my new confidence in the goblin's continued idiotic behavior, I triggered my warcry skill and charged. One of the goblins in the group was an archer, perhaps the one who had winged Annie on her last escape, but it had been hunched over with his bow behind him out of sight when I approached. My failure to see the archer could have been a worry as it restrung its bow in haste, but a taunt had it focused on me instead of my family. A comment about where he liked to store his arrows could do much to distract a goblin.

Emma's giggle, moments after my taunt, was evident even over the clanging of swords against armor and a goblin's grunt of pain. It was amazing what sounds would carry even during a life and death battle. Father had told a tale of a subordinate passing wind in fear during a cannon battle, flatulence perfectly timed between the roar of the single cannon, but I had thought it a jest to garner laughter from his daughters. Now I didn't think so. The idea that someone would giggle, or pass gas, or do any number of things during the chaos of battle, made perfect sense to me. Even the whimsy of musing about bodily functions while methodically removing limbs seemed normal now.

The crowd of goblins surrounding me, each attack doing small but persistent damage, was thrown back by Annie's explosive offense. Only one goblin seemed to be alive after the explosion, but Emma's lifetap spell of sickly red and green ended that before I could step forward. Our plan called for us to retreat the moment the goblins were dead. If the timing were perfect then Robert's large heal, beginning to be cast some time in the middle of the battle, would land as I was retreating to the group. With me being the only melee combatant, except for the skeleton, I would be ahead of the group, and they would remain further back. The hope was that they would be safe while I drew attention. Emma's main aim was to watch for approaching stragglers or patrols. If they found themselves attacked by a group of monsters while I was finishing up multiple enemies, things could be difficult. Emma and Annie's snare spells would be used to drag their attention away, and then we would quickly retreat. Utilizing the arena snare-and-retreat tactic was the backup plan.

Given the odd forgetfulness and the refusal to leave their camps, a retreat was always the first option. We could always let the goblins calm down and then return to try again. Whatever these Old Ones had done to these creatures, they had damaged their minds. They made useful cannon fodder in large numbers, but elite warriors they were not.

Then, the windows of information agreed. Only one of the goblins in the camp was an 'elite' like the ones in the Den. He was also named differently from the rest.

Shan-Dar Clan
Gibbles - Elite
Beast Tamer - Lvl 6
This opponent is beneath you.

I kept my eye on 'Gibbles' as we cleared camps. The grossest part about this goblin was not the drool dripping from his mouth, or the way he ate with both hands without tool or cutlery, it was what he was eating. We had found our traitor, and the poor cat had not received the reward it had desired. I should have felt vindicated that a traitor to my family was receiving just punishment, but the fact that it was just a small animal that wanted food: that hurt. Either way, that goblin was trouble, and we would need to end him the same as we would the rest of the camps.

Chapter 29

We continued our hunting throughout the night, the fact that we didn't need to sleep was pushed for all it was worth. Sometime around two in the morning, we had an event update.

Waves survived 1/10.

This update almost had me cheering, though I refrained since we had been working through killing the camps as silently as possible. It was silly; the goblins knew we were here -some even watched us as we killed off other camps- but it still felt like we should be silent. Using my war cry skill as quietly as possible had me making a weird coughing-bark sound.

I had worried that we could kill for the entire period of the timer and still not reduce the wave. The 'Cleansing' event had monsters appearing out of thin air. It was possible those creatures had been conjured from some far off plane of existence to our front walk, a terrifying idea. A far more disturbing idea was that those monsters had been created, ex nihilo, right there and then. The 'Old Ones' seemed curiously restricted in ways I couldn't define. It would be in line with previous restrictions if they were able to recreate the waves at the end of the preparation phase. The counter ticking off the wave gave me confidence that we were making progress. I silenced the little voice inside me that whispered that the wave could be reset to zero and the camps refilled when the timer ends. That would seem to fit the arbitrary rules as well.

At around six the first rays of light started to peek over the horizon and we were joined by the Colonel. I was discomforted to see him across the fields, a saber from the mansion's game room striking at beetles as he approached. When Annie had noticed him we had backed out of the forest to invite him to the group. He had explained that he needed to gain experience as well and had stationed Philip to guard the mansion. It was unlikely that any goblins would approach with us hunting them here, so it was a sound strategy.

There was an awkward moment when the Colonel tried to give us battle directions. Robert spent a few moments staring at his shoes being unwilling to correct his uncle but also clearly being unable to accept his instructions either. The Colonel had noticed the silence, but he seemed to want to bull through with sheer stubbornness. I could see his point of view. He was a veteran of multiple battles, he was the only one who had held a command, he must see us as little more than children. But as I kept having to remind myself, this was a new world.

"Colonel, this will sound rude to you, but we are the veterans of this new world," I said.

I tried to keep the frustration out of my voice. I had never suffered controlling men well and to have someone I cared for behaving this way caused me more angst than I would typically feel when dealing with such a man. There was no polite way to tell someone that they were acting the fool, but I wasn't going to fight a running retreat through the woods either. The Colonel's plan was perfect for the old world, I would agree wholeheartedly, but for this one where we could simply approach and attack, it was impractical.

Mainly since the number of camps had grown even as we killed.

The Colonel's mustache twitched at my criticism, but he remained silent.

"For the first camp, please watch, we will show you what we have been doing, and then you can join in on the next one. Before we begin, have you distributed your stat points?" I asked.

The quick nod to my plan told me the Colonel would play along with my actions, but at my question he looked into the distance, checking his character sheet I assumed before he focused back to me.

"They appear to have been assigned by this world without my attention. Some in agility, some in vitality, some in strength."

I winced at that but shrugged, that some of his stats had been assigned in agility was unfortunate, but we couldn't change it now. I would be sure to inform him of my distribution method when he leveled up next. Given the level of the monsters and the multitude, it was clear he would level eventually.

When we marched back towards the camps, the Colonel seemed to grow more and more wary, glancing at each of us as we unconcernedly approached the horde. I had been waiting for the Colonel to say something, but when we stepped under the shade of the trees, he set his face and held his saber to his side with a grim look. The Colonel seemed to have made up his mind to let me lead, and he would hold back while I did so. Some of the respect I had for the Colonel was returning. I might have had a rose-tinted view of him before, but not all of it was unjustified. Despite the worry he obviously had, the man was not a coward. Letting someone lead, someone you didn't entirely trust, that took bravery, though of a different sort.

None of the camps we had emptied had been refilled while we had been gone. The goblin horde was still pushing out along the tree line and setting up camps. The champion was still waiting at the campfire while eyeing us. Sitting on the ground, Gibbles' short legs splayed out in front of him, his hands resting on his rotund belly and his elbows resting on a log. Gibbles was the picture of a barbarian relaxed in repose.

We avoided the champion and instead targeted a different campfire nearby. We had discussed it and decided to clear out multiple camps around the champion's before we attacked Gibbles. We knew that unique enemies, and Gibbles was undoubtedly that, tended to pull surprises. The last thing we wanted was whatever surprise Gibbles would present combined with additional goblins from a camp.

Our plan worked without a hitch, I aggravated the goblins with a war cry and a few well-placed swipes, being sure to hit each goblin at least once. Moving backward while fighting the lower level goblins, I kept tagging each as I went. Emma would pick an enemy and use her skeleton to harass them while I chipped away at them in a round-robin fashion. Eventually whichever goblin Emma had attacked would become annoyed with the skeleton and turn to attack it instead of me. This was Annie's signal to drop a fireball at my feet. Whatever was left would almost invariably charge towards Annie. Emma would snare them, and I would taunt them. Robert would heal, and then we would repeat the process. Each fight was taking a minute or so, and we had fallen into a stable pattern. By this point we didn't even need to say anything, we just did it and then prepared for the next.

What I hadn't counted on was the Colonel's response to my taunt skill.

"What in god's name is wrong with you! I ignored your clothing, as needs must, but this is uncalled for!" the Colonel shouted after the last goblin was dead.

I didn't even bother to turn around, in my mind he was yelling at Annie for throwing a fireball at my feet. Trying to avoid chuckling I turned around to watch Annie's response when I realized the Colonel was staring at me. It took a moment of staring at the Colonel's outraged face before I understood what was upsetting him. By that point, I was blushing a deep red. I had long become used to the horrible things I said or did while using the skill and no longer even thought about them. They had become routine, an idea that would have horrified me before the apocalypse.

His tone of voice and the look of outrage is what caused me to do what I did next.

"Focus on me and use your taunt skill," I said in my sweetest voice.

The Colonel gave me a sour look, I would assume from my blatant ignoring of his question, but he then leaned forward while staring into my eyes. The next words that dripped from his mouth would have made the crudest of dockhand from London gag in disgust. Turning slightly green from the suggestion, I looked away and out to the campfires. It wouldn't have been so bad if he hadn't been staring into my eyes when he said it. My little prank on the Colonel ended up being on myself as well.

"I'm sorry," said the Colonel in a subdued voice.

"No, I'm sorry. That was uncalled for and I am ashamed by my behavior. Please excuse me," I said while stepping away and into the forest for a bit of fresh air.

Usually, Emma or Annie would approach me and try to comfort me after I was insulted or derided by a man, my masculine and offensive behavior being well-known and well-ridiculed. That is, they would approach and comfort me when I was *unfairly* harassed. This time I deserved it and would neither seek comfort nor accept it. My actions were uncouth, and I earned rebuke for them. The Colonel didn't deserve to be embarrassed in such a way, and it was my childish behavior which had led to it. Taking another deep cleansing breath and a few more seconds to stare into the brightening sky, I turned and marched back to my party in preparation for the next fight.

Looking to each of my party members I continued my apology, "Right, please everyone excuse my behavior. It was uncalled for, and I will try to do better."

Emma had nodded while trying to hide her smile. Robert had nodded as well, but I thought I could see a frown hiding behind his straight lipped look. I could understand that. Robert respected his uncle, and for a good reason, and of late I seemed to be unable to keep from butting heads with him. Annie just smiled as she watched the other camps. I don't think Annie really cared either way. In what little discussion we had while clearing camps, Annie had expressed more and more of a desire to experiment with her spells and to travel. The social conformist who had demurely navigated the turgid waters of London's social scene was officially gone.

"The only other warning I have for the taunt skill is to use it only when you need to, having it reserved to be able to grab the attention of a monster is vital. I think it's the entire point of the warrior class. We place our bodies between the creatures and our softer team members, drawing the fire of the enemy allows them to do the damage needed to win," I said.

Realizing that I had almost devolved into a lecture, I snapped my teeth closed and faced back towards another campfire.

"Very well, Colonel, I would have you assist on this next fight, though do try to avoid drawing them off of me, we are excessively leveled for these enemies while you are not."

Without waiting for a response, I moved forward and plunged back into combat.

Chapter 30

Without meeting anyone's eyes, the Colonel said, "This isn't working."

I was a bit bewildered by his statement. It had come after a few solid hours of silent killing where we had emptied camp after camp. We had made substantial progress. True, we hadn't seen another wave indicator change in the event window, but that was likely because we had not tackled the champion, Gibbles.

At my confused look, one that the others shared, the Colonel waved his hand to the side as if to cast away the confusion.

"Check the logs, our level difference causes an experience penalty for all of us," the Colonel said.

Checking my logs, something I had not done since the day before, I noticed he was right.

Victoria [Warrior lvl 9] - at level 10 NPC's will no longer be zone locked.
Victoria [Warrior lvl 9] - Grouping with low-level members (Markus) incurs an exp penalty.

The message repeated over and over again for each of our kills. When I checked my experience bar in my character sheet, I tried to work through where it was versus where it should be, but I couldn't determine how off it was. The hours had begun to blend together into a constant slog of killing.

Annie stared into space unseeing while biting her lip before she spoke, "He's right, we have only gained about half the experience we should have."

"I'm almost level four, when I hit it, I think I should return to the mansion and work on further defenses. I doubt that my gaining a level would be worth more than if all of you gain another."

The Colonel seemed calm with his announcement, but I could see the white knuckled grip on his saber. He was worried that we would see him as a coward, that it would look like he was running away from the fight.

Robert approached Markus while he was facing out towards the occupied campfires. This was a habit we had slowly started to mimic. No matter if we knew the enemy would only act in specific ways, keeping a watch on them was now routine. Grasping his uncle's shoulder tightly and giving him a slight shake Robert smiled at him and nodded. Of course, I was no longer constrained by nobility or his idiotic masculine avoidance of emotions. Instead of a refined pat on the shoulder, I ran over and hugged the Colonel around the stomach, lifting him in the air slightly and giving him a spin.

"All right! Ha! All right you! Put me down!" the Colonel shouted as he tried to seem upset by my outburst, though his deep manly chuckles belied that intent.

After the discussion, and the Colonel's departure, there was a period where our rhythm had been disrupted. My attacks didn't start at the perfect moment, Robert's heals had been mistimed, and Annie was a tad too eager to lob her fireballs into the enemies. But after a few fights, we settled and returned to our regular routine. This was something I would have to be prepared for in the future. Extra healing and caution were needed when starting and stopping after fighting for long periods. It takes time to return to a routine, and a routine can be easily disrupted. I had known it intellectually, but combat had a way of making someone viscerally aware of a fact.

Clearing through camps was quick, but even when the sun had reached its zenith, the event counter had failed to tick over.

I had become a bit tunnel visioned into killing more camps, but Annie brought me out of it. We had discussed this very situation though, Annie was designated the 'big picture' woman during our fights. If we become too focused on some detail of the battle, she would direct us into focusing on something else. Most of her time at the beginning of any fight was waiting to avoid angering the enemy early, before throwing out a massive explosion. This gave her time to watch for this kind of behavior.

"Vick, we need to think about this. We aren't making progress on the event."

Pulling my sword out of the skull of the last goblin, I jammed the tip onto the ground and then rested my head on the hilt.

Leaning my cheek on my sword, I eyeballed my teammates before I spoke, "Do you think it's because we haven't attacked the champions?" I asked.

Emma nodded then spoke up, "If the next wave can't start until the previous champion is defeated, that means we have to defeat the champion before the wave counter updates."

Straightening up I responded, "If that's true…what if we kill all the champions and then just leave the wave enemies? I'm sure we could handle groups of goblins even if a wave had double the number of these camps. If you snare, that is. We could repeat our actions as with the Arena Master."

Robert was smiling and nodding with the suggestion, "We might have to run around with the last enemy in the wave for a long time to regain mana, but we could string things out and fight at a pace we could survive. Worse case we fall back to the mansion and kill from the doorway like the Colonel's plan."

Just to confirm that everyone understood the idea I outlined the new plan, "So, we are agreed? We focus on killing towards each champion and leave these normal wave enemies till the end?"

The nods all around said we were all on the same page. I was uncomfortable trusting that we understood the logic of the event. As twisted as the logic was, it seemed to match what we experienced, and either way, killing the enemy was the plan so it could only help.

Gibbles was our first champion, and he was situated in a camp that we had cleared wide around. Sitting in his camp all alone he had eventually become bored watching us move around him and had fallen into a light dose, his body still resting against his log with his feet up and waiting. If I had known he was resting, we could have snuck up and attacked while he was sleeping, but we had made the mistake of stomping through the light underbrush on our return. When he noticed us focused on him, he rose and stretched in preparation. From a small bag at his side, Gibbles pulled out a massive club with metal bands. Resting his club on his shoulder, he grinned his sharp smile at us then scratched his back with his weapon.

I was still uncertain about the surrounding monsters, so I called for Emma to snare Gibbles and let him race toward us and away from the other campfires. If more monsters attacked, we would have a bit of distance to root, snare, or run.

When Emma's snare spell grasped onto Gibbles, he roared and sluggishly moved toward the necromancer.

Annie called out as Gibbles began his lethargic march, "We look to be clear, it's just him attacking."

As if to mock us, this was when Gibbles' pet dropped down from the trees above. The large scaly creature resembled a panther in structure but sported large triangular green scales, the edges of which were jagged and stiff. The large reptile landed behind me and casually swiped its barbed tail across the back of my legs in passing as it lunged at Emma. Our necromancer was surprisingly agile, she jumped backwards while sending her pet in to attack the creature.

I only had a moment to decide, should I attack Gibbles or his pet. With the champion approaching, I was tempted to attack him, but instead, I turned and engaged the panther-like creature. Triggering the details window for the pet failed to clear up its nature.

Shan-Dar Clan
Sud-re-kel - Pet - Elite
Warrior - Lvl 3
This opponent is beneath you.

"Emma! Keep Gibbles chasing you, I'll get the cat thing," I called out as I bashed my shield into the back of the cat as it tried to pry an arm bone off of Emma's skeleton.

"Got it!"

Spanking the cat with my shield garnered an instant response, the lizard-feline-thing spun around and tried to claw my face as it turned. Luckily, instead of catching me upside my head, my sword was up for a downward slice, and the sudden spin had me jerking back in surprise. The cat's claws met the edge of my sword instead of my face. I hadn't intended to slice the cat's paw as it spun, but I wasn't opposed to the red forty-five and the snare debuff the unprecedented attack gained me.

I was worried about the amount of damage the cat would do while I was in offensive stance, but I didn't dare switch to defensive because if it decided to attack another party member, it was unlikely I would be able to catch up to it. As a compromise, I switched to my neutral stance and hoped it would balance out the dangers. After taunting the cat by hissing at it, I struck it across the nose. Unfortunately, while a real cat would have had a soft button nose, this thing had a hard horn-like ridge for a nose, and my blow mostly bounced off of it. Despite the dismal damage numbers from my attack the cat still yowled and retreated with watery eyes.

A grunt, followed by rough words from Gibbles, distracted me for a moment. I recovered my focus when a green cloud floated past me and attached itself to the cat. The cat's eyes shifted from their black orbs into glowing pits while its claws began to shine a sickly green. I didn't know what was coming, but I could sense that it would be trouble. Ducking behind my shield was almost enough to save me from the frantic flailing of the cat's wild swings. One of the mad swipes had reached just beyond the shield, and when the cat pulled its paw back, the nails dug into my fingers as they gripped the shield's handle. The pain was surprisingly sharp and different from the normal strikes and bites I had become used to, and it caused me to holler and strike at the cat's hooked limb.

My spastic strikes had come at the cost at a few extra injuries from the cat trying to dislodge its claw, but my wild swings also severed the animal's limb. The cat creature hissed as it limped around me trying to rejoin its master, but I was unwilling to let it through. I wasn't sure why it wanted to meet up with Gibbles, but if it wanted to, then I was against it. After multiple false lunges and attempts to outmaneuver me the pet gathered its courage and tried to charge through my defense. I bashed the creature on the side of the face and knocked it off course. This proved to be the last straw as the animal lost its footing and landed on the stump of its severed limb. With the cat collapsed on the ground, the skeleton tackled it while Annie's spells tore away the last of its life.

When I looked to Gibbles all I could see was a mound of burnt goblin. Annie and Emma had finished Gibbles together and then turned to assist me. I felt a little self-conscious about not doing as much damage as the others, but I just had to remind myself that we all had roles and mine was to be there for my family.

With Gibbles dead, the Champion counter and the Wave counters both advanced, but that was nearly unimportant compared to what happened next. Annie's amputation debuff faded. When the debuff disappeared, her maximum health returned to normal, though she was still not fully healed. When Robert cast his heal spell, Annie's arm visibly regrew in seconds. Before she had been fully restored we surrounded my sister and began to cry and hug, even Robert appeared misty-eyed, though I doubted I could get him to admit it.

After a few minutes to regain our composure we turned to face the camps and look to find the next champion.

Chapter 31

Changing our plan to hunting champions, and leaving the non-elite monsters for when the event started, meant we had first to find each goblin champion then clear the camps where they were resting. At first, it was simple. A goblin that was double the size of any other tends to stands out. Once we fought our way to the second elite champion, we hesitated before attacking him. To our surprise, the warrior elite was no more a challenge than a regular elite inside the dungeon. This left us a little off-kilter wondering if something was going to jump out and surprise us while fighting. This concern only lasted as long as it took to end the next camp of goblins.

"Does this seem too easy to anyone else?" I asked in concern.

Emma gestured at me quickly, but to my apparent confusion, she sighed.

"Vick, one thing you learn is never to ask if things are too easy. That just gives the world a chance to notice and correct the mistake," Emma said with a much-aggrieved expression.

I nodded to Emma's concern but turned to the others, "Robert, Annie? You know what I mean though? It just feels like something will go wrong at any moment. This is just working too well."

They both agreed but didn't offer anything else in response to my concerns. I was sure that if they had a suggestion to ease my worries, they would say something, but the lack of response told me they could feel it as well. There were a lot of enemies, but they were low level, easy to kill, and all around us. The only creatures to give us any trouble had been the elites, and none of them even remotely compared to a boss within the dungeon.

With nothing but our vague unsettled feeling, all we could do was continue our rampage.

The third elite was a rogue and given our history with being backstabbed we tried to fight even more defensively than usual. We had the issue that the rogue was able to jump back and fade away. This wouldn't have been too problematic, especially in that he stayed targeted to me, but at one point, he began to run, and he ran directly into another group of monsters.

This was the only real difficult fight. Even then, Emma threw out an area snare spell and Annie bombarded them with fireballs. This tactic took longer and had Emma repeating her snare spell far more often than she was doing damage, but ultimately it was no real difficulty. Had we just leveled so far that this area was too easy for us? Were we destined to complete this event and throw back this part of the invasion? If so, that was a good sign for the rest of humanity if our small group was able to so quickly become capable.

About halfway to reaching the fourth elite, another goblin warrior, Annie demonstrated something that reduced the difficulty even further. We were slowly clearing out the camp of goblins. I had managed to gather them around me and sliced each of them to keep them focused on me when Annie dropped her fireball. Usually, this would have the monsters turning to attack her, and a few seconds later, her second fireball would land. This second fireball and the burning debuff would be enough to kill most of the enemies. Emma and I would take a few swipes at the ones that survived, and they would only survive long enough to take a few more steps.

This time was different

The first fireball landed like normal, but it was instantly followed by a second fireball which fell only a heartbeat after the other. The two explosions were so closely spaced that it sounded like rolling thunder. Only one goblin, which had been partially protected from the blast by one of the warriors, survived the fiery explosions. With a couple of careless swipes, I ended the charred enemy.

Emma asked the same question I had, "What did you do?"

Annie smiled and held up her hand to show off a forming fireball; after a second, the ball was floating above her hand.

"I kept wondering why casting a fireball had this step where the ball would form and then just hover over my hand until I focused on making it fly," she said while gently bouncing the ball in her hand.

Holding her hand stationary with the flaming ball resting above it, she continued. "It was so annoying. If I stop focusing, the fireball goes away. I recover some of the mana, but it was an extra step, and if I just lost focus for a moment, I would waste most of the mana!"

So saying her fireball glowed brighter for a moment and then unraveled in the air while part of the ball turned into little glowing motes of blue light that rushed into her hand.

Annie flipped her hand over as if showing off a stage trick. To be fair, even a few days earlier, I would have found her performance more magnificent than any I had seen at the grand shows of London.

Annie repeated her trick of forming a ball of fire and bouncing it into the air on her left hand before she focused on her right hand.

"But if I keep the first fireball in mind, I can form a second one and have two waiting to go. It's hard to keep my focus on two things at all times, but as long as I manage, I can throw two fireballs one after the other!"

With a wicked smile, she let both fireballs dissipate into the air as she had her first, the strain of focusing on both spells while talking to us had shown in her face. She had stared into space with a puckered expression, the tip of her tongue just barely pushed between her teeth, a look I hadn't seen since we had been little girls and she was learning arithmetic.

"The downside is that whatever mana I use to form a fireball is locked up into the spell, and I can't regenerate it until the fireball is cast or recovered."

With Annie's new trick with the dual fireballs, she was able to keep one spell ready at all moments even as she would form a second one. This only sped up her casting time by a few seconds, but a few seconds matter a great deal during a fight. With Annie's new fireball speed, Emma stopped trying to do damage at all. She just changed to casting the area snare spell and then Annie would throw her fireball into the group. This left the monsters burning and running towards Annie and had me smacking at their backs while she lobbed another fireball at the group. We went from killing a camp every few minutes to scything through them in half the time.

I was resisting the urge to complain about feeling useless, especially since this could only help us end the threat faster. By the look on Robert's face, I wasn't the only one feeling superfluous. Unfortunately, someone else agreed with our feelings.

Bonus Event!

"Uh…" Robert said.

I agreed with Roberts confusion. All of us hunched down and looked around, trying to figure out what was going on.

From across the swarm of camps came a scream of anger.

"You WORMS!"

Finding that whatever was coming was starting with words calmed me enough to stand straight and look towards the voice. Behind the groups was a stone platform, one I would have sworn an oath had not been there even moments before. The platform housed three large goblins, with the largest being a barrel-chested goblin with colored paint splashed across his body. The color wasn't in patterns or designs; they looked instead like someone had chucked open cans of paint at him. Next to him stood an old and hunched goblin. Unfortunately, more of the elder goblin was on display than with the larger one, namely, all of it. The wrinkled goblin was standing there without a stitch of clothing on while clutching a chest-high staff strewn with bones, feathers, and stones all tied to the stick with bits of leather. Near the two eye-catching goblins stood a smaller, but still more substantial than the average goblin elite. This goblin held the only shiny weapon I had seen in the camp. His weapon was a sizeable one-handed mace. Besides the standard loincloth leather armor, he also wore a rusted helmet with an open face guard.

The large goblin covered in paint stood on the highest step of the stone platform and screamed at us past the field of his followers.

"You think you can defeat the Shan-dar clan? Do you think greater strength will protect you? We have fought across the Fields of the Unbroken! We have decimated the Mind Flayers! We serve the Old Ones and have been set in this new world, with new lives, and we will travel over this land like a locust and consume it all!"

The large goblin's words continued in an unhinged rant, screaming about places their clan had been and the foes they had defeated. It took a few minutes, but even the old codger goblin seemed to have reached a limit. While the large goblin was screaming and yelling, foam flecking his lips, the naked goblin began to cast a spell. During this entire tirade, we just stood watching. Partially it was confusion, partly it was that there was a crowd of silent goblins between us and the chieftain on the podium, and partially it was that no one wanted to look in the general direction of an old naked goblin.

Once the spell began, the large goblin stopped his tirade about the might and conquest of the Shan-dar clan and changed over to a darker theme.

"Now, NOW! Begins my rise! MY clan is with me, and I am one with them! Through our worship of the Ancient of Sacrifice, we have been blessed with a power unlike any other. Show them Kul-det! Show them!" screamed the chieftain as the goblins from the different camps began to walk towards the podium.

The old goblin slammed his staff down on the ground, and from the top of it, a slender spearhead was exposed. The goblin with the helm kneeled in front of the naked elder and leaned backward with arms held wide. While the goblin was old, his body was made up of lean muscles, and he used those muscles to drive the spearhead into the heart of the kneeling goblin. With a prying motion, he expanded the hole and out gushed the dark fluid. With one hand, the old goblin smeared himself with blood and pressed it to the chest of the chief.

Champions defeated 4/5.

The chieftain stood aloft with his hands held wide, his teeth bared at the tribe while the spell's green filaments slowly edged in and out of the smear and through his chest and back to the shaman. The old shaman lifted the staff in the air, and the tribe dropped to their knees. The surrounding goblins began to emit a high pitched keening, a sound without words, and the spell shot out of the chieftain and into the surrounding goblins connecting to each of their hearts.

Slapping his chest and roaring the goblin chieftain continued, "Now I will rise with the power of my people! I will become a titan of destruction that will rampage upon this land, and the Ancient of Sacrifice will reward us with a new rebirth! Kneel my brethren! Kneel and fulfill my dest-"

Chief defeated 1/1.

The goblin chieftain's voice was cut short when the shaman drove the spearhead through the large goblin's neck. Clutching at his wound, the chieftain turned wide, wild eyes to the shaman who casually stabbed him in the heart — pulling the spearhead free from the injury he licked across the blade leaving his mouth smeared with crimson. The glowing green lines which had connected the tribe to the chieftain pulled back through the heart wound of the painted goblin and flowed into the elder. Visibly the clan began to wither and die, a pulsing light passing through the cords into the chieftain and then into the shaman. As each pulse passed through the spell the shaman's skin smoothed and his arms flexed with new strength, while the entire time the clan members kneeled and screamed in torment.

Turning back to my party, the no longer as old goblin smiled and spoke, "Sacrifices always return less than is given, but if I am the one to gain, what do I care? Tell me, how many sacrifices remain in *your* den?"

Ignoring the shaman, I attacked the nearest sacrificed goblin, whipping my sword around with a two-handed strike aimed at the goblin's neck. My swing cleaved the goblin's head from his shoulder, and the glowing line connecting him to the chieftain snapped and flailed around, leaking a green mist onto the ground. I had worried that killing the goblin would change nothing and all we could do was wait until the goblins had died and empowered the shaman, but it appeared that the goblins had to die slow painful deaths for the ritual. Putting them out of their misery would reduce the shaman's power.

Charging into the crowd while switching to my offense stance, I shouted: "Kill them all!"

Chapter 32

Screaming 'kill them all' and charging into battle was less a plan and more a reaction to our plan falling through. There was no way we could end all of the goblins, there were at least a thousand in the camps surrounding us. It wasn't the worst idea, the shaman was gaining power from the goblins, and when they died it robbed him of some that, it just wasn't the best plan.

"Head to the shaman!" Annie screamed while lobbing fireballs one after another into the crowds in front of the podium.

I didn't know what Annie was planning, but killing towards the shaman was a decent plan. Out of the corner of my eye, I noticed Emma was throwing out clouds of poison at further away goblin groups. Since her spells took time to kill, spreading her damage out over a more significant footprint was the best choice for the necromancer. My distraction cost me when I tripped over a goblin's dropped sword and slammed face down into the ground. Robert yanked me from the forest floor and pushed me forward while swinging his mace at the goblins as we passed.

Without a need for defense, I switched out my shield for my other sword. Using both my weapons at the same time while in offensive stance was a surreal experience. Instead of lines of attack and movement, the world seemed to glow with a swarm of interconnected threads, each of which knotted to another, and all of them were a way for me to deliver death. For a while, I lost myself in the dance. With the goblin horde unmoving in the grip of the ritual, I focused on only the lines of attack which lead to vital points. Lungs, necks, eyes, groins, hearts, each became the central focus of the movement of my blades. Once I was lining up only critical strikes, I switched to minimizing my movements, ensuring that my blades were continually flowing from wound to wound.

With so many targets I couldn't be sure how many I killed, but my trance was disrupted when my blade bounced off of what appeared to be air until my sword touched it. The impact vibrated up my arm and nearly cost me the grip on my weapon. When I looked around in a stupor, I could see the naked goblin grinning at me, the shaman's once paper-thin skin was now goblin green and youthful looking.

Licking his lips the goblin stared down at me, "Hmmm. The taste of youth. It's been centuries since I've felt this. My Master so does love sacrifice, and he shares the scraps from his table to his faithful."

Suddenly jumping forward the goblin's jagged teeth snapped in my face. With a shout of surprise, I swung my sword at the goblin, and again my sword rebounded from a glowing green shield that appeared between us. Leaning backward the naked shaman started cackling at my reaction.

Waves survived 2/10.
Waves survived 3/10.
Waves survived 4/10.
Waves survived 5/10.
Waves survived 6/10.
Waves survived 7/10.
Champions defeated 5/5.
Waves survived 8/10.
Waves survived 9/10.
Waves survived 10/10.

The event updates rolled in as goblins began to die all around us, the bulk of them focused through the ritual and into the shaman. Staring on the shaman, I requested his information.

Shan-Dar Clan
Avatar of Sacrifice - Boss
Shaman - Lvl 10
This would be an even fight.

The good news was that the shaman was at the same level as us, but the bad news was that he was a boss. The bosses within the dungeon had been significantly more dangerous than the elites, and they had been lower level as well.

When the last event update triggered, the sacrificed goblins faded away. With a swing of my sword, I could tell the shield was still surrounding the podium and protecting the shaman Avatar. While I checked the shield spell, my party members grouped up behind me. Switching my old sword for my shield, I changed over to a defensive stance. I had the feeling that I would need the extra protection for the next fight.

The shaman raised his hands into the air and began to shout a repeating phrase that felt like someone was trying to dig nails into my mind. While he was screaming his litany, the shield began to flash and flicker until it slowly collapsed and wrapped around the shaman in a green glow that covered him like clothing. Unfortunately, this clothing was still transparent leaving the now younger monster exposed.

Silencing his chant, the goblin smiled at us before continuing in a calm voice, "Ahhh, my sacrifice has gained me much. So nice."

Bonus Event!
Kill Avatar of Sacrifice 0/1.

The flashing update of the new event distracted me, and at a crucial moment. The goblin flung both his arms forward, and from his clawed hands, a cloud of insects formed and swarmed over our group. Most of the creatures were locusts and moths, but mixed into the swarm were wasps and bees. The insects landed on the exposed parts of my body and began to bite and crawl under my armor causing my skin to twitch. Robert shouted a spell that I had never heard him use before and a white glow spread around all of us, but nothing seemed to change.

Behind me, Robert shouted the bad news, "It's a curse, my dispel poison or disease spells won't cure it!"

While charging the shaman, I focused on the debuff to find out how troubling it was.

Debuff - Curse of the Crawlers.

15% Decreased Accuracy of Targeted Spells.
10% Decreased Accuracy of Melee.
15% Decreased Accuracy of Ranged Combat.
5 damage per six seconds.

The damage over time component was almost entirely ignorable. It wouldn't even overcome Annie's regeneration. The reduction in accuracy was the real purpose behind the curse. It was the fact that the debuff lacked a timer that seriously concerned me. My focus shifted away from the information panel and back to the combat when I reached the shaman. Throwing my whole weight behind my blow, I tried to drive the tip of my blade through the shaman.

The glowing shell around the shaman knocked me backward from my attack, deflecting my stab without the Avatar even stumbling. The absorption of my attack with the shield was what I expected. What I had not expected was the glowing blue eighty-five that rose above the shaman from my assault, nor the blue mana bar which appeared then dipped slightly. Watching the movement of the bar, I recovered my stance and delivered a flurry of attacks on the shaman, each dropping the goblin's mana bar slightly. The Avatar had a decent amount of health, nearly half of mine, and it's mana provided almost as much again to its shield. We would have to deplete the shaman's shield before we could attack him and reduce his health.

My gawking came at a cost, I failed to notice the shaman winding up for a two-handed strike and the attack landed across my face. If I had been slightly further from the goblin, the blade tip would have cut across my face, as it was I took the weighted end across my shoulder and temple. The pop of my shoulder snapping out of the socket, and the corresponding temporary stun, left me seeing stars and ducks. Before the stun could end, my world turned into a fiery inferno as Annie delivered a fireball practically across the back of my head. Unfortunately, her lack of accuracy had my body blocking much of the fireball's concussive force. While it only did minimal damage to the shaman's shield, it bought me enough time to regain my focus.

Emma was not idle during my attack, she had sent her goblin skeleton around behind the shaman and had it attack while the blast was incoming. I nearly cheered when the boney pet jumped to tackle the shaman. The pet's damage was minor, but its ability to act as a distraction, and crude disablement was a welcome addition to the team. My cheer choked in my throat as the shaman spun around and smacked the skeleton away with his staff before it could tangle the Avatar in a boney hug. I felt the heat rise up my cheeks when I realized that I had failed to use my taunt skill when I had been close. The shaman's attire, or lack thereof, and the goblin's unique abilities, had so distracted me that I had failed to perform my most basic and vital of jobs.

Your job is to anger him and take the abuse he delivers, not to kill him. Trust your team.

Still kneeling on the ground from the stun, I triggered my taunt skill. I thought that I had grown immune to the crudities of my skill, that I had adjusted to the words it used. I was wrong. Perhaps it was the Colonel's recent rebuke and surprise at my use of the skill. Maybe it was the fact that the goblin was still naked and I was near eye level with a part of his anatomy I had only heard tell of from the ladies at tea, but whatever was the direct cause, this taunt was more embarrassing than ever. The goblin seemed to find my crudity just as surprising because for a brief moment the battle became silent, my party did not cast, the goblin did not chant, and the skeleton stood with its jaw hanging open.

Ignoring the pause in the battle, I rose with a roar and slammed the edge of my shield into the goblin's chin and grinned at the blue damage numbers bursting from his shielding. My attack seemed to draw everyone back into the combat, and the noise returned to its previous levels. Sadly, the goblin recovered quickly from my attack, and he shouted a word of power as he swirled his bladed staff around. The new spell had a red glow appearing on all of us, and I ducked behind my shield as I focused on the debuff for a moment.

Debuff - Curse of Malaise.

5% Decreased Strength.
10% Decreased Attack Speed.
7 damage per six seconds.

This debuff was just as debilitating as the previous one, the damage was slightly more concerning because it combined with the debuff earlier, but the reduction in attack speed and the loss of my damage was a worry.

"Ah! Thank you for the sacrifice! Every little bit given, helps," the goblin said as he smiled in my face.

When I glanced up, I noticed that the goblin's mana bar had regained a significant amount; the debuff also recovered mana for the Avatar. That was a powerful capability and made this opponent far more dangerous than we had initially expected, but there was little we could do. We had no choice but to continue the attack and keep ahead of the goblin's spells.

Chapter 33

As the fight progressed, I became less worried about dying to the shaman and more concerned about not being able to kill him. We had been fighting the shaman for two minutes and had only removed a quarter of the shaman's mana shield. Two minutes is an eternity in a battle. While we had suffered multiple debuffs, each without a timer, none of them did severe damage. The little damage they did was quickly negated by Robert's weak group heal. The only spell the goblin had which did serious injury was a poison bolt type spell which he seemed to reserve for me alone. Luckily, Robert had learned the words to the goblin's poison spell, and when he heard it, he began casting his cure poison spell. The countenance of the shaman when the poison bolt was cured directly upon impact left me laughing in the green monsters face.

Genuine laughter at a monster's attack was nearly as useful as my taunt skill.

My laughter choked off as the shaman sprayed out gas from his mouth and directly into my own.

Debuff - Curse of Shortened Breath.

15% Increased Cast Time of Spoken Spells
10% Reduced Agility
5% Decreased Accuracy of Melee
3 damage per six seconds.

"Gah! Don't breath, uggh…any of that in!" the curse was well named, every sentence was a struggle, and the feeling of a massive beast standing on my chest was intolerable. The only real luck was that out of everyone, I was the target of this curse. Having problems using my warcry was a minor concern compared to slow heals or fireballs.

While I wasn't a caster, I had been paying attention to my party and how their spells worked. Annie's spells were big hitters, cost a lot of mana, and were blazing fast to cast. If she wanted to, she could pull attention to herself in short order since she did both the most damage per spell and could throw them the fastest. Emma's spells, on the other hand, were mana efficient, had a medium casting speed, and came with a unique utility like self-healing. Robert's, on the other hand, were either long casting and massively efficient, or fast casting and very expensive.

Why each class had such a difference in their spells was beyond me. Magic seemed to be wildly different for each class. Annie had mostly silently cast spells, requiring only a hand gesture in most cases. Emma had a mix of silent and spoken spells, while Robert had almost entirely spoken spells. There seemed to be no rhyme nor reason to the differences.

My musings on classes and the nature of spells almost cost me a punctured neck, the goblin Avatar having no qualms with using his bladed staff for melee combat instead of spell casting. Luckily, I was using my defensive stance, and I had been subconsciously following the cues, and it was all that saved me. Focusing back on the combat I triggered my taunt skill. The raspy wheezing taunt this time was not nearly as effective. It's hard to claim that your enemy is beneath you when you sound like a chimney sweep.

After I used my taunt, Annie changed spells. I had become used to the concussive blasts of fireballs, so the sudden shift to the blue-white flash of lightning and the roar of thunder disrupted the flow of my attacks for a moment. To my surprise, some of the electricity made it through the shield and sparked against the shaman! His life dipped only for a moment before more of the shield drained away, and his life rose, but this was the most significant shift we had seen in the fight.

After glancing down at the soot-stained section of his chest that had been struck by the lightning spell, the shaman looked to Annie and prepared to cast. This spell had a long windup involving multiple hand motions and a guttural incantation. This was new behavior, and if this new world had taught me anything, it was that new was bad.

Gasping through my debuff, I tried to shout to Annie, "Get…behind…cover!"

My gasping and choking were so disjointed that Annie couldn't understand me. I tried to use the chat system, but I was having trouble focusing on it through the feeling of choking and the need to continue wailing on the shaman's shield. When the shaman finished his spell, a glowing green orb flew from his hands and towards my sister. I tried to interpose my body and brace with my shield, but the spell passed through me as if I were immaterial.

When the orb impacted on my sister, a figure made out of sticks and plants formed. The semi-transparent green form jabbed its root-like hands into Annie's body. My sister arched her back and screamed in pain before she fell to one knee. When she raised her head she yelled and threw a new lightning bolt at the shaman. In the party window, Annie's health didn't drop, but her mana was plummeting. The wooden monster behind her was siphoning her mana away, but it didn't appear to be transferring it to the shaman.

I wasn't able to check the status of the translucent creature which was engulfing Annie, but I could see the debuff on my sister.

Debuff - Curse of the Green Man.

50% of Drained Mana transferred to Green Man as Health.
10% Mana Drain per six seconds.

Annie caught my eye before she began casting lightning blast after lightning blast into the shaman. Her mana was draining at an astounding rate. After the fourth lightning impact, the shaman tried to turn away from me and towards my sister. Most of my effort was in blocking, I was trying to stop the shaman's charge towards Annie. I was bashing my shield into the shaman and trying to push him from the side and from the front, I didn't dare get between Annie and the shaman entirely. While I wouldn't suffer damage from Annie's lightning, I couldn't afford to stop the electricity from impacting on the Avatar's shield.

Along with the impact from Annie's lightning, I had disrupted the shaman's charge enough to keep him a few meters away from my sister. Finally, Annie's mana ran dry, and the green man removed his translucent roots from my sister's body. Standing tall behind my sister, the tree-like green man slowly started to resolve into a solid form.

Emma noticed the transformation and charged with her skeleton pet. Her skeleton cackled as it raked its boney hand down the bark of the green man. The new enemy seemed to be frozen in distraction, its eyes pinched shut in its wooden face as it pulled its hunched form fully upright. When it snapped its eyes open, they were solid glowing green. Annie was not idle as Emma's skeleton attacked. The moment she felt the roots slither out of her body, she ran towards Robert.

Emma shouted to me as I was focused on keeping the Avatar away from Annie, "I'll keep him focused on me, keep on the Avatar!"

Without turning my head, I nodded and continued bashing at the shaman. My only focus was keeping him away from Annie.

Our damage against the shaman had dropped to almost nothing, and he was starting to regain mana, but we had to focus on keeping ourselves alive before we could worry about killing him. This battle had gone on so long that I was carefully balancing the stamina I had available as if it was my mana. Until this fight, my Warcry - Stamina skill had allowed me more than enough stamina regeneration to handle the short bursts of combat. With my focus on the shaman, my stamina, my foot placement, the few attacks the shaman made against me, as well where my family was, all of it had me stretched to my mental limits.

I nearly cried out in joy when my taunt skill finally recovered, and my stamina inched up enough for me to use it. The insult about the shaman's little wooden man barely registered on my consciousness compared to the sudden blows the shaman was throwing my way. Annie was standing somewhere behind me, precisely where wasn't clear, but the shaman had been focused her way. In front of me was Emma, running in circles with the green man chasing her, her skeleton smacking away from behind it. Giddy from getting the fight back under control, I couldn't help but imagine Emma playing a game of Ring around the Rosie with the green man.

By the time Emma had ended the green man, the shaman regained half of his mana. With Annie blasting him before we had reduced him to only a quarter left, but now we were back to halfway. My frustration was short lived as Annie began to cast her lightning spell again. While Emma had been running away and chasing the green man with her skeleton and I had been bashing at the shaman's shield, Annie had been biding her time and recovering her mana. Robert's mana had dipped low at one point, but my defensive posture and the green man being killed at range had given him time to regain it as well.

"We can do this! We have him!" Robert shouted from behind me.

Robert's excitement buoyed my flagging confidence, and I carefully began to weave strikes into my defensive movements. I erred on the side of caution, but I needed to retain the Avatar's focus while my party ended the threat. When the mana shield ended, a bright flash of blue light rippled outwards throwing me away from the Avatar. The naked shaman raised his hands into the air as his body started to distort and bulge. Annie's lightning bounced away from the shaman without damage. All we could do was watch and conserve our stamina and mana as the Avatar grew in size to look down on Robert. When the distortions ended, the Avatar's life had increased by thirty percent. The goblin was hunched over and breathing deeply after his growth.

Dashing towards the now oversized Avatar, I slammed my shield into the distorted goblin's chest. The stumbling goblin tried to reach over my shield with an overlong arm, the other clutching at his bladed staff to recover his footing. The moment the goblin's life dipped, proving that it was no longer capable of deflecting attacks like during its growth spurt, I triggered my taunt skill. To my surprise, instead of grinning a nasty smile at me as he had before, this new monster roared in rage, it's blood-shot eyes bulging from its face. The Avatar rose up, both arms held over its head, and slammed them down on my shield as I weathered the storm of its attack. The beast seemed to have forgotten the bladed staff that the shaman had so deftly used before and instead bashed away at my shield, the stick almost comically small in its hand. After the third impact, the staff broke from the abuse, though the creature failed to drop it. The monster foamed at the mouth as it continued its barrage on my shield.

The beast's latest swing deflected at an angle off my protection, the continuous roar of rage distorted from the sound of a fireball exploding above my shield. Taking my chance during the monster's distraction, I whipped my sword around as I held my shield above me, the impact of my blade against the creature's leg feeling like chopping into a tree. Before I could brace my sword hand behind my shield, the monster struck me a glancing blow, the guard ricocheting off of my head from the mostly deflected attacked. While it cost me health, it could have been worse, it could have stunned me and left me unprotected from the follow-up attack.

After pounding upon my shield for what felt like an eternity, the colossal monster stopped and gasped in exhaustion, its body visibly steaming from its exertion. During its exhausted state I returned to chopping at the creature's leg, all the while Annie and Emma bombarded the monster with poison and fire. Emma's skeleton had abandoned trying to climb the oversized creatures back, its bulk unlikely to be slowed by the lightweight pet.

With a grunt, the monster took a step forward, and instinctively I dodged. I wasn't sure what had clued me to the beast's plan, but I was happy I had moved. The naked creature charged in a straight line, its body slipping in the blood caked grass as it tried to stop and turn around. With a grunt, the monster stepped forward again and aimed itself at me. Without waiting for the creature to begin its charge, I dodged again. The monster blurred forward until it passed my position and then drove divots into the ground as it stopped. While the creature was in a hunched position trying to turn, I took advantage and swung as hard as I could at the Avatar's head. The impact against the skull of the enraged monster shook up my arm, but I was excited to see the now familiar stars and duck flashing around its face.

The still goblin looked befuddled as Annie's fireball exploded against his nose, ending his life.

After looking around at the forest of dead goblins, the gigantic Avatar which was slowly shrinking, and the smell of death, I plopped onto my backside and took a moment to breathe.

Chapter 34

When I was a little girl, I remember running as hard as my short legs could carry me through the fields behind the mansion. I would pump my chubby legs as hard as I could, driving my feet into the ground, and race across the grass and up the hills. The effort of running would leave me winded and red of face, and inevitably, I would collapse to the earth. It felt to me like the stress and excitement would leak out of me and into the ground. Whatever had burdened me would pale in comparison to the strain of throwing myself against the wind. Even the pain from my exertion would be oddly pleasant.

As I lay on the ground, my elbows propped up on my knees, and head held low, I could feel none of the sweet release from exhaustion. The strain and stress of moving my body beyond its limits were forever barred from me now. This world had taken something precious, something quintessentially human, and replaced it with a crude replacement. Despite its base nature, I still looked up when the happy completion event sound rang out, and the event list updated once more with our success.

Zone Event - Siege of the Mansion! (Bonus) Completed!
The Blythe mansion has been targeted by the Shan-Dar Goblin Clan. The goblins are amassing to attack the only near human settlement, the Blythe mansion. Gathering their horde outside their Den the Shan-Dar Goblin Clan prepares to march for war! Survive the goblin horde waves and defeat the Goblin champions and Chief!
(Bonus) Defeat the Avatar of Sacrifice.

Reward: 4035 exp, per participant Class Reward.

The feeling of the gold colored four thousand experience and the subsequent level up was glorious. I felt far more from this level then I had from any before it. The increase in feeling was so much more that I looked off into the distance as I tried to catalog the differences, entirely disconnected from the world around me. I was finally brought back to myself by Emma calling for me in concern.

To my surprise, none of the others had leveled. I was the only one. In my mind, this battle would result in all of us earning our freedom. The Avatar of Sacrifice had become more than just an enemy to defeat for the safety of the mansion. Instead, he represented everything wrong and bad about this world and the way to achieve everything I wanted in it as well. I chuckled at my silliness when I realized my mistake but raised my head quickly. We still had more to do to earn the rest of the party their freedom.

"How much do the rest of you need to level?" I asked.

Annie looked up at my question. She had been staring at the chest that had appeared upon the event's end.

"Hmm?" she distractedly responded before she stared into space for a moment and then continued, "I only need a few kills, maybe a couple of goblins? Do you think there are any other goblins in the forest?" she asked with a bit of concern.

"If not, we can keep looking and find something, even if it takes all night killing wolves we should be fine," Robert said as he joined the group huddling over the chest.

Emma chirped up at that point, "it really shouldn't take that many. We can probably get it before we finish walking back, we are far from the edge of the forest, after all."

I just sat watching as they opened the chest. Taking a moment without worry or fighting, without concern for the future or expectations seemed divine.

Each of them pulled items out of the chest, and when they had all grabbed their loot, they turned to smirk back at me and then looked into the chest again. A hint of concern started to drift through my weary mind at those looks. They weren't malicious, but they were filled with laughter. Laying back and ignoring their antics sounded terrific, but it wouldn't help them reach level ten, nor would it end their incessant tittering. Even Robert was trying to hold back his laugh. I could feel a sense of dread growing.

To forestall the issue, I tried to distract myself.

"What did you get from the event, Emma?" I asked, even as she kept glancing into the chest.

The wicked grin from Emma was odd to see on her usually kind face.

Venomous Bite
Non-Tradeable
AC: 1
Int: 5
Wis: -1
HP: 25
Mana: 25
Class: Necromancer
Slot: Ring

Worn Effect: Pets gain a venomous bite skill, (excluding pets without mouths).

Excluding pets without mouths? That was a creepy addendum.

"The bite applies a small poison debuff that works with my poison bolt," Emma said with a smile.

Annie shoved a giant glass ball under my nose before I could ask what her item was.

> *Orb of Ignition.*
> *Non-Tradeable*
> *Int: 6*
> *Mana: 25*
> *Class: Wizard*
> *Slot: Off-hand*
>
> *Worn Effect: Fire damage increased by 5%*
> *Triggered Effect: Next fire spell does double damage at triple the mana cost.*

"I think it's nice. I wonder if I can use my scarf at the same time? It's pretty, at least. Fashionable even. " Annie said, her face scrunching up with an effort to contain her laughter. Robert and Emma both smirked and looked away to try and hide their amusement.

Sighing, I turned to Robert, one last item to delay looking into the box and seeing how I was being made into a joke.

Robert looked off into the air for a moment until suddenly, a golden colored plate appeared around his chest. Delicate silver piping outlined the golden breastplate, but combined with his riding breeches and sitting above his dinner coat; the ensemble was a sight. Puffing up his chest, Robert looked off into the distance, turning back and forth as if to show off the different sides of his splendor.

Sputtering, I couldn't contain my laughter and released most of my tension in a loud, braying laugh. Robert smiled at my outburst and returned to his usual unflappable demeanor. Robert couldn't care in the slightest if he looked silly; he cared far more about practical things. His armor helped him, and if it had been baby blue or striped, he wouldn't have cared at all.

"Alright, well then, how does it compare to the rest?" I asked.

Robert just smiled again, then sent the description of the item to the party chat.

The Plate of the Indomitable
Non-Tradeable
Wis: 3
Mana: 65
Class: Cleric
Slot: Chest

Triggered Effect: Once every 24 hours, become invulnerable for 10 seconds. The effect ends upon any spell casting.

The bonuses from the chest piece were small, but the triggered effect was priceless. Once every twenty-four hours, Robert could become utterly immune to all damage. Sure, he wouldn't be able to cast while invulnerable, but the idea of being resistant to anything was an exciting idea.

Seeing the power Robert's item held, I was now eager to see my class item. Even if it was causing near paroxysms of laughter from the others. With a bit of trepidation, I approached the golden treasure chest. Peeking in, I could see a small collection of ring mail in a little bundle. The armor looked similar to the chest piece I was wearing, but this would cover a far smaller area. Focusing on the metal, I asked the world for the description.

Fallen Champion's Chainmail Leggings
Non-Tradeable
Armor Type: Chain
AC: 12
HP: 185
Class: Warrior
Slot: Legs

Worn Effect: Kicks provide a chance to apply a lame debuff.
Set Effect (2): Blocks have a chance to cause the next strike to be

a double attack.

"No. No. No. No!" I quickly repeated when I realized what it was at the bottom of the chest. Behind my back, the other three burst into laughter at my plight. Pulling the handful of chainmail out of the chest, I stuck it into my inventory before equipping the 'armor.' The sudden feel of the breeze on my legs and the renewal of the laughter told me the new armor was just as bad as I thought it would be. Looking down, I stared in confusion. How exactly was this supposed to protect my legs?

The chainmail ended roughly at my mid-thigh, the links strangely full and open, the skin of my legs clearly showing through. The metal loops became smaller and tighter as it reached my womanly region, the light no longer penetrating the rings as it reached the ever more provocative areas. Twisting and looking over my shoulder, I frowned as I realized that my backside was likewise covered. The rings cupped and outlined my rear in a way that metal should not have been able to do. Eventually, the others calmed down, and my frown was removed when Emma promised she would stitch a long tunic for me that would cover the most salacious bits. I would have been more appreciative if she hadn't said it after she caught Robert glancing at my legs then quickly looking away.

While we walked back to the mansion, we spent some time zig-zagging around the forest, killing the newly appearing wolves. While Emma and Annie committed a slaughter of the new canine population, Robert asked me about how it had felt to level to ten.

"It was odd, level ten feels…good. Different from the other times I've leveled up, that's for sure," I said as I watched the pyrotechnic fight. The two of them had fallen into an odd running battle where Emma would attack with her creeping slowing spell, then Annie would toss fireballs. Ever since Emma discovered the way to kill the Arena Master, this running fight technique had become her favorite method to kill difficult enemies.

Never taking his eyes off his childhood love, he leaned towards me before asking, "So, what did you get for level ten? I hope it wasn't another dud."

Perking up in excitement, I opened my log to check.

Level up!
Victoria [Warrior lvl 10] - Congratulations, you are no longer a zone-locked NPC.
New Skills!
Gained Skill - War Cry - Aggression.
Gained Skill - Area Taunt.
Gained Skill - Double Attack.
Gained Skill - Tricky Blow.

Grabbing on to Robert's arm, I started to chant and hop, "I've got four new skills! Four new skills! Four new skills!"

My excitement and chanting drew the other two over until they joined into hopping in a circle around Robert.

"Yes! Yes, alright! What are these skills though Vick!" Robert shouted over our giggling trio.

Glancing through my skills, I quickly summed up my new abilities.

"I have a new War Cry which makes things hate me more, an area taunt which works on groups of enemies," I started while ticking things off on my hand. Stuffing my sword into my armpit, I continued the count on my now free hand.

"Double attack, which says I will hit twice where normally someone would hit once, that one looks like it's an innate skill, it just happens some times? Finally, Tricky Blow which can cause new attack openings, which is also an innate skill, which means it can trigger automatically while fighting," I said while smiling at my party.

I was ecstatic with my new gains. With everyone else gaining new spells and abilities I had felt like I was being left behind. With my new skills, I would be right there helping everyone.

Awkwardly, I shifted my sword around until it was back in my grip, and then I charged the next wolf. We had time, but we still needed everyone to be level ten. My actions had nothing to do with being able to try out my new skills. Nothing at all! My new aggressive war cry was impressive. It was as much a growl as it was a scream. I wasn't worried about not having the stamina regeneration from the previous war cry, it might become a worry in more massive fights, but for single wolves, it was overkill.

We only found a few more wolves before we reached a part of the forest where the level of the wolves dropped below the point of giving us experience. We marched around at the edge of that zone and hunted the higher level beasts. It was slow, but every five minutes or so, a new wolf would appear and continue along one of the well-traveled paths. Eventually, we killed the last beast needed for everyone to level to ten. Watching my family level up through the unique level ten experience was educational. Everyone had broad smiles and a vacant expression, their gaze cast into the distance as they let the experience roll over them.

Of course, the moment everyone recovered, they returned to gazing into the distance, this time to check their new spells. I smiled as I watched them act in synchronicity, but my smile faded when Robert's face shifted to one of horror.

"Robert?" I asked, drawing everyone's attention.

Shaking his head, Robert looked to Emma with a haunted look as he linked one of his newest spells to chat.

Spell: Resurrection I

Cleric Spell: Level 10
Target: Other - Corpse
Mana: 205 mana
Effect: Returns a non-monster corpse to life. Returns 10% of lost experience and the resurrected will suffer from resurrection sickness for ten minutes.

The Clerics of the Fade were among those who perfected the Resurrection series of spells. In battle, the legions of the Fade were able to drag their most stalwart paladins to their clerics and return them to life. Every fight with the Fade became a battle of attrition. - Lore of the Faithful, by Ruth de Bloom.

Chapter 35

Emma was as hopeful and as horrified with the resurrection spell as any of the rest of us. The religious question of what such a spell meant was the first thing I considered, but I'm sure all of us were thinking about what it meant for us personally. Emma's mother was dead, our mother was dead, could such a spell be able to raise our family from the dead? If it could, should we?

That Robert could return one of us to life was a godsend, possibly literally, but we then had to ask the nature of this spell. Was this God offering providence, or was this something that came with hooks into our immortal souls? As Robert had once done for Emma, she now calmed Robert's upset.

"You should use it," Emma said, her skeleton standing behind her while the eye sockets stared us down to disagree.

"This world has changed, we need to survive and use what we can. But..." at this Emma looked down before continuing, "could we stop at Highgate Cemetery before we head to the continent?"

Father had paid for Sophia's burial in our family plot. Father had paid for multiple burial plots and reserved many for those who had served the household the longest. In part, it had been a trend to demonstrate wealth and prestige, partly it had been to retain workers -something Rebecca had ruined- and in part because of Fathers grief in the loss of our mother. When I was a child, I had enjoyed the stone statues and architecture of Highgate. The solemn atmosphere and dour mood of father after each visit had been upsetting, but the white marble, angels, and stone arches had been magical. It had only been after Sophia had died and been entombed that the sadness of the place had seeped into me. Emma had only recently stopped wearing her black morning dress, and now she was suggesting we try to return her mother from the dead. It was morbid, but I understood her desire for her mother.

Annie brought us out of our considerations and back to the needs of the moment.

"Let's wait until we return to London before we decide on what we should do. First, we need to return to the mansion and plan for the trip. I can't imagine the roads have gotten any safer."

This was a good point. There had been sporadic brigands on the roads from time to time, and with the 'cleansing' event wreaking havoc, things could only be more unsettled.

Our return to the mansion was mostly uneventful, though Annie and Emma's demonstration of their respective new levitation spells was an exciting sight. Annie's spell was simple and offered her the ability to hover over the ground by a foot or so, and to fall slowly from any height higher than that, while Emma's was the same except for one distinct difference. While Annie's spell simply caused her to rise and gently bob along as if she were adrift in a river, Emma's caused her body and eyes to turn ghost white and her hair to float as if in the wind. This was purely a cosmetic difference, the rigor like pallor and eye change had no effect on her vision or movements, but her changed visage was horrifying.

At the back door of the mansion was the Colonel waiting for our arrival. Emma had correctly deduced that her spell would be disconcerting while approaching the mansion and removed the buff, but Annie was enjoying the sensation of floating too much to follow suit. Markus eyed her as we approached but decided to remain silent about her change in movement.

While Markus and Robert discussed the event and its conclusion, I watched the interplay between the two men. Robert stood tall and stoic while he debriefed the Colonel. Markus leaned on his cane, his knuckles white from the effort of holding his balance and hiding his discomfort. While Robert stood upright without effort, Markus obviously struggled, which made his success all the more impressive. To me, my father was a mountain of a man, every memory I had as a little girl was looking up and imagining the world from his height, both figuratively and literally. While I never looked up to the Colonel to the same degree, if my father was a mountain, then the Colonel was an only slightly lower peak. But now I saw him clearly. He was a man. Flawed like any other, greater than many, lesser than some, and strained by the extreme conditions we found ourselves in.

My introspection was broken by an outburst by Robert. Suddenly focused on the discussion, I waited to discover what I had missed.

"You will follow orders, Robert! This is a matter of life and death. The mansion needs to be reinforced," the Colonel said.

Stepping backward slightly, Robert reached back and took Emma's hand. When the Colonel saw this, he pressed his lips together.

Holding my hands to my side, I tried to redirect the Colonel's focus.

"Colonel," I said as I approached.

I could understand his position, but we would not be staying here, we would help to fortify, but we would not remain.

"…Colonel, we aren't staying. We're going to check on the estates in London and eventually make way to my father. None of us will remain here indefinitely."

I could see the Colonel deflate as I explained the plan. He had to have known we were leveling to be free of this area and wouldn't remain, but I think this was his last attempt to keep control over what he could. Since the end of his military career, he had spent his time shepherding the Collingwood's fortune and Robert specifically. The family may no longer exist, what was left of the wealth was certainly gone, and Robert had grown into a man who while polite and non-confrontational, would stand up for what he wanted.

Running his hand over his face, the Colonel turned to me with a gentle smile, "I guess I knew that. Still, we need help, and your strength will come in handy. A basic palisade around the mansion would be enough."

"Colonel…" I wanted to tell him that the monsters walked paths and it was likely the goblins would never recover, but I didn't know this for certain. He could be right. Another goblin event could happen at any time, and a basic barricade would help. In the end, it would only take a day or two of effort for us to chop down enough trees and move them, my strength was more than enough to move the moderately sized logs of the forests and Annie could quickly destroy their trunks. In fact, the hardest part would be to put out the fires she would set while 'chopping' them down.

"Very well. We will stay, only for two days, and collect as much lumber as we can. With Mr. Nye here, you two should be able to build the fortifications after we harvest the wood," I said while staring Markus down.

"Agreed," he said as he looked me in the eye. If one good thing had come from this, the Colonel now at least saw me as a fighter and someone to respect for that reason.

So that was how we spent the next two days. Mr. Nye provided a wood ax for chopping firewood, and I put it to use decimating the edge of the forest. True to form, Annie spent her time trying to use lightning and fireballs to bring down slightly more distant trees. While Robert and Emma watched over us to protect from random animal attacks. Mr. Nye had initially thought to suggest he and Robert would do the foresting while perfunctorily suggesting the ladies could provide lunch, but his suggestion had been rejected outright. After watching my sister and I destroy a hundred trees in less than an hour, he had avoided looking us in the eyes. The most challenging part of the process was the hauling of the trees back to the mansion.

While we worked, the others stayed inside, with only Rufus peeking at us from the upper windows. Rebecca avoided us as well, hiding within her room. Only the Colonel and Owen seemed willing to interact with us beyond the work. For the Colonel, it was a matter of respect, for Owen, it sadly appeared that he was unaware that anything had changed. The gentleman who could remain straight-faced while smiling with only a twinkle of the eye, the man who snuck me treats when the weather stormed, that man was fading away before my eyes. I was becoming maudlin thinking about the people we would be leaving behind and all the things that had offered me a happy, if not free, life.

When we finished hauling trees, the stack almost reaching waist high and so broad as to take up a large portion of the back garden, we organized to head to London. We had hauled trees for an entire day and night, the lack of sleep no more hampering to us than it had been in the dungeon. We left at first light on four of our horses, we no longer had need of the carriage seeing as we had our inventories. We started down the front walk to the main road. The world sat before us, possibilities abounded, and the whole of it waited for us. London was merely the first stop.

A Special Thanks

<u>To those in my life who helped me during a trying time.</u>

To my wife, thank you for always supporting me.

To my mother-in-law, for putting up with my reading out loud.

To my father-in-law, can I call you 'Da-doo'!?

To one of my favorite authors, P.S. Power, for showing me that effort can be like a superpower.

<u>A special thanks to:</u>

Morgan O'Brien & Neil OHara

An extra coffee from the Patreon money doesn't sound like much, but it saved my mind!

About the Author

Alston Sleet resides in Portland Oregon with his lovely wife, takes care of his disabled mother-in-law, and dodges the antics of his father-in-law. By day he works as a computer programmer focused in the manufacturing industry, creating software to enhance the power of our future robotic overlords.

Since the age of four, he has known he always wanted to be a computer programmer. A strange child, who thought that 'going outside' was the thing our ancestors fought to overcome and 'why would we want to go back?'

Luckily, the forces of 'no computer' prevailed for his parents and Alston managed to learn to enjoy the outdoors. Occasionally. When it wasn't raining in Portland.

Along with the Wife, mother-in-law, father-in-law, dog, cat, two snakes, and three horses, he works tirelessly to understand how an introvert ended up with so many people who love him around.

Alston's first book was Digital Me a sci-fi/fantasy litRPG, all with a dash of political fun. The Dungeon Traveler follows the tale of a failure of a man being reincarnated into another world - as a stone.

If you have comments, questions, insults, or flame wars, the author can be contacted by email at AlstonSleet@gmail.com or through patreon at http://www.patreon.com/AlstonSleet